PRAISE FOR THE NOVELS
OF MARTA PERRY

"What a joy it is to read Marta Perry's novels! . . . Everything a reader could want—strong, well-defined characters; beautiful, realistic settings; and a thought-provoking plot. Readers of Amish fiction will surely be waiting anxiously for her next book."

—Shelley Shepard Gray, *New York Times* bestselling author of the Amish of Hart County series

"A born storyteller, Marta Perry skillfully weaves the past and present in a heart-stirring tale of love and forgiveness."

—Susan Meissner, author of *As Bright as Heaven*

"Sure to appeal to fans of Beverly Lewis."

—*Library Journal*

"Perry carefully balances the traditional life of the Amish with the contemporary world in an accessible, intriguing fashion."   —*Publishers Weekly* (starred review)

"Perry crafts characters with compassion yet with insecurities that make them relatable."   —RT Book Reviews

"[Perry] has once again captured my heart with the gentle wisdom and heartfelt faith of the Amish community."

—Fresh Fiction

HANNAH'S JOY

Pleasant Valley
BOOK SIX

MARTA PERRY

BERKLEY
New York

BERKLEY
An imprint of Penguin Random House LLC
1745 Broadway, New York, NY 10019

ISBN: 9780451491602

Berkley trade paperback edition / May 2012
Berkley mass-market edition / February 2019

Printed in the United States of America
1 3 5 7 9 10 8 6 4 2

Cover art by Shane Rebenschied
Book design by Tiffany Estreicher

*This story is dedicated
to my children and grandchildren,
with much love.
And, as always, to Brian.*

ACKNOWLEDGMENTS

I'd like to express my gratitude to those whose expertise, patience, and generosity helped me in the writing of this book: to Erik Wesner, whose *Amish America* newsletters are enormously helpful in visualizing aspects of daily life; to Donald Kraybill and John Hostetler, whose books are the definitive works on Amish life; to Louise Stoltzfus, Lovina Eicher, and numerous others who've shared what it means to be Amish; to my Mennonite friends, for helpful advice; and most of all to my family, for giving me a rich heritage upon which to draw.

LIST OF CHARACTERS

Hannah Conroy army widow

Jamie Conroy Hannah's son, twenty months old

Travis Conroy Hannah's deceased husband

Paula Schatz Hannah's aunt, Mennonite, runs Pleasant Valley's bakery

Leah Glick protagonist of *Leah's Choice*, wife of Daniel Glick; their children: Matthew, Elizabeth, Jonah, and Rachel Anna

William Brand woodworker, works in his cousin Caleb's shop

Caleb Brand furniture shop owner, engaged to Katie Miller

Katie Miller protagonist of *Katie's Way*, quilt shop owner

Rhoda Miller Katie's sixteen-year-old sister

Naomi Esch Amish, works in the bakery

Isaac Brand William's older brother, head of the family

Rachel Zook protagonist of *Rachel's Garden*, wife of Gideon Zook; their children: Becky, Joseph, Mary, and Josiah

Megan Townsend military wife, Hannah's friend

Robert Conroy retired military, Travis's father

Rebecca "Becky" Brand Caleb's niece

Joseph and Myra Beiler Leah's brother and sister-in-law

Anna Beiler Fisher protagonist of *Anna's Return*, wife of Samuel; their children: adopted daughter Grace and baby David

Barbara Beiler Leah's sister-in-law

Cliff Wainwright bookstore owner

Phil Russo local veteran, husband of Nancy

Ephraim Zimmerman Mennonite bishop, husband of Miriam

Ammon Esh barn builder

Emma and John Eichner William's older sister and brother-in-law

Sheila Downing attorney

CHAPTER ONE

A man in army fatigues stepped off a bus just down the street at the Pleasant Valley bus stop. Hannah Conroy clutched the stroller handle as an onslaught of dizziness hit her. She fought the irrational surge of joy that turned in an instant to ashes.

It wasn't Travis. It was a stranger, a young soldier, moving into the welcoming arms of his family—mother holding him, fighting back tears; father standing stiffly as if to deny his emotions; a girl of about ten waving a WEL-COME sign.

Not Travis. Travis had lain beneath a marker in Arlington National Cemetery for well over a year. He wasn't here on a warm September day in Pleasant Valley.

Two women in Plain dress stopped next to her on the sidewalk, their faces blurred by the tears she wouldn't let fall. One reached out a tentative hand.

"Are you all right? You are Hannah, ain't so? Paula Schatz's niece?"

She nodded. She couldn't cry. Jamie would be frightened if he saw his mother in tears. But he was almost asleep in the stroller, one chubby hand still grasping his toy dog.

"I'm fine." Hannah almost managed a smile. "Thank you."

"You're going into the bakery, ja? Let us help you get the stroller inside."

The woman motioned to the other . . . a girl in her early teens, Hannah saw now . . . who pulled the door open, setting the bell jangling. Together they maneuvered the stroller into Aunt Paula's bakery, where the aroma of fresh-baked bread surrounded her, easing the hurt.

"Thank you," she said again. The grief and pain ebbed, leaving her as lost as a leaf in the wind.

"It's nothing." The woman patted her arm with a feather-light touch, the girl nodded, and they were gone.

Aunt Paula, as round and comforting as one of her own dumplings, glanced up from the customer she was serving, her eyes clouding when she saw Hannah's face. By the time Hannah reached the kitchen door, Aunt Paula was there, wiping her hands on the white apron she wore over her traditional Old Order Mennonite dress, its tiny print faded from many washings.

"Hannah? Was ist letz?" Aunt Paula spoke English most of the time, but in moments of stress she was apt to slip into Pennsylvania Dutch. "What's wrong? I saw Leah Glick and her daughter helping you."

"Nothing." Hannah bent, the action hiding her face for a moment, and lifted Jamie from the stroller. He was relaxed and drowsy, a precious, heavy armload now at twenty months. "I'm fine."

She didn't want Aunt Paula worrying about her. It was enough that her aunt had made a home here for her and Jamie.

But Hannah couldn't stop herself from glancing at the window. The family, their faces animated with love, moved toward a car.

Aunt Paula followed her gaze. "Ach, I see." Her voice was soft. "I know. After your uncle passed, I'd see a man with wavy hair like his, or his way of walking, and my heart would stop, as if it reacted faster than my brain did."

"It's been almost a year and a half." Hannah cradled Jamie close, and he snuggled his face into her shoulder, his soft breath against her neck. "I'm better. But sometimes—"

"Ja. Sometimes." Aunt Paula patted her. "I know."

The bell jingled on the bakery door, and Aunt Paula turned to greet the man in Amish garb. In all the years since she'd lived here as a child, Hannah had nearly forgotten the peculiar mix of Amish, horse-and-buggy Mennonite, black bumper Mennonite, and English that made Pleasant Valley so unique.

William Brand was Amish, and he worked with his cousin Caleb in the cabinetry shop down the street. Hannah had learned that much from him, but it had taken persistence. William stuttered, and like many stutterers, he took refuge in silence much of the time.

Banishing thoughts of the past, Hannah moved to the counter, smiling. William was silent enough already. She didn't want him to think she was avoiding speaking to him.

"Good morning."

He ducked his head in a nod. Tall for an Amish man, and broad-shouldered, he wore the traditional Amish black broadfall trousers with a blue shirt and suspenders, the usual straw hat on his head. In his midtwenties, William was probably a year or two younger than she was, but his fresh color and the shyness in his blue eyes made him seem even younger. Next to him, she felt ancient.

And what did he make of her, with her denim skirt, pink lipstick, and curling ponytail? Did he find it odd that Paula Schatz had such a modern niece?

"H-H-Hannah," he managed, as if determined to say her name.

Then he looked at her son, and his face softened. He held out a work-roughened hand, and Jamie latched on to it, saying something that might have been an attempt at William's name.

"S-sleepy time, Jamie?"

Jamie shook his head vigorously, but the movement was interrupted by a huge yawn that showed every one of his baby teeth, and they both laughed.

Funny, how William's stutter seemed to ease when he spoke to Jamie. Once, a lifetime ago, she'd planned to become a speech therapist, and her interest stirred at the observation.

"He just doesn't want to admit he's tired. I thought he was going to fall asleep in the stroller," she said, reminding herself to speak naturally to William. Talking with a stutterer required more patience than many people had.

"H-h-he's a-afraid he'll m-m-miss something."

"That's for sure." She tickled Jamie's belly, loving the way he chuckled, eyes crinkling.

Aunt Paula returned to the counter, carrying two coffees in foam cups and a white bag. "There you are, William, your usual coffee, just the way you and Caleb like it. And a couple of crullers to tide you over until lunch."

"D-d-denke."

He handed her the money. With another smile for Jamie, he went out quickly, perhaps relieved not to have to engage in any further conversation. His straw hat shielded his face from Hannah's view as he passed the window.

She stood watching his tall figure for a moment, and then went to get Jamie's plastic cup of milk from the small refrigerator behind the counter. She focused her mind on him, trying not to let it stray toward those moments on the sidewalk.

"Has William always stuttered?"

Aunt Paula leaned against the display case, seeming ready for a comfortable gossip. "I don't know about always. You don't remember the Brands from when you were growing up?"

She shook her head. "I was only nine when we left, after all." She handed Jamie the cup.

Of course Aunt Paula knew that. How could Paula forget when her beloved younger sister had up and left the community, left the church, left her family, and incidentally left behind all Hannah's security?

"No reason you should, I guess," Aunt Paula said. "Anyway, it's a big family, and William is the youngest. His mamm and daad were both sickly off and on, and it seemed like William kind of got lost in the shuffle, what with his oldest brother, Isaac, taking over the farm and always barking orders at the younger ones. I'm not sure when the stuttering started, but it was before William went to school."

Hannah nodded, feeling a pang of sympathy. William hadn't had it easy. "That's typical. It's usually in those early years when a child is starting to talk. How did the family handle it? Did they get help for him?"

"Not that I know of." Aunt Paula frowned. "I think the schoolteacher tried to help him, but seems like the other kinder were always impatient, finishing his sentences for him, acting like he was . . . well, slow."

"I don't think he's that." She'd seen quick understanding in William's face in their few conversations, even when he didn't speak.

"Ach, William's bright enough, and the best thing that could have happened to him was going to work with his cousin Caleb in the shop. He's got a gift with his hands, so Caleb says, and Caleb's a master woodworker himself, so he'd know. The boy will maybe find a little respect for himself there."

"Not a boy," Hannah murmured, taking the cup from Jamie, who was nearly asleep on her shoulder. She rubbed his back, cherishing the feel of his small warm body against her.

"No, you're right. He's not." Aunt Paula touched Jamie's

brown curls in a quick caress. "William seems younger than he is, no doubt because of the stutter."

Hannah nodded, moving toward the stairs that led up to the apartment above the shop. She would put Jamie in his crib and—

"I'm nearly forgetting." Aunt Paula's voice lifted. "That's what you were studying in college, wasn't it? Before you got married, I mean?"

"Speech therapy."

She'd gotten interested when she'd babysat for a family with a child who stuttered. The Davises had been so helpful, encouraging her and aiding her with loan applications so she could go to school. That had been her only goal, until Travis came along.

But Travis had loved her. It had seemed meant to be, that they should love each other and get married and make a home together always.

Always hadn't lasted very long. Just a few short years of moving from one army base to another. She'd been pregnant when his unit shipped out to Afghanistan. Travis had never seen his son, and she'd quickly learned that a mother with a young child and an incomplete education had very little chance of making a home of any kind, even with the military's death benefits.

"You could help William." Aunt Paula, not able to follow Hannah's thoughts, smiled broadly. "I don't know why I didn't think of that before. You can teach William, help him get over his stutter."

"No, no, I couldn't," she said quickly. "I'm not qualified. I never finished school, and besides—"

"Well, you're as near to qualified as William is likely to get," Aunt Paula said briskly. "It would be an act of charity to help him." She said it as if that were the defining argument, as it probably was to anyone brought up Mennonite, accustomed as they were to the idea of service.

But Hannah hadn't been Mennonite since she was a

child, and as much as she'd like to help, her instincts told her it was a bad idea to get involved in William's problems.

"I really don't—"

"Just think about it." Aunt Paula patted her shoulder. "You'll see I'm right. It would be good for you, too, to make use of your education."

Hannah hesitated, but then she nodded. Agreeing to think about it was easy. Marshaling the arguments against it was more difficult.

Especially since she didn't want to use the strongest one—that she intended to go back to the outside world as soon as she could swing it financially.

The familiar worry settled on her, darkening the sunny day. How long could she go on staying here, accepting Aunt Paula's home and her help, without her aunt expecting Hannah to commit to her way of life?

"Paula had our coffee break all ready for us, ja?" William's cousin Caleb pulled a cruller from the bag, spilling a little powdered sugar on the maple bench he'd been polishing.

"You'd b-best not l-let K-Katie see you making such a m-mess," William teased.

"There, all better." Caleb wiped the sugar with a polishing cloth. "Katie's out talking to some of the sisters about plans for the fall charity auction. She'll never know."

Katie Miller, who owned the quilt shop that was attached to Caleb's cabinetmaking business, would be marrying Caleb this fall. It had been a long time since William had seen his cousin look as happy and settled as he did since Katie came into his life.

"W-women are always busy," William said, taking the top off his foam cup and blowing gently on the steaming coffee.

Funny, how easy it was to talk with Caleb—far easier

than talking to his own brother. But Isaac wasn't much of a listener, not like Caleb was.

Besides, working with wood just seemed to calm a person. As if he knew what William was thinking, Caleb ran a hand along the curved back of the bench that was William's latest project, his touch seeming as affectionate as if the wood were alive.

"Ja, women are," Caleb said. "Katie especially." His face warmed as it always did when he spoke of her.

"Katie especially what?" Quick, light footsteps accompanied the words, and Katie came through the archway that linked the two shops, smiling at Caleb in a way that suggested he was the only man in the world.

"Katie especially is busy, ain't so?" Caleb said, reaching out to link his fingers with hers. "If I'd known you'd be back this soon, Will could have brought you a cruller."

"I'll just have a bite of yours." She broke off a small piece, turning her smile on William. "You've been down to Paula's bakery already, I see. Was her niece there?"

"J-ja." Hannah's soft brown curls seemed to frame her heart-shaped face in his mind.

Katie nodded. "It's been a gut thing for Paula, having Hannah komm to stay. Paula was telling me yesterday how busy she's been."

"We've all been busy," Caleb reminded her. "You and the other merchants worked so hard this summer to bring more people to town—now you have to work harder to keep up with them."

"That's better than having no customers at all," Katie said, her tone teasing. "Where would you be without me?"

"All alone," William said. "A g-grumpy old b-bachelor."

Caleb grinned. "You're right about that, for sure. Still, I have to wonder sometimes if Katie won't be too busy even to marry me, come November."

"Just you try and get away." Katie raised their linked hands. "I won't let you go. William would help me hog-tie you, ain't so?"

William nodded, responding with a smile to their teasing. He liked seeing the two of them so happy. And he'd like to believe that someday he'd find what Caleb had with Katie.

But the years seemed to be slipping away, and it almost felt as if life was passing him by. As if he were intended always to be on the fringe of things, watching other people's lives.

That image of Hannah Conroy slid back into his mind. With her Englisch dress and manner, Hannah seemed out of place behind the counter at the Plain Good Bakery, as if she didn't quite belong, either.

"About Hannah," Katie said, almost as if she were reading his thoughts. "I heard something today that surprised me."

"J-ja?" He couldn't help the spark of interest he felt.

"Of course we knew that Hannah was a widow." Sympathy filled Katie's face. "Poor thing, so young and with a baby to care for, besides. But I'd never heard until today how her husband died." She hesitated, her forehead wrinkling. "He was a soldier, did you know that? Killed in combat, they say."

William absorbed that, trying to understand. A Mennonite woman married to a soldier? Mennonites and Amish shared a fundamental devotion to nonviolence, governing their lives by it. He understood the perplexity that underlay Katie's words. It just didn't seem possible.

"I d-d-didn't know." He saw again the strain written in the lines around Hannah's brown eyes. Maybe that explained, at least a little, the isolation he sensed in her.

"Hannah's parents left the valley when she was a child," Caleb said. "I suppose they might have left the church, as well. I do remember hearing Mamm talk about how sorry she was for Paula, losing the sister she was so close to."

"It's gut that she has Hannah back, I guess," Katie said. "With no kinder of her own, Paula needs someone to take care of. I've seen how she dotes on that little boy . . . so cute he is with those big brown eyes like his mammi's." Katie paused for a moment. "I just hope it works out for them. An Englisch woman and a soldier's widow, as well—it seems strange that she'd want to stay here."

"Ja," William said softly, thinking of the sorrow in Hannah's face, the innocent laughter of her little son. How hard her life must seem to her right now.

At least, with her aunt she'd found a resting place. A person didn't have to be interested in her to see that, to sympathize, and maybe to hope she'd stay.

Hannah stood for a few minutes by the crib that evening, listening to Jamie's soft, even breathing. His cheeks were rosy, and his soft brown hair, still damp from his bath, curled on his neck.

"God bless you, little man," she whispered. Giving him a final pat, she tiptoed out of the small room.

She eased the door closed. The monitor would tell her if Jamie woke, but he was a good sleeper, up in the night only when he was sick.

They were fortunate that Aunt Paula's apartment was large enough to give each of them a bedroom. When Hannah had stayed with her friend Megan and her family, she and Jamie had been cramped into a room hardly larger than a closet.

Not that she'd complained, of course. If Megan and Jeff hadn't taken her in when she'd had to move out of base housing, she wasn't sure what she'd have done.

Come here, maybe, as she had eventually anyway. She certainly hadn't belonged on the army base, even as a guest, once Travis was gone. When she'd finally been honest with Aunt Paula about her situation, her aunt had responded with two words. *Come home.* She'd never forget that, and never stop being grateful.

She walked out to the living room, finally getting used to the quiet after nearly two months here. Black bumper

Mennonites like Aunt Paula drove cars and allowed electricity and telephones in their homes, even computers, but not television or Internet access. She still hadn't quite figured out the reasons why one technology was okay and another banned, but as long as she lived with Aunt Paula, she'd follow her rules.

Those first months after Travis died she'd had the television on twenty-four hours a day, just for the sake of hearing another voice. But she was past that now. Her aunt must be down in the bakery kitchen, preparing for the next day. Picking up the baby monitor, Hannah hurried down the stairs.

At the sound of Hannah's footsteps, Aunt Paula looked up from the bread she was kneading. "Is he asleep then, the precious lamb?"

"Out like a light." Hannah set the monitor on the counter and washed her hands at the sink. "What can I do?"

Aunt Paula nodded toward the bowls draped with tea towels that sat atop the stove. "That rye dough should be ready for punching down and forming into loaves already."

Hannah nodded, tying one of the large white aprons over her clothes. Sure enough, the dough had risen well over the top of the bowl. She punched it down, turned it out onto a floured board, and set to work, moving in tandem with her aunt, working on the opposite side of the table. The risen dough had its own scent and texture, and she took pleasure in feeling it work under her hands.

At first she'd been virtually useless in the bakery, fit only for waiting on tables in the coffee shop section and making change. But desire was a great teacher. She wanted more than anything to pull her weight as long as she was here. Besides, it was fascinating. There was so much more to the bakery than she'd imagined, and her aunt made it all look almost effortless.

But Aunt Paula really did need her. Running the bakery was too much for one person, and the Amish women who worked for her came only during the day.

"Naomi Esch is coming in early tomorrow," Aunt Paula said, as if she'd been following Hannah's thoughts. "So you don't have to rush around in the morning. If you can just come down during our busiest time . . ."

"Of course I will," she said quickly. "Jamie will be fine while we're working."

They'd set up a corner of the shop with some of Jamie's favorite toys, turning it into a little tot lot where he'd be safe. For the most part, he played well enough, though he'd attempted to escape a few times.

That would only get worse as he grew older. It was a temporary solution, just as her being here was.

"I'd like to have Naomi work a few more hours a week through the fall." Aunt Paula prepared the dough for a second rising, patting it as if it were a child. "But if she can't—well, I don't need to tell you again what a relief it is to have you here to help."

Hannah's throat tightened. That was Aunt Paula, always making it sound as if Hannah were doing her a favor, instead of the other way around.

"You know we love being here. If you hadn't stepped in . . ."

She let that trail off, shaking her head. If she thought too much of those last few months, trying to find a job, trying to find someone reliable to watch Jamie when she worked, afraid all the time that she wouldn't be able to pay the rent . . . Well, it was best not to dwell on that.

Aunt Paula reached out a floury hand to clasp hers for a moment. "Let's chust say we both benefit, ja?" The Pennsylvania Dutch accent was more pronounced, as if emotion brought it out. "Having you here is like having my little sister back again."

Hannah tensed, as she always did when Aunt Paula wanted to talk about Mom. The woman Paula remembered as her little sister didn't seem to bear any resemblance to Hannah's mother.

She struggled not to show her feelings. "You still miss her, don't you?"

"Miss her. Remember her. I'd begun to give up on the idea of having a sister by the time she was born, after all those boys in between. And then Elizabeth came along." She smiled, her eyes misty. "It was almost like she was my baby. She followed me everywhere. I never thought anything could change how close we were."

Hannah wasn't sure what to say. Her mother had depended on her big sister—that much was obvious. Maybe losing touch with her when they'd moved away had contributed to her downward slide. Or maybe it would have happened anyway, no matter where she'd been.

Aunt Paula set the dough back for a second rising and began helping Hannah form the rye dough into the round loaves that were one of her specialties. She sighed, and Hannah knew she was still thinking of that little sister.

"I never understood it." Her aunt's hands worked the dough automatically, as if she could do it in her sleep. "It always seemed as if Elizabeth was looking for something she couldn't find." She looked searchingly at Hannah. "Did she find it out there, in the outside world?"

Hannah shook her head. "No. I don't think so." Whatever it was Mom had hoped to find had probably been swamped by the depression that took over her life.

Took over Hannah's life, too, in a way. Dad had come home less and less, not able to cope with his wife's illness. Finally he'd stopped coming at all.

And Hannah's childhood had been measured by how well her mother was. There'd been the bright days, when Mom had gotten up and dressed and put food on the table and talked about how Hannah was doing in school. And the bad days, when she hadn't gotten out of bed at all.

"I'm sorry," Aunt Paula said softly. "I shouldn't have reminded you."

Hannah shook her head. "It's all right."

"No, it's not. You had to deal with your mother's illness all alone after your daad left. If I'd known . . . if she'd stayed here . . ."

If her parents had stayed here in Pleasant Valley, what would her life have been? Maybe she'd have worked here in the bakery with Aunt Paula, just as she was doing now. Or maybe she'd have married early and have a houseful of children by this time.

Either way, she'd have known what it was to feel secure. That was what had been missing in her life from the day they'd moved away—that sense of having a safe, certain home.

That was what she had to give Jamie, no matter what the cost. Her heart clenched. She must never let him feel as lost as she had.

But this life was too restricted. That was probably why her parents had left. Jamie's future wasn't here, and neither was hers.

"We have worship this Sunday," Aunt Paula said, with a change of subject that startled her.

"Yes, I know." The small churchhouse where Aunt Paula's Mennonite congregation worshipped was shared on alternate Sundays with another Mennonite group, the horse-and-buggy Mennonites, from whom they'd split years ago. It seemed strange to her, the two groups sharing a building, but everyone in Pleasant Valley seemed to take it for granted.

"I was wondering . . . I was thinking . . ." Aunt Paula seemed to be having trouble getting it out, whatever it was.

"Yes? Is there something you want me to do for church?"

"I wondered if you'd consider starting to wear Mennonite dress." Aunt Paula said the words all in a rush, indicating her print dress with a wave of her hand.

Words failed Hannah. There it was—the pressure she'd feared, her aunt's expectation that she would commit to a life here.

She couldn't. She'd attended worship with Aunt Paula

since she'd arrived, even finding comfort in the simple, quiet services. But that was as far as it could go.

"I'm not asking that you be baptized or anything." Aunt Paula's tone was worried. "I don't want you to think that I'm putting conditions on you. It's just . . ."

"You'd feel more comfortable if your niece looked less like an outsider," Hannah said, finishing the thought for her.

Hannah had known this moment would come, but she still wasn't prepared for it. She'd dressed Plain when she was a child, of course. Maybe even for the first few months after they'd left the valley. But that had worn off, just as the other things that once seemed an immutable part of their lives had gone.

"I've spoken too soon," Aunt Paula said. "I shouldn't have asked it."

"It's all right. I just . . ."

I can't. That was what she wanted to say. Dressing Plain was too much of a commitment. Too close to saying that she was here for good. She couldn't do that.

And yet how could she say no? When she thought of all she owed her aunt, how could she?

She'd left the outside world out of desperation, feeling caught in a trap of never having enough money, enough security, unless she dipped into the death gratuity benefit, which she was trying to save for her son's future, always afraid of what the next day would bring.

But maybe, in its own way, Pleasant Valley could be a trap, too.

Chapter Two

Hannah smoothed the denim jumper down over her waist, frowning at herself in the mirror. She'd always dressed modestly, never been comfortable with the idea of super-short skirts and navel-baring tops. Still, that wasn't really what had brought up Aunt Paula's request, was it?

For her aunt, dressing like the other women in her church was showing that you were a part of that community. How you dressed was a reflection of who you were.

That wasn't who Hannah was, and it hadn't been for a long time. At some point during a mostly sleepless night she'd almost convinced herself that agreeing would be like wearing a uniform, something you did to fit in at your job. Almost, but not quite.

The clatter of blocks falling announced that Jamie was tired of the tower she'd helped him build. He toddled over to her and grasped the skirt of her jumper, pulling on it.

"In a minute, sweetheart. Let Mommy fix her hair.

Then we'll go downstairs with Aunt Paula. You'll like that, won't you?"

By way of an answer, Jamie scurried to the baby gate she'd stretched across the bedroom door. He shook it, a prisoner trying to get out of his jail.

"Yes, yes, in a minute," she repeated. She pulled her hair back in a ponytail and twisted it into the bun she wore when she worked in the bakery. Too bad she'd had her hair cut in layers the last time she'd had it done. Given the way her hair wanted to curl, getting the smooth look achieved so easily by Plain women was virtually impossible.

She paused, hairpin in her hand, struck by a memory she hadn't known was there. Her mother stood in front of a mirror, just as she was doing, while a small Hannah sat on the bed, swinging her legs and watching. Mammi put her prayer kapp in place over her hair, and the little girl Hannah had been reached up to pat her own.

"Some people don't wear kapps," she'd said.

"Ja, that's so." Mammi turned from the mirror to smile at her. "But we do."

"Why?" she'd persisted.

Mammi sat down next to her. "The Bible says that a woman should have her head covered when she prays. I might want to pray anytime of the day, ain't so?" She patted Hannah's cheek. "Besides, it shows where we belong."

The adult Hannah put her hand on her cheek, almost imagining she could feel her mother's touch. An unpleasant idea pricked at her mind. She'd thought, so often, of what it had done to her when her parents took her away from Pleasant Valley. Maybe she should have considered what it had done to Mammi.

She went quickly to the door and opened the gate. At least her parents had had a choice. She hadn't.

Hannah held Jamie's hand as they walked down the stairs, encouraging him to grasp the spindles with each step. She'd get there faster if she carried him, but he'd never lived in a house with stairs before, and he had to learn to master them safely.

The morning rush was well under way, with the usual mix of Amish, Mennonite, and English sharing the news of the day or comments about the weather. Several people were lined up at the counter, and three of the five round tables were filled.

Hannah guided Jamie to his play yard and lifted him in, nodding to Naomi Esch, the Amish woman who worked for Aunt Paula. Naomi had a nod for her and a warm smile for Jamie as she bent to tickle him, saying something softly in Pennsylvania Dutch. Jamie giggled, making a grab for her kapp strings.

"He loves you," Hannah said impulsively. "You'd be a good mother, Naomi."

A shadow crossed Naomi's face, making Hannah wish she hadn't spoken. Then it was gone, and Naomi was smiling.

"Ja, I had lots of practice raising my little brothers and sisters," she said. "Do you want to take the tables, and I'll help Paula behind the counter?"

It was obviously a change of subject, and Hannah nodded. Tying an apron over her jumper, she picked up the coffeepot and began refilling cups, talking to the regular customers as she did.

She glanced again at Naomi, busy now behind the counter. Naomi was probably close to Hannah in age, and most Amish women were married by then. According to Aunt Paula, Naomi had taken over her younger siblings when her mother died, and her father still kept her close to home, even now that the younger ones were grown. If that bothered Naomi, it couldn't be read on her serene, pleasant face.

Difficult parents. Hannah's thoughts flickered to her own again. She hadn't had a monopoly on that, had she? She turned back to her work, trying to forget.

The bakery had emptied out by midmorning when

William Brand came in. Did he time it that way deliberately, so he wouldn't have to talk to people? The thought bothered her, reminding her of Aunt Paula's suggestion about her working with William.

Not that she needed a reminder, with her aunt sending her a meaningful glance, which she tried to ignore. Instead, she watched William, who detoured as usual to speak to Jamie.

William's face relaxed when he knelt by the plastic barrier. It wasn't just that William stuttered less when he spoke to Jamie. He let down his guard, too. Did he even recognize how wary he looked sometimes, at least around strangers? That was gone now, his strong-boned face gentled by a smile and his blue eyes warm with laughter over something Jamie was babbling.

Aunt Paula elbowed her. "Talk to him," she murmured.

Sending her aunt an exasperated look, Hannah moved to the counter as William approached it. But before she could say anything, the bell over the door jingled.

The Amish man who entered was solid and middle-aged, with eyes as blue as William's but a beard that reached below his collar.

"Good morning." She nodded to him. "I'll be with you in a moment."

She turned to William, but the other man was elbowing him out of the way.

"Ach, my brother will wait, I know." He nodded to Paula and Naomi, who were busying themselves behind the counter. "I am Isaac Brand. You must be Paula's niece, ja?"

Hannah nodded, smiling automatically. So this was William's older brother. What had Aunt Paula said about him? That he liked snapping orders and had a scant supply of patience?

"I'll be with you as soon as I've finished William's order." She picked up a sheet of the waxed paper they used to handle the pastries. "Crullers again today, William? Or would you and Caleb prefer donuts?"

"I-it's okay," he stammered, stepping to the side. "You c-c-can t-t-take c-c-care of—"

"You see?" Isaac interrupted him. "My brother doesn't mind, and I must get on with my business. A large coffee with cream and sugar. And I'll have one of those Bavarians, ja?"

Hannah opened her mouth to argue, but a quick glance at William's face told her that her defense wouldn't be welcomed. And Aunt Paula was already coming to the counter with coffees.

"Here you are, Isaac, and William, here is yours and Caleb's. Hannah, will you see to the pastries while I ring them up?"

She nodded, bending to the pastry case so that no one would see the indignation in her face.

"We'll be cutting hay in the south field tomorrow." Isaac glanced at his brother. "Tell Caleb I'll need you then."

William nodded, his face expressionless.

It's not your business, she reminded herself. Anyway, William was probably used to the way Isaac spoke to him.

Somehow those rationalizations didn't help. She handed William the bag with his purchases, their fingers brushing. He nodded his thanks and turned away, face averted.

She watched as the brothers went out, parting ways on the sidewalk in front of the shop.

"That's Isaac," Aunt Paula said, unnecessarily. "He's a gut enough man in his way, I suppose, but he never sees anyone's viewpoint but his own."

"Does William live with him?" She regretted the show of interest the moment she said the words. Aunt Paula didn't need any encouragement.

"Ja," Naomi said, joining them at the counter. "Well, not exactly *with* him. He lives in the grossdaadi house on the family farm. He helps out there, besides working with Caleb."

"That must keep him busy," Hannah commented, wondering if Naomi would say more.

Naomi frowned a little. "Isaac has sons of his own big enough to help, and folks thought maybe William would go in full-time with Caleb. But I guess Isaac still needs him."

Or liked having William on call. Hannah reminded herself again that it wasn't her business.

Still, it rankled, the way Isaac had pushed William aside and interrupted him. If all his family showed such disregard for him, it was small wonder that William found it difficult to speak for himself.

Before she was even aware of having made up her mind, she was taking the apron off. She glanced at her aunt. "Do you mind if I take Jamie out for a little walk while it's quiet?"

"That's fine." Aunt Paula had a knowing look in her eyes. "Where are you planning to go?" she asked, all innocence.

Hannah suppressed the urge to say that her aunt already knew. "I think I'll go and have a little talk with William," she said.

Maybe he'd want the limited help she had to offer. Maybe he'd reject her, feeling embarrassed or offended. She didn't know. But she had to try.

Jamie bounced eagerly in the stroller when they started down the street, hanging on to the tray as if it were a steering wheel. "Go," he announced.

A woman who was passing slowed, smiling at him. "Hi there, sweetheart." She gave a friendly nod to Hannah and moved on.

That sort of thing happened all the time in Pleasant Valley, and Hannah still hadn't gotten used to it. She wasn't sure whether people were just naturally friendly or whether they knew who she was and connected her with Aunt Paula.

She wheeled the stroller past the hardware store and glanced in the window of the harness shop run by Bishop

Mose, leader of the local Amish. She could see him at the counter, white beard flowing to his chest.

Memory stirred. She had walked down this street as a child, probably been wheeled down it in a stroller even earlier, just as Jamie was. Maybe it wasn't so odd that people seemed to know her.

She hesitated in front of the frame building that housed the cabinetry shop on one side and the quilt shop on the other. It wasn't too late to turn around and walk back.

Don't be such a coward, she lectured herself. *All he can do is say no. That might hurt your pride, but nothing else.*

She pulled the door open and maneuvered the stroller inside, and paused again to figure out a path through the furniture pieces displayed in hospitable-looking groupings. Maybe she should have left the stroller on the sidewalk.

"Komm in, komm in." An Amish woman stood at the counter, talking to a man behind it who must be William's cousin. "Can I help you with the stroller?" She was already coming toward them, smiling. "I am Katie Miller. You must be Paula's niece."

She must. It was what everyone said. Hannah nodded, returning the woman's smile. "I'm Hannah Conroy. Everybody seems to know that."

"Ach, I remember that feeling very well. I was the newcomer for a while, and it seemed so strange that everyone knew me when I didn't know them." Katie knelt, face-to-face with Jamie. "This fine big boy must be Jamie. I have heard about you from William."

Jamie chuckled, standing in the stroller and banging on the tray. He raised his arms in an unmistakable gesture. "Up!" he demanded.

"Jamie, she doesn't want—" Hannah began.

But Katie was already lifting him in her arms. "For sure I do want," she said. "Look, Jamie, here is Caleb."

She carried him to the counter with Hannah following.

"Wilkom, Jamie." He smiled, holding out a hand to the baby. "And wilkom to your mammi, too."

Caleb didn't share William's blue eyes and fair coloring, but Hannah thought she might have picked them out as relatives. Something in the strong bone structure of the faces was very similar.

"It's nice to meet you both." She glanced from Caleb to Katie, who was bouncing Jamie in her arms. Hadn't Aunt Paula said something about the two of them getting married? Through the archway she could see the bright colors of Katie's quilts. Maybe sharing the building had brought them together.

"Can we help you with something?" Caleb asked. "We make a few wooden children's toys, but nothing is on display right now."

"No, I . . . actually I wanted to speak to William for a moment. Is he here?" She'd nearly had as much difficulty getting the words out as William might.

"Ja, for sure. He's upstairs in the workroom." Caleb gestured toward a flight of steps. "Go right on up."

"I would love to watch Jamie while you talk, if you think he will stay with me," Katie said.

Since Jamie was pounding on the counter enthusiastically with a wooden dowel Katie had handed him, there didn't seem to be any doubt about that. And it certainly would be easier to have an adult conversation without his noisy presence.

"Thanks so much. I'll just be a few minutes." She waved at Jamie and hurried to the steps.

It might be a very few minutes if William were embarrassed by what she'd come to say. After all, he was an adult. He'd apparently learned to function well in his world despite his speech difficulty. Maybe she was being presumptuous.

By the time she'd reached that point in her thoughts, she emerged into a bright open space at the top of the stairs. William was at a workbench, but he'd obviously heard her coming, and he looked at her with a question in his bright blue eyes.

She took a breath, trying to think how best to start. "So this is where you spend your time." She glanced around the room, its worktables home to various pieces of William and Caleb's craftsmanship: rocking chairs, a quilt rack, a child's doll cradle.

"J-ja." William put down the wooden handle he'd been holding. "W-what d-do you want, Hannah?"

She didn't think he'd meant to be rude by the abrupt question. He'd figured out how to say things in the shortest way possible—that was all.

She took another breath. Just get it out.

"I wanted to ask you something, but I think I have to explain a little bit first." She touched her fingertips to the workbench, as if that would help. "Before I was married, when I was in college, I studied speech therapy."

She hesitated. He understood, she was sure. As Aunt Paula had said, William was bright enough.

"Anyway, I should say that I didn't finish school, so I'm not really a qualified speech therapist, but—"

"W-why?" he asked, his gaze steady on her face.

"Why didn't I finish?" The question had thrown her off her stride. "I . . . Well, I met Travis Conroy." She tried to smile. "We fell in love and got married, but he was transferred to another army base, so I had to drop out of school to go with him."

"I'm s-s-sorry. A-about your husband." The sympathy in his face was so great that it was almost like a touch.

Her throat tightened. Maybe eventually she'd get over that reaction to sympathy, but not yet.

"Thank you." She shook her head slightly. "I suppose everyone in town knows about me, don't they? That my husband was killed in the war in Afghanistan, I mean?"

"Maybe n-not everybody," he said.

The flicker of humor surprised her into a smile. "I guess that sounded self-centered, didn't it? Well, anyway, even though I don't have a degree, I do know a little about working with people who stutter. And I wondered if I could help you."

William's face tightened into immobility. He had to have guessed where she was headed with this conversation, but he still seemed unprepared for the direct offer. He didn't say anything, and the very silence pushed her into speech again.

"I'm sure you could find someone more qualified if you were willing to travel to a bigger town, but I'm here in Pleasant Valley. Aunt Paula suggested it, and I know she wouldn't mind letting me off work a few hours a week to help you. While Jamie is napping in the afternoon, for instance, if that would work for you."

She had the feeling she was starting to babble, but his continued silence unnerved her. She couldn't tell what he was thinking, whether he was upset by the suggestion, or—

"D-denke," he said. He stared down at his hands, braced on the worktable, frowning a little. "I d-d-don't k-know if that's a g-gut idea."

She'd thought she might be relieved if William turned her down. Then she would have made the offer but wouldn't have to follow through. Instead she wanted to bombard him with arguments to persuade him.

"Do you think I wouldn't be able to help you? Is that it? I can't guarantee anything, of course, but most stutterers can be helped by therapy. Even learning a few techniques might make it easier for you to express yourself."

His lips pressed firmly together. It was almost as if—

"Don't you want to speak more easily?" The question was out before she realized that some might consider it unfeeling.

William shrugged, not looking at her. She recognized the gesture. When she and her classmates had helped in an after-school program at a community center, there'd been one teenager who'd reacted in just that way. They never had gotten through to him.

She didn't want that to happen with William. The depth of her feeling surprised her. She hardly knew him, and she'd tried to get out of offering assistance. But when it looked as if she'd get her wish, she knew just how much she wanted to help him.

Hannah put her hand on his sleeve, feeling the warmth and strength of the muscles beneath the fabric.

"I'm sorry, William. I shouldn't have said that. Look, let's leave it for now. If you decide you want my help, just let me know. Otherwise, I won't bother you about it."

Still he didn't speak. She turned away. That was that, it seemed. She hadn't wanted to do it anyway. So why was she so upset?

When Hannah had gone, William lingered in the workshop. He'd have to face Caleb's and Katie's questions soon enough, but not yet.

What was wrong with him? Why hadn't he responded to Hannah's offer? It was a simple matter to say yes or no. Even he could manage that.

He hadn't known what to say, and that was the truth. All this time he'd been pleased by her attention when he'd gone into the bakery. It looked as if what he'd thought was interest in him was actually interest in his stutter.

Foolishness on his part anyway, to think an Englisch woman could be attracted to him. No good could come of that. He wasn't one who could leave his faith behind because of a woman.

The bell on the door downstairs rang, followed by a familiar voice. Isaac. Ready or not, he headed down the stairs.

Isaac glanced at him as he greeted Caleb and Katie. Then he nodded toward the door. "I saw that Englisch woman, Hannah Conroy, leaving. Must be hard on Paula, having her close blood relative be a woman like that."

The careless words were like a slap. Before William could respond, Katie had planted herself in front of Isaac.

"What exactly do you mean, Isaac? A woman like what?"

Katie's cheeks were flying red flags, and any smart man would know that meant danger. Katie wasn't one to stand for what she would be sure to call foolishness, and unkind besides.

Isaac looked startled at a female calling him to order. "Well, I just meant it's obvious she's not Mennonite anymore."

"That doesn't mean she's not a perfectly fine woman." Katie's voice was crisp.

If William looked at Caleb, he'd probably see laughter in his eyes, so for the sake of family peace, he'd not risk it. Anyway, Katie was handling Isaac better than anyone had in a long time.

"Ja, well, I wouldn't know. Just seems to me that Paula must be feeling bad, her niece not being in the faith, and married to a soldier, too." He shook his head. "Well, knowing Hannah's parents, I'm not surprised."

"W-w-what about th-them?" William hadn't realized his oldest brother would be of an age to remember Hannah's parents.

"Elizabeth was a pretty girl, for sure." Isaac leaned on the counter, back to being sure of himself. "But spoiled. The baby of the family, the girl coming along after a bunch of boys. As for John Zercher—well, he was a fence-jumper from the day he was born."

"Amish, wasn't he?" Caleb frowned, as if trying to remember. "Were they the family that moved out to Ohio after the parents died?"

"Ja, that's them. John was always trying to get away with things. His parents probably breathed a sigh of relief when he was safely married, even though he went up to the Mennonites to do it. And then just when folks thought he was settled, he goes off to the city with his wife and daughter."

"Did Hannah and her mother want to go?" Katie's expression was one of instinctive sympathy.

Isaac shrugged. "They must have, since they stayed away." He shook his head. "What am I doing, standing here gossiping about old times? I came in to remind William that I need him tomorrow, and maybe the next day, too." He glanced at Caleb. "Hope that's not an inconvenience."

Katie looked as if she were about to speak again, but Caleb beat her to it.

"Seems to me that is for William to decide." He folded his arms across his chest, looking at William.

"Ach, I don't need to think twice about that." Isaac clapped William on the shoulder. "William's always ready to help me out. He hasn't forgotten what he owes his family. Or how I stood by him when he was so foolish over Rachel."

William's stomach clenched as if he'd been hit, but he managed to keep his face expressionless. Isaac would bring that up, of course, as if William needed help remembering. He'd thought himself in love with Rachel, his other brother's widow, and he'd done a lot of foolish things while trying to show her how he felt.

Rachel was married to Gideon Zook now, but she still behaved as if he were the little brother he'd always been. She and Gideon had long since forgiven him, as had everyone else. Except, maybe, himself.

"Well, I must get on home." Isaac's hand tightened on William's shoulder. "I'll see you at supper."

He nodded. There was nothing else to say.

Katie didn't seem to agree. The moment the door had closed behind Isaac, she let out an exasperated noise.

"Ach, William, I hate the way you let Isaac boss you around. When are you going to stand up to him?"

Caleb touched her lightly. "That's not up to us, ain't so?" He glanced at William. "Did Hannah have a project she wanted us to work on?"

"N-no. N-n-not exactly." He paused, but there was no reason not to tell them. And he could trust Caleb to give him good advice. "She kn-knows a lot about s-stuttering. Studied it in school, I g-guess. Offered to h-help me."

"Is that so? Are you going to do it?" Caleb leaned forward, face interested.

William looked away, shrugging.

"Well, are you?" Caleb asked.

"Sounds like a wonderful idea," Katie added. "How nice of her to think of it."

William held his silence for a few minutes. "I . . . I d-don't think so."

"Why not?" Katie demanded, heedless of Caleb's hand on her arm.

"Just d-don't feel r-right about it. Folks might t-talk." And Hannah, like Rachel, was an older woman with a family already. He didn't need to make that mistake again.

"I wouldn't refuse on that account," Caleb said mildly. "But it's up to you." He gave Katie a quelling look when she seemed about to argue.

William shrugged again. "I'm supposed t-to let her know. But I d-don't think so."

He headed for the stairs. He'd go back to the workshop and lose himself in the new quilt rack design he was developing. That was the best thing for him.

But he couldn't help hearing Katie's remark as he went up the stairs.

"It's too bad he won't do it. Getting over his stuttering would be a good thing if it gave William enough of a voice to stand up to Isaac."

Chapter Three

Supper on Saturday was a relaxing time at Aunt Paula's. The bakery was closed on Sundays, of course, so there was no need to set bread to rise or start making piecrusts.

"There you are, Jamie." Aunt Paula set a bowl on the tray of the wooden highchair she'd borrowed for his use. "See how you like chicken and dumplings."

"He'll make a mess." Hannah was resigned to that by now. Jamie had to learn to feed himself, but his efforts didn't make a pretty sight.

"Ach, that's fine," Paula said, sliding into her chair. She bowed her head for a silent prayer.

Hannah followed suit, reaching out to pat Jamie when he started to bang his spoon on the tray. To her surprise, he actually got quiet, only to resume the pounding when the prayer ended.

"Enough," Hannah said. She took the spoon away.

"This is for eating with. See?" She lifted a bite of dumpling with the spoon and advanced it toward his mouth.

Jamie turned his head away, pressing his lips together.

"Komm, now," Aunt Paula said. "This is gut stuff." She broke off a piece of dumpling. When he turned at the sound of her voice, she popped it into his mouth.

His threatened wail turned into an expression of pleased surprise, and he took a fistful of dumpling and shoved it into his mouth.

Aunt Paula chuckled. "You see? Gut, ja?"

"Who wouldn't like this?" Hannah took a forkful of soft dumpling and tender chicken. She had fallen into the habit of eating quickly, knowing that Jamie's patience for a relaxed supper would be short-lived, but a meal like this deserved more attention.

"Don't you hurry yourself with eating," Aunt Paula said. "Tonight I will give Jamie his bath and get him ready for bed, all right? You can have a little break."

"You don't need to do that. You work so hard all week, you should—"

"But it will give me pleasure," Aunt Paula said, interrupting. Her eyes softened when they rested on Jamie, who seemed to be trying to see how much he could fit in his mouth at once. "It has always been a sorrow to me, having no children, knowing there would never be grandchildren to love." She shook her head, her cheeks flushing. "You'll think me foolish, talking like this, but having you and Jamie here . . . well, it makes me happy."

Hannah wiped her eyes. "You'll have us both crying in a minute. I just wish . . ." She stopped, not sure she wanted to reveal her thoughts.

"What?" Aunt Paula paused, spoon poised over the bowl of freshly made applesauce.

"Do you know that Travis's father hasn't seen Jamie since the funeral? He was only three months old then." She tried to keep the pain from her voice. "I know he and

Travis had their differences, and Robert does live clear across the country. But you'd think he'd want more than the pictures I send. His wife passed away when Travis was a teenager, so Jamie is his only family."

Aunt Paula put out a hand toward Jamie, almost as if wanting to protect him. "It makes no sense to me at all. Surely the quarrel between him and his son was buried with Travis."

"You'd think so, wouldn't you? Maybe it's not that. Maybe he's just not interested."

"You've done all you can." Aunt Paula smiled at Jamie. "That poor man is the loser. Nobody could look at this precious boy and not love him."

"I think you might be prejudiced," she teased, but the instant bond that had formed between Paula and Jamie was precious to her. She'd had nightmares sometimes, in those early months of Jamie's life, thinking about what would become of Jamie if something happened to her.

Jamie had family now, thanks to Aunt Paula. Hannah's throat tightened. Paula didn't ask anything in return for her kindness and support. But Hannah knew one thing that would make her happy, if she could bring herself to do it.

She cleared her throat, trying to find a way to bring up the subject. "I was thinking . . . remembering, I guess. About Mammi, and the day she told me what the prayer kapp means." She tried to smile. "I couldn't have been much more than six or seven, sitting in the bedroom watching her fix her hair."

Aunt Paula nodded, eyes growing misty. "Elizabeth had beautiful hair. When she was little I'd brush it for her. I remember when she first started wearing the kapp. She was so pleased, thinking it made her look like a grown-up woman."

"I'm glad you have some happy memories of her," Hannah said softly.

"I wish . . ." Paula stopped, sighing. "Well, there is no

point in wishing to undo the past. I could not keep my baby sister with me forever."

"No, I guess not." Paula couldn't have prevented their going away, even though it grieved her. But if they'd stayed, if Mammi had had family and religion and tradition to rely on, maybe she would not have slipped so far into the depression, where no one could reach her.

"I don't mean to make you sad." Aunt Paula reached across the table to pat Hannah's hand. "Now, what were you saying about the kapp?"

It was a small thing to do, wasn't it? And it would make Aunt Paula happy.

"I was thinking that perhaps I should go back to wearing one. If you think it appropriate."

Aunt Paula beamed. "Appropriate? Ja, of course. Women in more progressive churches than ours wear them with Englisch dress." She sobered, looking at Hannah searchingly. "But don't think I'm pushing you to do this, my Hannah. It's for you to decide."

"I know. And I have decided." She touched a stray strand ruefully. "But it's a job to keep my hair back. I don't want to look foolish."

"There's nothing foolish about it. It's a sign of devotion. Now, I can lend you some kapps, for sure. But it would be wonderful gut if we could make some for you." Aunt Paula's mind seemed to be racing, but the thoughts clearly pleased her. "Why don't you walk down to Katie's shop after supper? She carries the organdy for kapps and will know just what you need. We can work on it after Jamie is in bed."

"Katie won't be open, will she?" Hannah bent to rescue the spoon Jamie had thrown on the floor.

"No, but she and her sister always stay on Saturday to make sure everything is cleaned up and ready for the next week. I'm sure she'll be happy to see you. And Jamie and I will have a nice little time together."

It was fairly obvious that Paula wanted some time

alone with Jamie. Hannah's heart warmed. Jamie might be missing a father and grandparent, but he did have people who loved him.

As she walked down Main Street, Hannah realized she had another goal besides getting the material for her prayer coverings.

Katie and Caleb seemed to be close to William. Perhaps he'd told them about her offer to help with his stammer. Maybe Katie would have some insight into William's attitude.

His reaction had unsettled Hannah. In fact, it still did.

William had shut her out. That look of reserve sat strangely on his open, friendly face, but maybe it shouldn't have surprised her. She'd realized that he might have been embarrassed, even hurt at her directing so much attention to what he probably saw as a defect. If she'd hurt him— well, she'd have to find some way to make amends.

She frowned a little, thinking about that conversation. Why on earth had she told him so much about her marriage? She'd never intended that, but somehow the words had slipped out. Maybe she'd mistaken William's silence for empathy.

The sign on the quilt shop door had been turned to Closed, but she could see figures moving inside. She knocked, hoping Aunt Paula had been right.

"Hannah," Katie exclaimed, pulling the door wide. "This is nice, for sure. Komm." Her hand swept in a welcoming gesture.

"I hope you don't mind that I've come by after you're closed. Aunt Paula seemed to think it wouldn't be a problem, but . . ."

"Paula is right, as always, and I'm happy to see you. Here is my sister Rhoda, who helps me in the shop."

The girl who smiled and nodded must have been about sixteen or seventeen. She wore the sober Amish dress, but her face was pert and lively, making Hannah wonder how many young Amish hearts she'd be breaking.

"What can we do for you?" Katie asked. "Were you wanting some fabric?"

"That's it. I need to make some prayer coverings—or rather, I should say that Aunt Paula will teach me how to make them. I haven't worn one since I was nine, and I certainly don't remember how to make them."

She touched the clasp that held her hair at the nape of her neck. Would an Amish woman find it odd that she proposed to wear a prayer covering? Or even be offended? In the face of Aunt Paula's enthusiasm, she hadn't even considered that.

But Katie didn't seem to find it odd, and Rhoda was already pulling out a bolt of white fabric.

"Ach, that's right." Katie led the way to the counter. "I was forgetting that you were once a part of the community. You are coming home, ain't so?"

"I guess I am." That was certainly how her aunt thought about it.

Hannah wasn't so certain. She remembered this life more and more, the longer she stayed. But it still seemed distant to her, as if the sometimes bitter years that followed had created an impassable barrier.

Katie was measuring the fabric with a practiced hand. "How many kapps were you wanting to make?"

"Just give me enough fabric for three." If she needed more, she could come back. And if she found wearing a kapp too uncomfortable . . . well, that would disappoint her aunt more than if Hannah had never brought it up.

Trying to distract herself, she glanced around the shop while Katie cut the fabric. Colorful quilts and table runners glowed from every available surface, and the rows of fabric bolts tempted even someone as inept with a needle as she was.

"The shop is wonderful. I love your quilts."

Katie's cheeks flushed with pleasure. "Denke. My

mother has a quilt shop back home, and this was always my dream."

"You've certainly made your dream a reality. Back home? You're not from Pleasant Valley, then?"

Katie shook her head. "Columbia County. I'd been here a number of times to visit my cousins, and when the opportunity came to open my shop, I thought I'd stay. And then I got to know Caleb, and that was even more of a reason to stay." Katie's face seemed to glow with love as she glanced toward the shop on the other side of the archway.

It was dark, Hannah realized. "Caleb isn't working late, like you?" Or did she really want to ask about William?

"Not tonight. Rhoda and I went to have supper with him and his mother, but we needed to clear up a bit once we got back."

"Katie has several quilt groups and classes that meet here," Rhoda said. "Do you like to quilt?"

Hannah smiled, taking the bag Katie held out to her. "I'm afraid I don't have time for it, with my work at the bakery and a baby to take care of."

"Katie said you have a little boy." Rhoda's eyes sparkled. "I love babies. If you need anyone to watch him sometime, I'd love it."

"Thanks. That's good to know." Though where she'd go that she'd need a sitter, she couldn't imagine. Even if she could afford to hire one.

With an inward shudder she thought of the last sitter she'd hired to watch Jamie while she worked. The woman had come with wonderful references, but Hannah had quickly discovered that she left Jamie to cry in his crib while she watched daytime television. Hannah still had nightmares about Jamie crying and no one coming.

"Anytime," Rhoda said. She glanced at her sister. "I'll finish the back room, ja?"

"Sounds gut." Katie waited until her sister had disappeared through a door at the back. "She really is fine with kinder. You could trust her. But I think you did not come just to buy fabric or to talk about my sister."

The kindness and understanding in Katie's eyes were reassuring. Hannah nodded.

"You've guessed, then. I was worried that I had offended William earlier. I thought you would know."

"Ja, he told us about your offer to help him with his stammer. That was ser kind of you, and I don't think he was offended."

"But he didn't say yes," Hannah pointed out.

Katie hesitated, as if choosing her words. "It seemed to me that William wanted to accept. For sure, Caleb and I think it a fine idea. But William . . . he seems to be afraid it might set people talking."

Hannah blinked. That was certainly the last reason she'd expected. "But why? It's not as if we'd be doing anything wrong. I would just work with him in the afternoon, when Jamie was napping."

She wasn't sure whether to laugh or be upset. Did William think her offer was a means of flirting with him?

"Ach, you don't need to tell me there would be nothing wrong. Or William either, for that matter. But . . ." She hesitated and then shook her head. "You will not understand unless I tell you a bit more about William."

Hannah would think that William, of all people, would have a life like an open book. "If it's something private—"

"I'm sure most people in the valley know of it, though Will probably wishes they didn't." Katie shook her head as if exasperated with herself. "It's this way, you see. There was a brother between Isaac and William, and when he died in an accident, it was natural for William to start helping his widow, Rachel, and her kinder. Maybe natural, too, that he grew to think himself in love with her."

Hannah hadn't expected that. "If they loved each other, surely—"

"William is several years younger than Rachel, you see. I wasn't here at the time, but Rachel is a friend, and she has told me about it. She loved him like a brother, not like a man." She shook her head, smiling slightly. "And William was young and foolish. He did some things . . . oh, nothing bad. Just some little accidents, so that he could come to the rescue and Rachel would see how much she needed him. Foolish, as I say, and when it came out, William was mortified and ashamed. He had to confess to the church, even."

"It must have been so hard on him. And on Rachel, for that matter." Hannah tried to imagine the shame William must have felt.

"Ja. They are friends now, and Rachel is married again. But still, I think William is sensitive about what happened. Maybe he fears that if people see him getting close to another older woman . . ." Katie spread her hands wide. "Well, you can understand. Someone with more confidence than William wouldn't give it a second thought, I'm sure, but because of his stammer, he does."

"I understand. I don't want to do anything that would make his life more difficult."

Katie reached across the counter to pat Hannah's hand, and for a moment they seemed to be allies. Friends. "I'd like to see William get over these feelings. I'll do what I can to persuade him to say yes."

"Thank you." But given the pain that was behind William's reasons, Hannah doubted anything would work.

"This is a gut thing you're offering," Katie said. "Don't give up on him."

"I won't." She smiled at Katie, feeling the understanding between them.

At least one good thing had come out of her effort. It seemed she'd found a friend.

Amish worship on Sunday morning had been at Rachel and Gideon Zook's barn, and William had lingered after the lunch to help with the cleanup and spend a little time with his nieces and nephew.

Worship sometimes left him feeling a bit unsettled, and today had been one of those days. He couldn't help but notice, when he sat in worship, that most of the boys he'd grown up with now wore the beards of married men. They'd also been baptized, so that they were full members of the church.

But not him. Most folks decided to be baptized when they were ready to marry, and he had never been at that point. Not that he couldn't have asked to be baptized anyway, but somehow the time had never seemed right. If he were baptized into the church, maybe then he'd feel as if he weren't on the outside looking in, but that seemed a poor reason for making such a serious decision.

"That's the last of them," Gideon said, and he swung shut the door of the wagon that carried benches from house to house or barn to barn for worship every other Sunday. "Denke, William."

"G-gut to have it d-done, ja?" Most folks liked hosting worship, but felt relief at knowing their turn wouldn't come around again for a year.

"For sure," Gideon said. "Maybe Rachel will stop her cleaning now. She even wanted to shine every window in the greenhouses."

"L-looks fine." Rachel had started with one small greenhouse for her plants, but her business had gone well and now there were two.

"I did that, Onkel Will." Joseph, Rachel's boy, had approached in time to hear what his stepfather had said. "I shined every window. Even the high ones."

"You're g-getting so big you'll soon d-do it without a ladder."

He smiled at the boy, but with a small pang in his heart. Joseph was almost nine now, and it seemed he looked more like his daad each year that passed. In his blue shirt and black vest, he was a replica of Ezra dressed for worship at that age.

"You did a fine job, Joseph," Gideon said, snatching

off Joseph's straw hat to ruffle his fine hair, and then plop-
ping it back on again. "You made your mamm happy."

Joseph, who had a tender heart, looked gratified at
that, and he leaned against Gideon for a moment.

It was a fine thing, that Gideon was so close to his
stepchildren. Fine, too, that he always made William feel
he was still part of the family. Some men would not be so
generous.

"I'm going to check on my goats," Joseph announced.
"And Mammi said to tell you there's more lemonade on the
porch. You'll see the goats before you go, Onkel Will, ja?"

"For sure," William said, turning to follow Gideon toward the house.

"Stay and have supper after the rest of the folks leave,"
Gideon urged. "The kinder want to spend time with you."

"D-denke." They passed a small knot of men, Isaac
included, still talking. "Y-y-you are g-g-gut to include m-
me." His tongue always seemed to get tangled when he
tried to say what he felt. "D-denke."

Gideon seemed to understand what he was trying to
say. "I love them," he said simply. "How could I be jealous
of someone who loves them, too?"

"S-some would."

Gideon shook his head. "Then I'd feel sorry for them,
to be so selfish."

Rachel came out on the porch, carrying the baby, and
Gideon's face lit up. He covered the distance in one long
stride and tickled his son under the chin. Josiah chuckled,
the sound surprisingly deep for a baby. Gideon looked at
Rachel and a message seemed to pass between them,
something that didn't need words. He went on into the
house, leaving William with Rachel.

"Josiah, here is Onkel William." Rachel bounced the
boppli and then plopped him in William's arms.

He automatically tightened his grip on the fat little
bundle. "Not r-really h-his onkel," he said.

"Don't talk so foolish." Rachel's soft smile took any

sting from the words. "You are my little bruder, just like always. You know that, don't you?"

His heart warmed. "Ja."

"Is something wrong?" A small line appeared between her eyes.

He shrugged. Sitting on the porch rail, he bounced the boppli on his knee, and Josiah squealed. "Just b-busy."

Rachel nodded. "I heard Isaac's been working you a lot lately. Is it causing trouble with Caleb?"

"Caleb's f-fine. I just w-wish . . ." He let that die away, because there was no point in it.

"You'd like to be working full-time with Caleb, wouldn't you? I know Caleb would like that, too. He's always saying what gut work you do." Rachel usually seemed able to guess what he was thinking. "Why don't you tell Isaac that?"

He shrugged again, not wanting to say anything that sounded like a criticism of his brother.

"Isaac is a gut man," Rachel said carefully. "I could never forget how he helped me when I needed it. But I would not let him decide what my life should be."

No, Rachel wouldn't do that. Gentle and peaceable as she was, Rachel had stood firm against Isaac's plan for her to sell the farm to his son. Maybe she had more courage than he did.

"H-he's my b-brother. I l-live in his house. I w-want to help." Even if sometimes Isaac was telling him to do a chore that one of the boys could as easily attend to.

"Caleb says you have a gift as a carpenter." Rachel put a gentle hand on his arm. "If that's so, maybe that's what God wants you to do. And maybe Isaac needs to see that your work is important, too." She patted him as she would one of the children. "You deserve your own dreams, William. Don't forget that."

CHAPTER FOUR

You were such a gut boy this morning." Aunt Paula patted Jamie's cheek as Hannah lifted him into the stroller after church.

"He was, wasn't he?" Hannah couldn't help the relief in her voice. A two-hour service felt long to her even for the adults, but apparently not to people who were raised to it. The other toddlers were mostly content to sit quietly on their mothers' laps, but Jamie seemed born to squirm. Still, today had been the best yet.

Around them, people in Plain dress filed out of the simple white frame churchhouse where Pleasant Valley's Mennonite population worshipped. Many stopped to exchange greetings with them.

Was Hannah imagining it, or were the smiles a bit warmer today? Perhaps Aunt Paula wasn't the only person who was relieved because she was wearing a proper prayer covering.

She waited until they'd walked out of earshot of the

congregation before she spoke. "When I came to worship without a kapp . . . did other people think I was disrespectful?"

"Of course not." Her aunt said the words quickly, but she also glanced away just as quickly. Then she shrugged. "I don't know. Some, maybe, but that's forgotten already. After all, you haven't been baptized into the church."

No, she hadn't. She hadn't even considered herself a Mennonite since she'd been ten or eleven.

Her aunt had made her and Jamie welcome here. She'd hate to think that had cost Paula in any way.

Or maybe she'd be more honest with herself if she admitted that she hadn't considered that aspect of the situation. She'd been so worried about providing a home for Jamie, and so relieved by Aunt Paula's invitation . . .

"If it's been awkward for you with the church, having me here, I'm sorry."

Aunt Paula patted her hand where it wrapped around the stroller handle. "Don't be foolish. Most people understand. And they all rejoice with me that you are back where you belong."

The love in Aunt Paula's voice was unmistakable. But so was the sense of finality. As far as she was concerned, having Hannah here was like having her little sister back. She was picturing Hannah and Jamie here for life.

A flicker of panic brushed Hannah's nerves, and she took a deep, steadying breath. She'd been honest with Aunt Paula up front, hadn't she? She'd told her that first evening that this was only a temporary solution to her problems. That when Jamie was old enough, she'd have to go back to the outside world. How else could she raise him the way his father would have wanted?

Maybe adopting the kapp had been a mistake. Hannah had thought only to fit in, to please her aunt, maybe to honor the person her mother had once been. But if Aunt Paula took that to mean she intended to stay for good—

Love could trap you in a difficult situation, with no

way out unless you were willing to hurt someone. She knew that well enough. Her father had reached that point, and she'd never forget the pain she'd felt when she'd realized that he wasn't coming back.

"A fall Sunday is a fine thing," Aunt Paula said, smiling at the wooden barrels filled with chrysanthemums on the walk outside the gift shop. "Peaceful."

"It is." Hannah forced herself to respond in what she hoped was a normal tone. "It's still warm enough for summer most days, though."

Pleasant Valley seemed to doze in the slanting autumn sunshine. The shops were closed for the most part, with even the Englisch merchants following the custom of their Amish and Mennonite neighbors.

Peaceful was the right word. In the places she'd lived in recent years, it had been hard to tell which day was the Sabbath.

Her aunt picked up a mum blossom that had been broken off. She tickled Jamie's chin with it. He made a grab for the russet flower and promptly tried to stick it in his mouth.

"No, no, little man." Aunt Paula handed him the soggy teething biscuit he'd been chewing on. "Flowers are not for eating."

"He'll taste a few more before he figures that out," Hannah said.

She'd grown philosophical about the things that found their way into a toddler's mouth. Once Jamie had started to walk, it had become impossible to protect him from everything his chubby fingers wanted to explore.

But there were bigger dangers from which she did have to protect him, and the panic she'd experienced when she was alone in the world with a child stirred again. She hadn't felt it in over a month. She'd gotten used to the sense of security that surrounded her here. But she couldn't let that need for security push her into making the wrong decision.

The telephone was ringing when they reached the top of the stairs at the apartment. Aunt Paula gave the instrument a frowning glance, and Hannah had no trouble reading her thoughts. No one would call her aunt on a Sunday unless it was an emergency.

"I'll get it." Hannah moved quickly to silence the ringing, picking up the receiver. "This is Paula Schatz's house," she said.

"Hannah? Is that you?" A light voice with the hint of a Southern drawl . . . it was Megan Townsend, Hannah's best friend and constant support when their husbands had been deployed. But Megan's husband had come back.

"Megan. It's so nice to hear your voice." Hannah glanced at Aunt Paula. Her aunt nodded, gesturing toward the kitchen.

"I'll get Jamie something to eat," she said. "You visit with your friend."

"I was beginning to think you'd fallen off the face of the earth," Megan exclaimed. "Where have you been?" The urgency in her tone suggested that Hannah had vanished into the Sahara.

"I'm right here in Pennsylvania with my aunt, remember?"

Smiling, she settled into the rocking chair. Hearing Megan's voice reminded her of countless times when Megan had overreacted to the smallest incident and Hannah, by nature less volatile, had had to talk her down.

"Well, obviously, since I called this number. But I must have sent you a hundred e-mails and texts, and you haven't responded to a single one."

"I'm sorry." She should have realized that would be Megan's preferred method of contacting her. "I should have told you that my aunt doesn't have an Internet connection."

"Well, you get one, sugar." Megan must be relaxing because she'd dropped into her drawl. "It won't cost that much, and you have to have some way to stay in touch."

"I can't." She tried to think how to explain her aunt's church ban on the Internet and didn't come up with anything Megan would understand. "It is her house, and she wouldn't like it."

She'd lowered her voice, hoping it didn't carry into the kitchen. Since Jamie seemed to be banging the high chair tray with his spoon, that probably didn't matter.

"Old-fashioned, is she?" Megan arrived at her own conclusion. "There must be an Internet café someplace."

Sure, if she wanted to go all the way to Lewisburg. "This is a small town, remember? A really small town."

Megan chuckled, the sound a warm memory of all the afternoons they'd sat talking while their children played. "All right, I get you. Probably like the town in Georgia where my grandmamma lives. No movie theater and a bowling alley that closes at eleven."

"Not even a bowling alley. And I wouldn't have time to bowl if we had one."

"Is that aunt of yours working you too hard?" Megan's tone sharpened a little. "You know you can always come back here and stay with us if you don't like it there."

Hannah's heart clutched at the thought. Life on an army base had been, oddly enough, similar in some ways to living in Pleasant Valley. They'd all been in the same boat, and they'd supported each other.

But that had ended for her when Travis died, and she couldn't go back.

"Nothing like that." She put some energy into her voice, almost feeling Megan's concern through the phone, as if she sat next to her. "My aunt is the kindest person in the world. But working in the bakery and watching a toddler at the same time takes all my attention, believe me. Now that Jamie is walking, I can't take my eyes off him for a minute."

"My goodness, you ought to see the twins." That deflected Megan, as Hannah had known it would. "Cindy's walking all over the place, and Becca refuses to try. Thinks she can get where she wants to go by crawling faster, I guess. Yesterday she pulled every single thing off the end table. Lucky she didn't knock herself in the head with it."

"Did she get hurt at all?" Hannah could tell the baby hadn't by the half-laughing tone of Megan's voice.

"Not a scratch. She sat there laughing until she saw me, and then she crawled away as fast as those fat little knees would move."

Hannah laughed with her. She and Megan had gotten through their pregnancies together, shared tears over colic and fears over fevers, helped each other through every step. Megan was the closest friend she'd ever had, and she missed her.

"I wish I could see all of you," she said impulsively.

"Come for a visit," Megan said promptly. "Your aunt can get along without you for a week, can't she?"

"She could, but I couldn't." Hannah's throat tightened, her voice went husky. "I'm not ready to be back on the base. You understand."

Megan gave a wordless murmur of sympathy. "Well, then, I guess I'll have to come to you."

"You what?" She'd never thought . . .

"Come to see you," Megan said. "Listen, I deserve a break, don't I? Just give me some time to set it up and then get ready for fun, girlfriend. I'm coming to see this new life of yours for myself."

By the time she hung up, Hannah was finally convinced that Megan meant it. She'd really come. Hannah suspected she'd be walking around with a silly grin on her face for days.

But there was an edge to her excitement. Megan was a friend, a good friend. Hannah touched the prayer kapp on her hair. But could Megan possibly understand the life Hannah was living now?

She shook off the unwelcome thought. Megan would understand. Or if she didn't, she'd accept. That was the kind of friendship they had.

She went back into the kitchen, and Aunt Paula glanced up from giving Jamie his snack. She obviously expected to hear about the call.

Privacy was a missing element here. Hannah knew her aunt's curiosity arose from love, but she wasn't used to sharing quite so much. Sometimes the sense that other people knew so much about her made her uneasy. There was something to be said for the anonymity of a city.

"That was my friend Megan, calling to see how we are."

"Ja, you mentioned her before, I think. She is the one who has twins?"

Hannah nodded. "Girls, just a little older than Jamie. We were pregnant at the same time, so we've been through plenty. And Megan has a little boy who's five, so she was the one I turned to when I needed advice." She smiled. "Which was often. It's tough to read an answer in a book when you're juggling a crying baby."

"And all on your own." Aunt Paula wiped applesauce from Jamie's face. "That must be so hard, not having family around to help."

"Living on an army base was almost like having family." Hannah suspected she sounded a bit defensive. "People did look out for each other."

"I'm glad." Paula's face clouded. "If your mammi had been alive . . ." She let that trail off, shaking her head.

Hannah tried to dismiss a flicker of irritation. Paula was still remembering the little sister she loved, and maybe forgetting the woman she'd turned into.

Hannah poured milk in Jamie's sippy cup, gave it to him, and lifted him in her arms. "Nap time, sweetheart."

He leaned his head against her shoulder.

Some of Hannah's excitement over Megan's visit had slipped away, and she tried to regain it. "Megan had some good news for me," she said. "She's making arrangements to come for a visit."

"Here?" Aunt Paula's voice was sharp.

Hannah looked at her in surprise. "Yes. Not right away.

She'll have to work out a time when her husband can be with the children. It'll take some doing, but when Megan is determined, no one can hold out against her." She smiled, remembering.

Aunt Paula turned toward the sink, rinsing a plate with concentrated care. "If she comes, when would that be?"

If?

"Not right away. As I said, she'll have to make arrangements. Are you concerned that it will be a busy time for us? Megan is very adaptable. She won't get in the way."

"Well, but . . . where would we put her? I don't have another bedroom."

"She can share with me. She won't mind." Hannah wanted to see her aunt's face, but Paula kept it averted. Uneasiness sent a ripple down her spine. "Is something wrong?"

Her aunt shrugged. "I chust think that someone like her won't be used to our way of living. She won't like it here."

"Megan is coming to see me. She won't care—" The message in her aunt's stiff figure got through to her. "You don't want her to come, do you?" Obviously she should have asked, not simply announced it.

"It's not that." Aunt Paula's tone was unconvincing. "But how would an outsider fit in here?"

Hannah's breath caught. The fear and uncertainty that hadn't gone far since Travis died swept over her, and the floor was uncertain beneath her feet.

"Haven't I fit in here?"

"That's different. You are not an outsider. You are my niece, coming back where you belong." Aunt Paula shook her head, the lines of her face seeming to deepen. "I thought . . . I hoped . . . you were content here."

"I am. But that doesn't mean I have to forget my friends, does it?" The words came out strangled. Jamie seemed to sense her tension and stirred against her, making a fretful sound that was not quite a cry.

Aunt Paula shook her head. "I suppose not. But I can't help thinking you'd be better off without reminders of that other life." She shrugged, turning away again and busying herself at the sink. "But your friend will be welcome if she comes."

Hannah could only stand there, holding Jamie, feeling as if the few feet between her and her aunt had stretched to a mile, leaving her startled and surprised. And alone.

William had been watching for Hannah from the window of the workshop, trying not to be obvious about it. Caleb probably noticed, but he didn't say anything.

Unless it was raining, Hannah took Jamie for a walk in the stroller before his afternoon nap. Sometimes she went to the right out of the bakery, headed for the post office or the drugstore on an errand. More often she turned to the left, walking to the small playground that overlooked the stream.

He wanted to catch her for a talk, and he'd rather do it where neither his relatives nor hers were around to overhear. Easier said than done, he knew.

Caleb looked up from his work, stretching, and then nodded at the quilt rack William had been working on. "That new design is ser gut. We've sold two in the last week. Too bad the tourist season will end soon. We'd sell a lot more, for sure, if we had the customers coming in."

William nodded, distracted from the window. "If y-you w-won't need me s-so much then—"

"Ach, no, that's not what I meant," Caleb said quickly. "I'd like it fine if you were here full-time. I just wish we had more of an outlet for our business."

Caleb was right. Business would slow down for the shop as the weather grew colder. Stores in the bigger towns around probably weren't so affected. An idea stirred in William's mind, but then it skittered away as he glanced out the window.

There was Hannah, pushing the stroller, headed for the playground. Good. It would most likely be deserted this time of day.

He waited a few minutes just in case Caleb had seen her, too. Then he took a step back from the workbench, stretching as he moved out of the patch of sunlight that poured through the window.

"Think I'll t-t-take a b-break."

"Sure thing." Caleb didn't look up from the chair he was working on. "I'm going to do the same, once I set this glue to dry."

William went quickly down the stairs, smiling at his cousin Becky, who was minding the shop. "B-b-back soon."

Once he was out on the street, he had to force himself to slow down. Might as well give Hannah a chance to get settled, first.

Nothing wrong with giving himself a chance to think about what he was doing, either.

Still, he'd made up his mind, hadn't he? Hannah had offered him a chance that might never come again.

He passed two more shops and came to the grassy stretch that sloped gently down toward the creek, which was shallow at this time of year. The playground was small . . . a swing set, two slides, monkey bars, and a sandbox. But that was enough to keep a child occupied.

Jamie was already in the sandbox. Hannah had said once that it was his favorite. She sat on the edge, where the wooden frame formed a narrow seat, bending forward to talk to Jamie, or maybe encourage his play.

William walked across the grass toward them, trying to plan what he would say. That made it easier, when he could think things out and find the fewest words to use.

Hannah's voice reached him. ". . . I'll figure it out, sweetheart. Mommy will take care of you."

He stopped, realizing she didn't know he was there. Realizing, too, that she probably wouldn't want anyone to hear that.

He stood for a moment, not sure what to do. Jamie pushed a small tractor in the sand, making noises meant to sound like a motor. Hannah had fallen silent, her elbow on her knee, hand cradling her cheek.

He moved again. His shadow must have fallen across her line of vision, and she jerked back, turning her head.

"William. I didn't hear you." She was smiling, but it seemed to him that he could see fresh lines of strain in her face.

He blinked. "Y-you are w-w-wearing a k-kapp."

Nodding, she patted the rough wooden bench. "Join us. Jamie is always glad to see you. Look, Jamie, it's William."

Jamie threw his hands up, spraying sand in all directions. Laughing at him made it easier for William to sit down, keeping a careful space between himself and Hannah.

Hannah gave him a sideways glance. "You're surprised by the kapp, aren't you?"

"A l-little." Actually, a lot. Hannah dressed simply enough, but for sure not Plain. Still, all the different groups of Mennonites had their own traditions.

"I thought . . ." She let that trail off. "I remember my mother telling me about the kapp when I was little. About how it made sure our heads were covered when we wanted to pray." Her lips curved a little, as if that was a nice memory.

"Ja. I r-remember m-my mamm s-saying that t-t-to one of my s-sisters." So much for his planning what he was going to say. This talk had gone in a different direction before he'd even gotten started. "S-so that's why?" He indicated the kapp, white against the rich brown of her hair.

"I guess." She sounded as if there was more, but she didn't go on.

He bent, picking up a plastic horse and sending it galloping toward Jamie's tractor. Jamie giggled and grabbed for it. Rachel used to say, when her kids were this age, that toddlers thought everything they touched belonged to them.

"I thought it would make my aunt happy." Hannah's voice was so soft that she might have been talking to herself. "I didn't realize . . ."

"W-what?" He tried to keep his voice as low as hers, his gaze on Jamie.

Hannah sighed, putting her hand to her cheek again as if to comfort herself. "She thought that meant I would stay, join the church, be what she thinks is best for me."

The words set up an echo in his mind. A lot of people seemed to think they knew what was best for someone else.

"D-don't you w-w-want to?"

Hannah had seemed happy here, and Jamie was thriving. What was in the outside world that made staying here seem impossible?

If he could speak like most folks, he could say all that to her. But he couldn't. He'd have to trust she understood what he was thinking.

He buried his fingers in the sand and then popped them up, making Jamie laugh. He immediately tried to bury his own little hand, and William helped him.

"It's so hard." Hannah almost sounded as if she were talking to herself. "Travis . . . I owe him so much. I have to bring Jamie up the way he would want. He gave his life for his country."

Did she think that the Anabaptist belief in nonviolence was a betrayal of her husband?

She moved slightly, drawing his gaze. "You understand, don't you? I have to bring Jamie up to admire and respect his father's memory."

"J-ja." He did understand. She thought the only way she could be true to her husband's memory was to turn away from her own heritage.

"So I'll have to go sometime." She straightened her slim shoulders, as if preparing to carry a burden. "I'll have to."

"S-sometime," he said. "I h-hope not t-t-too soon. I w-wanted to s-say yes."

Her smile dispelled the clouds. "You're going to let me help you?"

"J-ja. Afternoons okay?"

She nodded, looking as if he'd given her a present, instead of the other way around. "Let's start tomorrow. Say Tuesday and Thursday around two. Will that work?"

"J-ja. Unless I h-h-have to h-help my brother."

He didn't want to tell Isaac he couldn't help on the farm because he was working on his stammer. In fact, it would be better if Isaac didn't know anything about the lessons. He didn't want to be answering a lot of questions about them.

She glanced at him, and he noticed that a strand of brown hair had pulled loose from her bun to curl against her cheek. It made him want to touch it.

"Is Isaac why you want to do this?" she asked quietly.

He shrugged. That was his usual response when he didn't want to talk about something. But maybe that was unfair to Hannah, who was going out of her way to help him when she had troubles enough of her own.

"E-everyone t-tells me what I sh-should be d-doing. S-seems like a grown-up sh-should figure that out h-h-himself."

She stared at him for a long moment, as if his words had struck something in her. "Yes," she said finally. "A grown-up should."

CHAPTER FIVE

The disagreement with Aunt Paula the previous day seemed to have shaken her aunt nearly as much as it had Hannah. All morning they'd been carefully polite to each other, so much so that Naomi had given them a curious look now and then.

Coming back downstairs after settling Jamie for his nap, Hannah clutched the notebook in which she'd designed a simple outline for her first session with William. He'd be arriving soon, but there was one thing yet to be settled.

Aunt Paula glanced at the notebook. "You're ready to start, ja?" She sounded more nearly herself than she had all morning. "This is a gut thing you're doing, Hannah."

"I hope so." She pressed her hand against her midsection, where a troupe of butterflies seemed to be fluttering. "I'm as nervous as if I were facing a final exam."

"You'll do fine." Aunt Paula wiped her hands on her apron and then patted her shoulder. "Have faith."

"I'm trying," she said. "Is it okay if we work upstairs?"

The instant she said the words her aunt's lips tightened, and she knew she'd made a misstep.

"That would not be suitable." Aunt Paula gestured toward the round tables. "Why can't you work here?"

Paula's house, Paula's rules, Hannah reminded herself. Something that would seem perfectly harmless in the outside world wasn't proper in Paula's view.

"I don't think William would be comfortable working with me where anyone looking in the windows might see. If he doesn't relax and feel at ease, we won't get anywhere."

Aunt Paula looked ready to argue the point, but Naomi intervened.

"What about the bakery kitchen?" she asked. "We won't have to go back there this time of day, so you and William can work in peace."

Hannah looked at her aunt. Was their disagreement over Megan's visit going to color everything she wanted to do?

"Ja, that sounds fine." Aunt Paula's expression eased. "Naomi is right."

Hannah shot Naomi a look of thanks. "Great. I'll go and set up." She glanced at the clock. "William should be here in about fifteen minutes. Jamie went down for his nap a little faster than I thought he might."

Naomi smiled. "He tired himself out this morning, I think."

Naomi had brought Jamie a small wooden wagon this morning, one she said her brothers had played with when they were small. Jamie had been entranced, filling it up with blocks, wheeling it around, tipping them out, and then doing it all over again.

"He loves the wagon, all right. That was so kind of you, Naomi." She'd learned that complimenting an Amish person was a tricky thing to do, since they didn't want to appear prideful about something they'd done.

Naomi smiled, ducking her head a little in that typically Amish gesture that might mean almost anything.

William did that, as well, Hannah realized, and the words he'd said yesterday seemed to echo in her mind again. He was struggling his way toward some form of independence.

Still holding the notebook, she walked into the bakery kitchen, which was still warm from the heat of the large ovens. They could sit at the table—a homey, familiar situation, with the comforting aroma of bread-baking still filling the air.

She set the chairs at right angles to each other. The little she'd learned of William's home life, the encounter with his brother Isaac, his stammer . . . those factors certainly suggested that making decisions for himself was a struggle for William.

And what is your excuse? A small voice in the back of her mind voiced what she knew was true. She had done her own share of drifting, of letting others make up her mind for her. Her parents, her teachers, Travis, Megan . . . even Aunt Paula, in a way.

She glanced at the monitor on the counter, its light flickering a little when Jamie moved, rustling the sheets in his crib. She was the only one responsible for Jamie. She had to make decisions for both of them.

Hannah moved restlessly, hands working on the back of the chair. What if she made the wrong decision, the way she had when she'd hired that babysitter? What if she let her son down again?

Travis had been her rock. Now he was gone, and she had been left to go on alone.

Her throat tightened, and she shook her head, impatient with herself. Now was not the time to dwell on her doubts. She had a job to do.

The swinging door moved, and her nerves jumped. It was time—

But it was Aunt Paula, holding a handful of envelopes. The postman must have just come.

Her aunt held out one envelope, her expression clouded. "This just came. For you. It looks like it's from Jamie's grandfather."

Hannah held it for a moment, studying the return address. Arizona, where Robert Conroy had settled after retiring from the army. He wrote so seldom that she couldn't remember the last time she'd seen his handwriting.

"I should leave you alone . . ." Aunt Paula made a movement toward the door.

"No, it's all right. Stay." She stared at the envelope, reluctant to move.

"Aren't you going to open it?" Aunt Paula prompted her.

Hannah blew out a breath. "Yes, of course." Somehow the return address seemed to bring Conroy's stiff, frowning presence into the room. They'd met only twice . . . once when Travis took her to visit after they were married and again at the funeral. Robert hadn't seemed especially approving of her on either occasion.

She ripped open the envelope and unfolded the single sheet she found inside. The note was brief.

I thought you'd want a copy of this. I heard you hadn't been back to the cemetery.

His name was signed in angular black letters that seemed vaguely angry.

She picked up the photo, knowing what it must be and reluctant to see it. She handed the letter to her aunt.

"It's not much of a letter, that's for sure." Aunt Paula sounded miffed, as if the rudeness had been directed at her. "What does he mean?"

Hannah turned over the photo. Smooth, even green grass carpeted the ground, dotted with straight rows of white crosses. She could read the lettering on the one nearest to the camera.

The photo wavered in her fingers, and she thrust it at her aunt.

"It's where Travis is buried." She tried to sound calm, tried to sound like a mature woman who'd dealt with loss and could cope with being left behind.

But inside she knew it wasn't true, and the pep talk she'd been giving herself was a mocking echo in her mind.

He shouldn't have come. William turned to the bakery door, the words repeating themselves in his mind. This was a mistake. Someone would see him, would start to talk.

And they'd remember. Sometimes he thought no one in Pleasant Valley ever forgot anything.

The bell jingled as he opened the door, the familiar sound calming him. After all, what was so unusual in his coming here? He came to the bakery most days, enjoying the welcoming aromas and the sight of the loaves filling wire baskets. No one would think anything of his being there.

The tables were empty at this hour, and no customers lined up in front of the counter. Naomi Esch smiled at him from behind the glass-fronted case that held pastries. "Hannah is back in the kitchen." She nodded toward the swinging door. "Go on in."

Naomi probably knew why he was here, but her face didn't hold any open curiosity. Naomi was a sensible woman, not a blabbermaul like some.

He moved between the tables, pushed open the swinging door, and stepped into the kitchen. And stopped. Paula stood close to Hannah, her arm around the younger woman. Hannah held a paper crumpled in her hand, and her brown eyes were bright with tears.

"Th-this is a b-bad time. I'll g-go." He turned toward the door, relief mixing with pity. Hannah was having trouble, and it seemed as good a reason as any for him to back away from this commitment.

"No, don't." Hannah said the words before he could push the door open. "I'm all right. Please, sit down."

He hesitated, but Paula nodded at him.

"That's right, William. Chust sit now. I'll leave you two alone." She patted Hannah's hand and went quickly back into the bakery.

"You d-don't w-w-want me here—" he began.

"Sit down." Hannah almost snapped the words and then gave him a watery smile. "I'm sorry, William. I am upset, but I'd rather work. It will take my mind off things. Coffee? Iced tea?"

He didn't want anything, but he suspected fixing it would give her a moment to calm herself.

"Ja, tea would be gut."

Hannah turned to the refrigerator, maybe glad of a reason to hide her face for a moment. She took her time over getting out glasses and putting a few cookies on a plate.

William sat in the chair she'd indicated, his gaze drawn by what lay on the table. Even without touching it, he could see what the photograph showed—her husband's headstone. The picture lay next to a torn envelope, which meant she'd just received it. No wonder she was upset.

Hannah put glasses on the table. She picked up the picture, shoving it into the envelope, her fingers fumbling with it.

Questions formed in his mind, but he wasn't going to ask them. He took a long swallow from the glass of tea.

Hannah slipped the envelope into the pocket of her skirt and sat down. Her lips moved in what was probably meant for a smile.

"You know, William, sometimes your silence says a lot."

He wasn't sure how to answer that, so he didn't.

She let out a little sigh, clasping her hands around the glass. "The picture was from my father-in-law. Jamie's grandfather. I . . . I hadn't seen the permanent marker until now."

"I'm s-s-sorry." Seeing it must have brought her grief.

She nodded, moving her glass in little circles on the tabletop. "Travis is buried in a national cemetery. They . . . It was a military funeral. His father had been in the army, too, so he took care of the arrangements."

"It w-was g-g-gut that you h-had h-his help." At least, William thought it would be. But there had been an undertone in Hannah's voice when she said the words. Maybe they had disagreed about the arrangements.

"I think he's upset that I haven't visited the cemetery since then." The words seemed to burst out, as if Hannah couldn't hold them back. "He hardly says two sentences in his note."

William had never met the man. He couldn't even guess at his motives. But this was upsetting Hannah.

He couldn't touch her to comfort her. He'd have to use words, and he wasn't good at that. Inadequate, as always.

"M-maybe he's a m-man of f-f-few w-words. Like me."

A smile tugged at her lips, chasing some of the sorrow away. "Maybe so. Well, that's not why we're here. I'm glad you said yes, William. I'm looking forward to working with you."

If he was going to back out, this was his last chance. But with her gaze hopeful on his face, he couldn't do it. Instead he nodded.

"Right, let's start, then." She opened a notebook that lay on the table. She hesitated, her hands flat on its pages. "I feel as if I ought to say this again. I never finished my studies. I'm not certified, and if you . . ."

He shook his head to stop her. "Y-y-you told m-me before. It's f-f-fine." He wanted to say more, to reassure her, but as always, he didn't have the words. But she was smiling, so maybe she knew.

"Good." She blew out a breath. "Now, I'll bet people have tried to help you by telling you to relax, or take a deep breath, or start over again."

He nodded. He'd heard that plenty of times. He'd tried,

but none of it worked, and he'd ended up feeling like he'd failed.

"I know." She was looking at him with a kind of gentle sympathy in those soft brown eyes. "It just made you feel worse, didn't it? People like that are trying to help. They don't understand that those techniques aren't usually successful."

He looked down at his hands, clasped around the glass. "D-d-does a-anything?"

"Yes, it does. You have to believe that." She reached out and touched his wrist, and the warmth of her fingers startled him. She might be able to feel his pulse thud against her palm.

A moment passed. Hannah's gaze moved, as if she'd lost her place and was looking for it. Then she took her hand away.

"There are some techniques that work with most people who stutter. Not a cure, exactly. Just something to make it easier to say what you want."

He nodded to show he understood, not sure he believed that anything would really help, but willing to try.

"I want you to put your hand on your stomach." She laid her palm against herself to illustrate, and he copied her. "Notice the way you're breathing, small breaths, slow and relaxed."

He listened intently, trying to hear what she'd indicated.

"That's a good way to start lessening the stuttering. It seems odd, because you feel as if you want to take a deep breath to talk. If you keep breathing slow and relaxed, you won't have the breath for long sentences. But you don't want to talk in long sentences anyway, do you?"

She smiled as she asked the question, and he smiled back. Hannah's face was intent, her eyes alight with interest, and it made him feel good to see her that way, after she'd been upset.

This was something she cared about, and it was giving her pleasure to work with him. "Now we're going to practice some breathing exercises, learning to move slowly into the words. Don't be fooled. It's hard work to concentrate," she warned.

Hannah was as good as her word. She led him through the exercises, her voice gentle, praising him sometimes, making him repeat sometimes, but always with that quiet patience.

By the time they'd practiced for an hour, William was as tired as if he'd been cutting hay. He felt as if he needed to duck his head under the pump to clear his mind. He was about to suggest they quit when the small white monitor on the counter came to life with a bit of static and a whimper.

"Mama, Mama, Mama." Something rattled, as if Jamie were shaking the crib bars. "Mama!"

Hannah smiled, closing the notebook. "When he's awake, he wants up. We'll have to stop for today. But I'll see you Thursday?" She made it a question, as if wanting the assurance that he'd be back.

"Ja. D-d-denke." He hesitated, not wanting to say more, but needing to. "Jamie." He jerked his head toward the monitor. "Bringing h-h-him up w-well is the b-b-best memorial to your h-husband."

Hannah's eyes filled with tears, and she blinked several times. "Thank you, William." She whirled and hurried up the stairs.

"*You* have us so curious, Hannah." Aunt Paula peered at her over a forkful of egg salad. "How did it go with William yesterday? You haven't said a word, ain't so?"

Hannah sat with her aunt and Naomi at one of the round tables, having their own meal after the lunch rush was over and Jamie was tucked up for his nap. She hesitated, considering her words. Aunt Paula had contained her curiosity for nearly a full day, but now it was bursting out.

"We made a good start," she said, knowing that wouldn't be enough to satisfy her aunt. "It's much too soon to know how successful we'll be."

"But what did you do? What did William say?" Her aunt's glasses wore a light dusting of flour, but her blue eyes sparkled behind them.

Naomi put down her soup spoon with a little clink. "Maybe it's not right for Hannah to talk about it to us," she said. "Like a doctor wouldn't talk about you to someone else."

Naomi's quiet understanding continued to surprise Hannah.

"Yes, it is something like that," she said, grateful. "One of the first things they teach you before they let you near a client is the importance of privacy. Even a child would be upset if he knew you were talking to someone else about his treatment."

She carefully didn't say the word *gossip*, afraid of offending.

Aunt Paula looked on the verge of objecting, probably to say that working with William had been her idea, after all. But Naomi nipped in again before she could speak.

"It wonders me how people ought to speak to someone like Will. Probably we do all the wrong things, ain't so?"

"That's sometimes true," Hannah said, relieved to turn the talk in that direction. "The most important thing is just to listen in a relaxed way and wait for the person to finish, not try to complete the person's thoughts yourself."

Naomi nodded. "I remember William's sisters always tried to finish his sentences for him when they were younger." She paused, glancing down at what remained of her chicken noodle soup. "He's a gut man. I hope this helps him."

Aunt Paula nodded. "It would be nice to see William taking part in life, instead of watching. It's time he found himself someone to love."

"Ja, it is," Naomi said, punctuating the words with a nod.

Did Naomi see herself in that role? The thought hit Hannah with a disturbing suddenness, and she was dismayed to find herself reacting negatively.

She had no right to feel that way. It wasn't any of her business who was interested in William. Naomi was a lovely person, and she and William shared the same faith. They both seemed lonely, in a way. Surely it would be good if they got together.

Hannah had a feeling she was coming up with too many arguments. She barely knew William, after all.

But he had done something yesterday that more than repaid whatever she might do for him. He'd said that bringing Jamie up right was the best memorial to Travis, and the words had been echoing in her mind ever since.

He was right. She'd had her chance at love, and it had been a wonderful experience. She might grieve how soon it had ended, but in a way, it made her future more clear. Her only job now was Jamie, and he was a full-time occupation.

"Ach, look at the time." Aunt Paula stood, gathering up her used dishes. "We should get busy. And there's the supply order still to do this afternoon."

Hannah noticed the frown lines gathering between her aunt's eyebrows. Aunt Paula always seemed to look harassed when it came time to deal with the supply orders. She seemed to love everything about running the bakery except the paperwork.

"Would you like me to take care of the orders?" Hannah spoke impulsively, and as quickly wondered if her aunt would think she'd presumed too much.

But Paula's face expressed only relief. "You would do the orders for me? Ach, it would be so nice."

"I'd be happy to." It was a simple way to repay her aunt's kindness, and the record-keeping would be easy for her. "I'll double-check the amounts with you before I call the order in. All right?"

"Ja, ser gut." The frown lines had disappeared. Aunt

Paula turned to Naomi. "Naomi, you'll be able to mind the bakery on Saturday, ja? I want to be sure I can take Hannah to the work day."

"That is fine." Naomi rose, too. "I have told my daad already. You will have a gut time together with all the sisters, ja?"

Hannah was a step behind. The other two obviously knew what they were talking about, but she didn't. "Work day?"

"Didn't I tell you about that?" Her aunt tossed the question back over her shoulder as they headed for the kitchen. "I thought I had. We . . . all the women from Pleasant Valley who are interested . . . have one Saturday a month when we meet at the fire hall to work on quilts and other crafts for the benefit auction."

"What is the benefit auction?" It sounded vaguely familiar, but Hannah didn't recall discussing it.

Her aunt glanced at her. "Ach, sometimes I forget you haven't been here forever. The big auctions we have spring and fall for charity. I've told you about that, surely."

"I guess I'd forgotten." Hannah started water running in the sink to wash up their few dishes from lunch. "When is the auction?"

"Next month." Her aunt shook her head in dismay. "I don't know how it's come around again so soon already. I haven't finished half the things I'd intended to make to sell, and the needs are so great this year, with all those tornadoes and then the floods."

Hannah remembered now. Her aunt had talked about the money the community had raised in the spring, and how they'd sent teams out west to help with rebuilding after the tornadoes.

"You said you'd raised a lot of money in the spring sale, didn't you?" She pushed her sleeves back before plunging her hands into the hot, soapy water.

"Ja, for sure, but it's never enough. The Mennonite Central Committee has been swamped with appeals this year, so I've heard." Aunt Paula began filling a tray with more loaves of bread to replace those they'd sold that morning.

"So everyone, even those who aren't Mennonite, helps with the sales?" Hannah asked. For such a small corner of the world, Pleasant Valley seemed to be involved in a great deal.

"Ja, that's how it's done. The Amish want to help, for sure, and they don't have a central organization to support outside charity, like the Central Committee and its Mennonite Disaster Fund. And lots of the Englisch help, too. They know the money will be well spent." Aunt Paula picked up the tray. "Besides, it is a lot of fun, working together. You'll see for yourself on Saturday."

"But, Aunt Paula, maybe it would be better if I watched the bakery so that Naomi can go." Naomi probably had many more skills to contribute than she did.

"No, no, we have it all set. Naomi doesn't mind, and we usually trade off anyway. I want you to go. There's no better way to get to know people than by working beside them, and some of the teenage girls will be there to watch the kinder."

Aunt Paula never liked having her arrangements upset, but in this case . . .

"But I wouldn't know what to do," Hannah confessed. "I don't know how to quilt or knit or sew."

Aunt Paula's busy hands stilled, and she stared at Hannah, her blue eyes round behind her glasses. "How could you not know how to sew, at least?"

"No one ever taught me." This must be a pretty big gap in her education, to judge by her aunt's expression of dismay. She began to feel embarrassed. "I'm sorry."

"But your mamm was wonderful gut at all those things. She had such an eye for color in quilt patterns, even when she was hardly old enough to reach across a quilting frame. You must remember that."

Must she? A vague memory teased at the back of Hannah's mind . . . an image of her mother bending over a quilting frame, sunlight streaming through the window to bring out the jewel-like tones of the fabric, Mammi's needle swooping up and down. But that had to have been long before they went away.

"I guess," she said. "A long time ago. I think my mother must have given it up after we left Pleasant Valley." As she'd given up so many interests, letting them fall away from her, one after another, until there seemed to be nothing left except the fear inside her mind.

The tray clattered onto the countertop. "I wouldn't have believed it." Aunt Paula seemed almost to be talking to herself. "She loved it so much." She shook her head slowly, as if mourning the loss of all that her sister had loved.

"I'm sorry." There didn't seem to be anything else to say.

"Your mammi started teaching you when you were just a tot." Aunt Paula gave her a challenging look. "You've just forgotten. You're Elizabeth's daughter. You'll have her gifts."

Hannah set a plate in the drainer, trying not to slam it down. "I don't," she said shortly. "Life doesn't work that way sometimes."

"But you must. Try to remember." The urgency in her aunt's voice was real. What was driving this insistence that Hannah be like her mother?

"I don't." Hannah's careful control snapped. "I don't think I want to remember. Or to be like her. Not if it means letting down my own child."

She put a soapy hand to her mouth, horrified at the words that had spilled out. "I'm sorry. I didn't mean to say that."

Aunt Paula shook her head slowly. Heavily. "Don't. We'd best not talk about it anymore."

Or we'll say even more that we regret, Hannah thought, finishing the sentence for her aunt.

What had possessed her? She couldn't blurt such things

out to Aunt Paula. Her aunt still had such a cherished image of who her little sister had been.

Paula picked up the tray again, heading for the door. She stopped just before she reached it and turned. She cleared her throat, and it seemed to Hannah that she was trying to find something to say.

"I should not push." She hesitated, staring at the bread as if she'd forgotten what she was doing with it. "I hope you will come on Saturday. I think you would like it."

There was a lump in Hannah's throat. Her aunt was trying, and she'd have to find a way to do the same. "Yes. I'd like to go with you."

"Gut." Her aunt paused again, ready to push the door with the tray. "In the attic there are some things of your mamm's. A trunk, some boxes. Some of the things she made, if you ever want to see them." The door swung as she went through.

Hannah stood at the sink, drying her hands on the towel, the movements automatic. Her head was light, as dizzy as if she hadn't eaten.

She didn't want to see her mother's things. She didn't want to delve back into a past that her aunt obviously remembered far differently than she did. And she definitely didn't want Aunt Paula to look at her as if she were her mother.

CHAPTER SIX

*T*he number of cars and buggies parked at the fire hall on Saturday certainly indicated that the work day was a popular event. Hannah lifted Jamie from his car seat and hefted the diaper bag onto her shoulder. She carried so much stuff around that it was a wonder one shoulder wasn't lower than the other, but whatever she left behind was sure to be the very thing that she needed.

"All set?" Aunt Paula, pulling a work bag from the backseat, looked eager to get going.

"We're ready." Hannah fell into step with her aunt, Jamie on her hip. "Looks like a good turnout."

Hannah made an effort to sound as enthusiastic as her aunt obviously was. She could only hope her participation would help to mend the breach between them. She loved Aunt Paula, and she also depended on her. Her aunt provided the only stability in their lives right now.

Please . . .

Hannah wasn't sure what she was praying for. She only knew she needed some assurance.

The chatter of women's voices, punctuated by laughter, filled the large room, bouncing off the cement block walls. Groups of women gathered around tables, working busily, while two quilt frames, set up in one corner, were also surrounded by chairs full of women. Hannah hesitated, taking it all in, not sure where to turn first.

"The children are over this way." Her aunt surged off to the right, obviously expecting her to follow. "You don't need to worry. They'll take fine care of Jamie."

Hannah trailed after Paula, Jamie clinging to her, probably a little spooked by all the people and noise. Whether he was going to let go or not was a good question.

"Here we are," Aunt Paula said. "Do you want me to wait while you get Jamie settled and introduce you around?"

Her aunt seemed eager to start, so Hannah shook her head. "You go ahead. I'll look around a little and see what I can work on." If anything, she added silently.

"Gut, gut. I'm helping with a quilt, so I should get over there." Aunt Paula paused long enough to smile at her and pat Jamie. "I'm glad you came, Hannah. You'll have fun. You'll see."

She didn't wait for a response, just hurried off toward the quilt frames at the far end of the room.

One corner of the room had been fenced off into a kiddie yard, complete with toys and a couple of portable cribs. Hannah started in that direction and then stopped, her attention arrested by a large framed poster on the wall. It was a listing of fire company volunteers, and somehow she wasn't surprised to see William's name listed under the heading of those who'd served for more than ten years. Obviously he didn't let his stutter hold him back from doing the important things.

Smiling a little, she went on to the child care area. To her relief, she recognized Katie's sister Rhoda, the one she'd met at the quilt shop.

"I was hoping you would bring Jamie today. He's a fine boy, for sure." Rhoda's pert face was lit with pleasure, and Hannah felt an answering warmth. The way to a mother's heart was to praise her child—that was certain.

"It's nice to see you, Rhoda. Are you watching the children?"

Rhoda nodded, holding a stuffed lion out to Jamie. "Ja, my friend Becky and I are babysitting." She gestured toward another teenager, also in Amish dress, who was sitting on the floor building a block tower with several small children. At the sound of her name, the girl looked up with a shy smile.

"Becky is Caleb's niece," Rhoda said. "When her onkel Caleb and my sister Katie get married, we'll be . . ." She paused, obviously not sure.

"Maybe cousins," Hannah suggested. She suspected most of the Pleasant Valley Amish were cousins of some description, if they traced their families back far enough.

Jamie bounced in her arm, reaching for the toy lion, and Rhoda made it jump, laughing a little.

"Want the lion, Jamie? Komm see me, then." Rhoda held out her arms.

To Hannah's surprise, Jamie lunged into them, grabbing for Rhoda's kapp strings.

"Jamie, don't . . ." Hannah began, but Rhoda was already untangling his fingers.

"Kinder always do that," she said. "Look, Jamie, let's fly over here and show everyone the lion." She swooped Jamie through the air and landed him next to the other toddlers.

Hannah took a step back. Could she actually get away without tears?

"I think he will be happy," a soft voice said.

She turned to find an Amish woman next to her.

"I hope so. I wouldn't want him to cry and get the others started."

"They'll be fine," the woman said. "Just see how well Rhoda and Becky handle them. That is my little Anna." She nodded to a tiny blonde girl leaning against Becky, and Hannah's stomach lurched. Anna was a Down's syndrome child. While Hannah watched, the little girl handed a block to Jamie.

"How sweet," she murmured.

Anna's mother nodded. "I believe God gives some of His children a bit of extra sweetness to make up for other things." For an instant, sorrow tinged her loving expression, and as quickly vanished. "I am Myra Beiler." She smiled. "A distant cousin of yours."

"You are?" Obviously Myra knew who she was, so Hannah didn't bother to say her name. "How are we related?" She didn't even know she had any Amish relatives.

"Well, your father was a Zercher, ja? And, let me see, I think it was his father that was cousins with my grossdaadi."

Suddenly acquiring a cousin was a bit disorienting. "I did know my father was Amish before he married my mother."

"Ja. He went up the ladder to the Mennonites." Myra laughed softly at Hannah's expression. "Up the ladder is moving to a Plain group that is less strict. That's what we say, anyway."

"Aunt Paula told me I'd make some friends here today. She didn't mention I'd find a cousin."

Funny, that she'd just been thinking about the web of relationships among the Amish. Apparently the Mennonites were included in it, as well.

"If you haven't already decided what you're working on, maybe you'd like to join my table," Myra suggested. Her voice went up at the end of the sentence, as if she weren't sure how Hannah might react.

"Only if it's something a person with no skill at all can do." She'd better confess that right away, before she got entangled with some of the experts. "Aunt Paula insists I ought to be able to remember how to sew, but I don't."

"Komm," Myra said. "We'll find a job for you, ja?"

Hannah followed her newfound cousin to a table spread with soft stuffed dolls in various stages of construction. She was about to remind her that she couldn't sew, but Myra was already introducing her.

"Here is my sister-in-law, another Anna, and our friend Rachel. This is Hannah, Paula's niece. I thought she could dress the dolls for us."

Well, that she could do. She slipped into a chair, nodding at the other women's greetings and wondering if she was the only person confused by the remarkable similarity among Amish women.

It wasn't just that they were dressed alike, although brown-haired Rachel wore a burgundy dress and apron while Anna, with flaxen hair, wore blue, which matched her eyes. Their manner was very similar, a sort of calm acceptance that seemed to say they knew who they were and where they belonged.

"We have a bunch ready to be dressed, so I hope you really want to do this." Anna smiled, nodding toward a stack of dolls. She had a quick smile and an air of assurance that contrasted with her sister-in-law's shy, gentle expression. "Has Rhoda taken over your little boy already?" She reached out to pat the infant sleeping in a buggy next to her.

"She has." Hannah glanced toward the corner, but everyone seemed to be playing happily. "I hope he won't cause any problems. He hasn't had much opportunity to play with other children his age."

"He'll be fine," Rachel assured her. "And if he does fuss, it's not as if we haven't all heard it before."

The other women smiled, and Hannah recognized the instant fraternity of young mothers. She'd known that before, on the base, where other young mothers were the ones who really understood.

She picked up one of the soft, faceless rag dolls and began to put on the tiny Amish dress. "I imagine these will sell well."

"For sure they will," Rachel said. "If only we have a warm day for the auction, so we get a crowd."

"We can't help being excited. It's our big event of the fall." Anna stitched yarn into place for a doll's hair. "Once winter comes, things get quiet here in Pleasant Valley."

Was there an implication that Hannah might find it boring? If they imagined she'd led an exciting life before she came here, they couldn't be more wrong.

"That sounds fine to me. I'm too busy for much outside activity anyway."

"It can't be easy, raising a small child without a husband's help." Myra's voice was soft, her brown eyes sympathetic.

"Especially out there." Anna gave a jerk of the head that seemed to indicate the English world. "I know, you see. I lived there for three years, and it was a struggle to take care of myself and my little Gracie." She hesitated, her gaze on Hannah's face. "I wanted you to know, in case you need someone who understands."

The lump in Hannah's throat made it difficult to answer. Anna had just handed her a gift, it seemed, and she didn't even know her.

"Thank you," she murmured. "I appreciate that."

The others resumed work, talking or falling silent with the easy familiarity of people who knew one another well. The apprehension Hannah had felt at fitting in had disappeared, almost without her noticing. This was like one of the wives groups on the base—women concentrating on a task while talking about teething and potty training and the best treatment for colic.

She glanced across the room to the quilting frames, where Aunt Paula was seated. Paula looked up at the same time, and their gazes met. Hannah smiled. Aunt Paula had been right. Despite Hannah's lack of skill, she'd found something worthwhile here.

"William tells me you are helping him with his speech." Rachel finished the seam she was stitching and reached for another doll. "I'm so glad."

"Yes, I . . ."

Hannah stopped, unable to come up with the rest of a casual response. *Rachel.* She hadn't realized. This was the woman Katie had told her about, the older sister-in-law William had fallen in love with. Apparently Rachel was still close to William.

Maybe it was better not to let on that she knew about William's feelings for Rachel, but she sensed her face had already given her away.

Before she could come up with something to say, another Amish woman, carrying a tray of cupcakes toward the kitchen, stopped behind Anna. She looked at Hannah with curiosity in her round, red-cheeked face.

"This is Paula Schatz's niece, ja?"

Hannah nodded. She was beginning to accept the fact that everyone here could identify her. "Yes, I'm Hannah Conroy."

"This is my sister-in-law Barbara Beiler," Anna said. "My oldest brother's wife."

All Barbara's interest focused on Hannah. "You are the one helping William Brand with his talking, then."

She nodded. If William had hoped to keep that fact quiet, he'd obviously failed. How did the Amish spread news so quickly, even without the help of telephones?

"It's wonderful kind of Hannah to do that," Rachel said quickly.

"It certainly is," Anna added. Oddly, there seemed to be a warning in her voice, as if . . .

"Ja, I'm sure that's so," Barbara said. "It's chust too bad that everyone doesn't see it that way."

"Barbara . . ." Anna began.

"What do you mean?" Hannah felt as if she'd missed a step in the dark and come down hard.

"Some folks are saying that William is as God made him. That he should be satisfied with that and not be trying to change."

"Barbara, that's not a thing you ought to be repeating." Rachel spoke sharply, the tone a contrast to the gentleness in her face.

"I'm not saying I think that," Barbara said. "Just that some folks are saying it."

"That doesn't mean you should tell Hannah such a thing." Anna's fair skin had flushed, as if her sister-in-law had embarrassed her, and Myra, also a sister-in-law, looked as if she wanted to crawl under the table.

"Well, I didn't mean anything." Barbara looked genuinely surprised by their reaction to her words. "Guess I'd best get these cupcakes to the kitchen." She hurried off, as if she couldn't get away fast enough.

There was an awkward silence in Barbara's wake.

Rachel hurried into speech. "Don't heed what a few foolish people think, Hannah. Please. You are doing a gut thing for William. He should have a chance to speak for himself."

"Barbara means well." Anna's expression was rueful. "I have to remind myself of that a half-dozen times a day. It's just too bad that everything she thinks comes out of her mouth."

"It's all right." Hannah tried to muster a normal-looking smile. "I was a little taken aback, but what William wants is all that matters."

But was it? She couldn't help but remember what Katie had said—that William was upset about the thought that people would gossip about them.

Now it was happening. How would he react? Would he feel that working with her wasn't worth the hassle?

That was his decision, Hannah reminded herself. But the possibility made her more uneasy than it should.

On the off Sunday, when they didn't have church, most Amish visited friends or relatives. William supposed the Mennonites did the same, making him wonder for a moment where Hannah and her little boy would spend the day. Paula had a flock of relatives in Pleasant Valley, so they were probably visiting someone.

He'd been invited to Myra and Joseph Beiler's for supper. When he'd stopped by the machine shop that Joseph ran with Samuel Weaver to pick up a mower piece Isaac needed, Myra had hurried out to the buggy before he left to invite him. A kind thought, that was, inviting him by himself instead of assuming he'd be going somewhere with Isaac's family.

The lane to Joseph and Myra's place ran between two properties, with the Beiler house on the left and the home of Samuel and Anna Weaver on the right, beyond a fenced paddock. Samuel had a gift with horses, and he was often training an animal or two for someone, besides doing his work in the machine shop.

It wasn't unusual these days for a man with a family to support to be working at more than one job. Myra had said Samuel and his family would be over for supper as well. It would be nice to get a glimpse of their little son.

William came to a stop short of the hitching post, making the horse turn its head, as if to ask what he was doing. That elderly black car belonged to Paula Schatz. It looked as if he had the answer to where Hannah and Jamie were spending their Sunday afternoon.

Clucking to the horse to step up, he jumped down and went to tend the animal while questions buzzed around in his head. Was this a coincidence, Myra inviting him when she had Hannah here? Maybe. Or maybe she thought that since he and Hannah were working together, it would be a kindness. Either way, he wasn't sure it was a good idea.

Joseph was in the backyard at the charcoal grill, holding his palm out to check the temperature, it seemed. He glanced at William and grinned.

"Myra keeps asking me if the grill is ready yet. She's afraid it won't be hot in time to cook the burgers and sausages, and she's determined not to carry the other stuff out until it is."

"L-looks like it's c-coming along fine." The coals weren't white yet, he guessed, but they soon would be. "I s-see you have other c-company." He nodded toward the car.

"Ja, Myra got to know Hannah at the work day yesterday. It turns out they are relatives of some sort through Hannah's father, so Myra wants to be sure Hannah feels welcome here."

"The Z-Z-Zercher family, that w-would be." William ran his thoughts back over the tangle of family trees in Pleasant Valley. Sometimes he thought it must be hard to live here if you weren't related to somebody or other.

"That's it." Joseph rearranged the coals with a long fork. "Myra has the family Bible out, showing her. I told them best to keep the little ones inside for now. I don't want anybody getting too close to the grill."

Joseph was a careful father to his little girls, gentle but firm. The kind of daadi William would like to be, if he ever had the chance.

The screen door on the back porch swung open, and Myra leaned out. "William, I'm glad you're here. Wilkom. Joseph, is the fire ready yet? I see Samuel and Anna and the kinder walking over."

Sure enough, Samuel and his family were skirting the paddock on their way, with Samuel carrying an infant seat. The single horse in the paddock tossed his head and then trotted along beside them. It looked like little Gracie was talking to the animal.

In minutes, everyone was clustering in the backyard,

the other women helping Myra carry food out to the picnic table, while Samuel tried to corral the young ones a safe distance from the grill. William went to help just in time to intercept Jamie making a wobbly run toward it.

"Whoa, l-little Jamie." He lifted the boy in his arms, loving the instant grin that showed the dimples in Jamie's cheeks. "No r-running to the fire. Hot," he said with emphasis. He pointed to the grill. "Hot," he said again.

Jamie wiggled his fingers, his brown eyes round. Obviously he'd heard that word before, what with the bakery ovens heated much of the time.

Carrying Jamie, William walked around the end of the picnic table to where Samuel was spreading out a blanket on the other side. Samuel upended a basket of toys, and the little girls dived in, giggling. William plopped Jamie down in the middle of them.

"S-so this is your l-little one." He smiled down at the small bundle. Samuel and Anna's little boy slept intently, his tiny hand against his cheek.

"Six weeks old today," Samuel said, beaming as only a new father could. "This is our David."

"A g-gut baby, f-for sure."

"Ja, for sure. Eats gut, sleeps, cries." Samuel grinned, nodding toward Gracie, who was cradling a baby doll. "Gracie wants him to stay awake longer, I think. She'll probably be regretting that when he's old enough to grab her toys."

William was still nodding in reply when he realized that Jamie had taken off again, toward the paddock this time. He caught up with the boy in a few long strides.

Jamie wiggled in his grasp. "Horsie. Horsie!" he demanded, pointing. "Horsie!"

"Ach, y-you want to see him. All r-right."

He swung Jamie onto his shoulder and headed for the paddock. Better to let him see the animal than have to keep chasing him, he'd think.

They reached the fence. The gelding, a handsome bay

with a white star on its forehead, sidled up to them. Holding Jamie firmly out of reach, William patted the glossy neck, running his hand along the muzzle to be sure the animal was quiet before he'd let Jamie near.

"There, now. He's a n-nice boy." He kept his voice soft, soothing.

"Horsie," Jamie whispered, imitating him.

"Ja, horsie." William took the small hand in his and helped Jamie pat the horse's neck. "Nice, g-gentle. Gut boy."

He heard a step and turned to see Hannah behind them, watching with a smile.

"You like the horsie, Jamie?" She came closer, but made no move to take her son from William. "He's nice, isn't he?"

"Horsie," Jamie said again. He might not have a very big vocabulary, but he could make his wants understood.

"Thanks for showing him," Hannah said.

William nodded, feeling her gaze on his face as if she were touching him. "H-he w-was d-determined."

"Do you know that you barely stammer at all when you talk to Jamie?" She kept her voice low and even, as if what she said didn't matter at all.

He considered. "J-Jamie d-doesn't judge me."

"No, children don't, do they? Neither do I."

She leaned on the fence next to him, watching the horse, which had dropped its head to crop at the grass. "I heard something yesterday," she said abruptly.

Not something good, he'd guess. "W-what?"

"A woman at the work day said that some people . . . some Amish, I think she meant . . . didn't approve of my helping you with your speech. They're apparently saying that God made you the way you are, and we shouldn't try to change that."

He kept silent for a moment, but there was a bitter taste in his mouth. He thought he could probably put a name to who was saying those things. Amish weren't saints, just people, and there were always those who were a little mean-spirited.

"Does it bother you?" Hannah asked. Her forehead crinkled, and her warm brown eyes looked apprehensive.

"N-no." He was surprised to realize that was true. "I d-don't l-like to be t-talked about, b-but it d-doesn't change my mind."

"Good." She said the word on a sigh of relief. "I'd hate to see you stop because of a foolish comment. That's what Anna said it was. Foolish."

"Anna w-was there?" Who else had heard?

"I was working with Anna and Myra. And their friend Rachel." Her gaze slid away from his.

She knew, then. Someone had already told her about him and Rachel.

"R-Rachel was m-my sister-in-law," he said. "My b-brother Ezra's w-widow."

And to Rachel, he was still her younger brother. Would anyone else understand that?

"Yes, I know. It made Rachel angry, that people had been talking that way and that someone repeated it to me." Hannah hesitated. "I wasn't going to say anything, but I thought you should know. In case it made a difference to you."

"It d-doesn't," he said shortly. "B-but you have heard m-more about R-Rachel, ja?"

The color came up in Hannah's cheeks. "I'm sorry if it upsets you. It wasn't gossip. Katie just wanted me to understand why you might be reluctant to work with me."

Hannah reached out to touch his hand, a feather-light brush of the fingertips that he seemed to feel down deep in his bones. "Katie and Caleb care about you. She was trying to help."

He nodded. Katie cared. And she meant well. He'd like to forget what was past, but that wasn't easy to do when you lived in a place like Pleasant Valley.

"I guess I should have told you about it before now, but

I didn't know how to bring it up. I didn't want to put any embarrassment between us." She looked up at him, frowning a little. "Are we okay?"

He nodded. "J-ja. Okay."

Joseph called his name just then, and when William looked toward him, Joseph waved his spatula. "Food's ready," he called.

William waved back. "W-we better g-go."

They walked back toward the group gathering around the picnic table, and William struggled with his thoughts.

It wasn't Hannah's fault that he was in this position. Still, he wished she didn't know. Or at least, that he had been the one to tell her.

CHAPTER SEVEN

Hannah sorted bread loaves into the wire baskets behind the counter, hurrying a little. Naomi wasn't working today, and Hannah wanted to be sure she'd done all she could before William came for his session that afternoon.

At least, she trusted he'd come. She slid a cinnamon loaf into place, noting how quickly they'd been selling out. Aunt Paula might want to think about making more. Maybe she ought to start keeping a record of what was selling when. Like the supply orders, it would be simple enough for her to do, and it would help her aunt.

Maybe it had been a mistake to tell William what she'd heard at the work day on Saturday. Still, he had seemed more resigned than upset. Perhaps he'd anticipated that reaction from some people.

She smiled, thinking of how Jamie had responded to the horse. He'd been playing horsie ever since, and at the moment he was attempting to ride the large stuffed horse that Megan and her husband had given him for his birthday.

Aunt Paula paused at her elbow. "Goodness, is that all we have left of the cinnamon bread?"

Hannah nodded, putting the last loaf in its place. "I was just thinking that we . . . you might want to make more of those, since they're so popular."

"We should," her aunt said, smiling, with a slight stress on the pronoun.

Encouraged, Hannah went on. "It occurred to me that I might keep a record of how the different types sell and when they sell best. Doing so might help you with planning what to make." Her tone grew a little diffident toward the end of the sentence. Aunt Paula might feel that her methods didn't need improvement.

But her aunt was smiling. "Ach, you see, I need you to help me stay up-to-date, my Hannah." She squeezed Hannah's hand. "I'm glad to see you take such an interest in the business."

Before Hannah could reply, the owner of the bookstore across the street came to the counter, looking around a bit absentmindedly, as if he'd forgotten why he'd come in.

"May I help you, Mr. Wainwright?" Hannah stepped to the counter. "Would you like a sticky bun with your coffee today?" She'd already noticed that he had a weakness for the sweet, sticky rolls.

"Thank you, Hannah. That will do nicely. When are you coming over to visit my shop?" That had been a running joke between them for weeks now.

"Soon," she promised. Reading was a pleasure she didn't really have time to indulge in very often, but Cliff Wainwright was such a good customer that she thought she should stop by. The trouble was that once she got into a novel, she wouldn't want to put it down.

Once Mr. Wainwright had left, Aunt Paula resumed

their conversation. "I was chust thinking that we want to be certain-sure you have some time off when your friend arrives tomorrow."

"You don't need—" Hannah began, but Aunt Paula was already shaking her head.

"Don't argue, now. I've already asked Naomi to work some extra days while Mrs. Townsend is here. I want you to enjoy her visit, and not be worrying over what's happening in the bakery."

Maybe that was meant as an apology for the fact that Aunt Paula hadn't wanted Megan to come in the first place. If so, Hannah should accept with gratitude.

"That's good of you. It would be nice to have some extra time to catch up on all the news. It seems so long since I've seen her."

Maybe Megan would have changed. She and her husband were at a new post in Georgia now, so she'd have found new friends, probably new activities, too, since her oldest had started kindergarten.

Wiping the countertop, Hannah caught a glimpse of her reflection in the toaster, the kapp looking very white against her brown hair. More likely Megan would think she was the one who had changed.

The prayer covering was bound to look strange to someone who wasn't familiar with the custom. Hannah hadn't quite gotten used to seeing it on herself. Maybe she ought to stop wearing it while Megan was here . . .

No, she couldn't do that. She wouldn't be that hypocritical. Wearing the kapp meant something to her, and surely her friend could understand that. Megan was used to the transient life of a military wife, transferred here and there at a moment's notice, her friends and substitute family drawn from other military people.

But how was Megan going to react to the setting in which she found Hannah? Everything here, from the bakery to the Plain dress of people here to the rural countryside and the village where everyone knew everyone, would seem strange to her.

The bell over the door jingled, and Hannah looked toward the sound, smiling automatically. And then gaping. Megan was here.

"Megan!" She scurried around the end of the counter as her friend rushed forward, and in a moment they were hugging, and everything else was forgotten.

"It is so good to see you. I couldn't wait." Megan gave her another squeeze. "I decided not to stop at my cousin's in Baltimore after all. I just drove straight through."

"I didn't expect you until tomorrow." Hannah grinned, unable to restrain the joy that swept through her. She'd never, before or since, had a friend with whom she shared as much as she had with Megan.

Same red curls and sparkling green eyes, same dimpled smile: Megan didn't look a bit different. Or a day older, for that matter.

Megan seemed to be assessing her in the same way. Hannah thought her friend's eyes narrowed a bit when they rested on the prayer covering, but she didn't mention it.

"You look great." Megan patted her cheek. "Rested and not so thin and strained. This place must agree with you."

"That's thanks to my aunt." Hannah took her hand and led her to the counter, breathing a silent prayer that these two women, so important to her, would get along.

"Aunt Paula, this is my friend Megan Townsend. Megan, my aunt, Paula Schatz."

Megan seemed to suppress any surprise she felt at Aunt Paula's Plain dress. She smiled, holding out her hand. "I'm so glad to meet you, Mrs. Schatz. Thank you for having me in your home."

"You are wilkom." There was a touch of stiffness in Aunt Paula's manner, but Hannah hoped Megan didn't notice it. "Hannah has been looking forward to your coming."

"No more than I have," Megan said. She whirled toward Jamie's play yard in the corner beyond the tables. "And to see that big boy. Just look how much he's grown."

She swept across the room with one of her impetuous movements and knelt beside the plastic barrier. "Jamie, I can't believe how big you are. Remember me? Remember Auntie Megan?"

Jamie stared at her, one finger in his mouth, brown eyes round.

"I'm afraid he's too little to remember," Hannah said. To Jamie, the time they'd spent here already had been a big portion of his life.

"I'll bet he does." Megan stood, holding out her hands temptingly. "Come to Megan, Jamie."

Jamie burbled something and reached up to her, and Megan lifted him into her arms. "There, see?" She grinned at Hannah. "He remembers."

"Or he just wants to get out of his little prison," Hannah said, smiling back. "Isn't that right, Jamie?"

Jamie patted Megan's face, and then wiggled to get down.

"Don't put him down," Hannah warned, "or we'll never get him back in."

Megan glanced around as the bell jingled and two shopkeepers came in, probably for lunch. "Can we go somewhere and talk?"

"Not right now," Hannah said, regretting it. She'd like to get Megan settled and hear all about her family, but this wasn't a good time. "Our lunch rush is just starting, and the other woman who works for my aunt is off today. I can't leave Aunt Paula alone to deal with the counter and wait tables."

"I'll help you, then. I've waited tables plenty in my time."

"I can't ask you to help. You're a guest."

But Megan was already putting Jamie back into his

pen and distracting him with the stuffed horse. "You're not asking. I'm volunteering. It'll be fun." She reached out to clasp Hannah's hand, her expression changing. "Just tell me quick. How are you, really?"

The tone of Megan's voice, the knowledge behind it, touched something deep inside Hannah. Megan knew. Other people might express sympathy, might feel for her, but Megan actually knew what the past two years had been like.

A lump formed in her throat, and she struggled to speak around it. "All right," she managed to say. "Better for seeing you, that's certain."

William took his time as he walked toward the bakery that Tuesday afternoon for his session with Hannah. He hadn't seen her since they'd talked on Sunday, and it wondered him how much that incident with the gossip had bothered her.

As for him, well, it hadn't really surprised him. Everyone knew who the blabbermauls were.

Barbara Beiler, for instance. She was a good woman, always first in line to offer help. But her tongue flapped at both ends, as his mamm used to say.

Well, so some people thought he was wrong to try to change himself. They would probably be quick enough to get a hearing aid if they needed it. Why shouldn't he have help to talk? Unless it was the bishop telling him what he was doing was wrong, he didn't figure he needed to listen.

It was amazing, but the sessions with Hannah were helping him already. He understood better now what was involved in stuttering, even understood some simple steps he could take to improve.

Putting those tools into practice, that was the hard part. It would take time, but he had that.

He found his steps quickening as he neared the bakery.

In a few minutes he'd see Hannah. That shouldn't have anything to do with his lessons, but there was no point in denying the truth. It was a lot more pleasant being taught by Hannah than by her aunt Paula, for instance. He grinned at the thought as he opened the bakery door.

Hannah wasn't waiting as she had been, each time they'd had a session before. Paula, busy behind the counter, looked up at him. Pushing her glasses up her nose, she left a flour mark on the lens.

"Ach, William, I didn't realize—" She turned, heading for the stairs. "Just let me call up to Hannah."

"Ja, d-d-denke."

She leaned into the stairwell. "Hannah? William is here for his lesson."

For a moment there was no response, and then he heard the clatter of feet on the wooden treads as Hannah came hurrying down. She reached the bottom, cheeks flushed.

"William, I'm so sorry. My friend arrived for her visit a day early, and I was so excited that I forgot what day it was. It will just take me a few minutes to get ready."

"Th-that's okay." Would she rather cancel today? If she had a visitor, maybe so. "If y-you w-want . . ."

Before he could get the words out, another woman came down the stairs behind Hannah. An Englisch woman.

He tried not to stare. She was very modern for a friend of Hannah's, with her cropped pants, bright red toenails, and dangling earrings. Not that he hadn't seen Englisch women dressed that way before, but . . .

Or was that the way Hannah had dressed, out in the world?

The woman sent him a curious glance before she turned to Hannah. "What's up? You ran out of the room so fast I thought something was wrong."

"No, not at all." Hannah looked a bit flustered. "I just forgot that William was coming today."

The woman looked at him, her eyebrows lifting. "William?"

"William Brand, Megan Townsend," Hannah said. "William and I are working on his speech two afternoons a week, and we meet on Tuesdays."

"I . . . I d-don't h-have t-t-to—" Of course his stammer would get worse in front of this unknown woman.

"I'm sure William doesn't mind skipping today," Mrs. Townsend said. "After all, I just got here. We haven't even had time to talk yet."

"J-j-ja." He managed to get that much out. "F-f-f-f . . ." He wanted to say fine. He felt the breath of the word moving across his lip, but he couldn't manage to get it out.

Instead he nodded and headed for the door, eager to get away from the woman's judgmental gaze.

"But I shouldn't cancel . . ." Hannah was saying as he opened the door.

"You heard him." The other woman's voice carried clearly. "The boy doesn't mind."

He shut the door firmly and walked away, shoulders stiff. *The boy*. He'd thought that Hannah, at least, didn't think of him that way.

Well, be fair. Hannah hadn't said the hurtful words. She had always treated him like a friend. All the same, he wished he hadn't come today.

It didn't help his disposition to see his brother coming toward him down the sidewalk.

"William." Isaac stopped, looking at him with a question in his gaze. "What are you doing here? I heard from Caleb that you were meeting with Paula's niece this afternoon."

"N-n-n-no." He ought to be able to talk to his own brother without tripping over his tongue. "Sh-she i-is b-busy." He wanted to keep on walking, but he couldn't do that.

"That's just as well, ja?" Isaac put a hand on his shoulder. "You don't need some Englischer trying to teach you to talk different. Folks are used to you. They don't mind."

He minded, but he didn't suppose Isaac would understand that. "It's j-just t-t-today she's b-busy. With c-company."

It didn't mean he was giving up. Or that Hannah was, either.

She would have gone ahead with their session in spite of her company, not that he would have agreed. Hannah had a guest. It was only right that she have the time to enjoy that. She hadn't had anyone come to visit her since she got here.

"I see." Isaac took his hand away, frowning. "Just remember, William. God made you the way you are for a reason. It's not up to us to change that." He shrugged his heavy shoulders. "Think about it, ja? You'll see I'm right. This business isn't for you."

"I-I-I d-don't—"

The rest of the words, the ones that would show Isaac how important the lessons were to him, wouldn't come out. They got stuck, like they always did when something was important to him.

"Go on along to the shop." Isaac turned away, speaking back over his shoulder. "I'll see you at supper, ja?" He left without waiting for a response.

William strode toward the shop, fists clenching. *I can make up my own mind about what's right for me.* That was what he wanted to say.

Too bad he couldn't.

"You're mad at me, aren't you?" Megan walked next to Hannah as she pushed Jamie in his stroller toward the playground.

Hannah blinked. "No, of course not. Why should I be?"

"I interfered between you and your student." Megan spread her hands wide. "You know me, always jumping before I think."

"It's all right." True, Hannah wasn't happy about it, but William had obviously intended to beg off anyway once he realized she had a guest.

"I think the boy understood . . ." Megan began.

"He's a man." Hannah's temper flared. "William's a grown man, only a year or two younger than we are. He's hampered by his stammer. Helping him is . . . well, it's the first chance I've had since I got married to use my training. It's as important to me as it is to him."

Hannah reached down to adjust Jamie's hat, not sure she wanted to see Megan's expression, a little embarrassed that she had responded so strongly to what was an innocent mistake on Megan's part.

But Megan patted her hand where it gripped the stroller handle. "I'm sorry. I guess I wasn't thinking of anything but how glad I am to see you. I didn't realize how much teaching William meant to you. I don't remember ever hearing you say that you were sorry not to have finished school."

They'd reached the playground, and Hannah began pushing the stroller across the grass, Jamie squealing at the bumps. The minute he saw the sandbox he stood up, eager to get there.

"Just a minute, little boy," she said, stopping to lift him out. She let him run the last few yards, watching him climb over the low wall.

"Look at him go," Megan said, smiling. "I know how much mine have grown and changed since the last time we saw you, with Tommy in kindergarten already, but somehow I still pictured Jamie as that chubby little baby."

"I know. It's almost scary how fast he's growing." Hannah put Jamie's sand pail and shovel into the sandbox, and he immediately began filling the pail with sand, spilling as much as he got in. She sat down next to Megan on the bench facing the sandbox.

"When you said I'd never regretted not finishing school," Hannah said slowly, "I guess that was true at the time. When Travis and I got married, I left school willingly to go with him. I figured there'd be plenty of opportu-

nities later to go back and get my degree." She hesitated.
"But it didn't work out that way."

"I know." Megan's voice was soft. "I'm sorry."

Hannah shrugged. "Well, I've moved on, and I accept
that I'll probably never have that chance. But if I can help
William, I'll feel that maybe I haven't wasted what I
learned."

"Maybe the opportunity will still come up for you to
finish," Megan said.

"Maybe." But Hannah couldn't envision how that would
happen. "But Jamie and I have a good place here with my
aunt. And she loves having us, so it's working out."

For the most part, it was working out, anyway.

"Pleasant Valley isn't what I expected." Megan smiled,
shaking her head. "I don't know what I did expect. But the
clothes, the horses and buggies . . ." She nodded toward
an Amish couple driving past in their buggy, two small
children peering out the back. "I feel as if I've wandered
onto a movie set."

"They're for real, I promise," Hannah said. "They're
just ordinary people trying to live the way they think God
wants them to."

"Driving a horse and buggy?" Megan's voice went
up in disbelief. "But your aunt drives a car. You mentioned that."

"Those are two different groups." The thought of trying to explain Anabaptists in a few words was daunting.
"The Amish are a fairly strict church. They try hard to
live separate from the world, and they stay away from any
technology that they think will intrude on family and
community life, like cars and telephones and computers."

"And your aunt?"

"Aunt Paula is a Plain Mennonite. They share a lot of
beliefs with the Amish, but my aunt's church allows
things like electricity and telephones in the home."

"What about that cap on your head? Did your aunt insist you wear it?"

She'd known Megan wouldn't be able to keep quiet about that for long. "Prayer covering," Hannah said. "Or kapp. My aunt wouldn't insist on anything. But it's . . ." She struggled, trying to find the words.

It had seemed natural, remembering her mother, being here where people took the kapp for granted. But Megan had brought a breath of that other world with her, and it wasn't so easy to translate.

"Women in the Plain groups wear prayer coverings. My mother did. I did when I was young. It just seemed very natural to go back to that once I was living here."

Megan shook her head. "Strange, that's all I can say. I sure couldn't live like this. Doesn't it bother you, all these rules?"

"Not as much as I thought it would," Hannah said, a little surprised to realize it was true. "After all, I lived this way until I was nine. To me, it's more like coming home."

"But it's not . . . normal," Megan protested.

Hannah had to laugh at her expression. "Lots of people wouldn't think life on an army base was normal, either. Remember all the rules and regulations there? You can't leave kids' toys out in the yard, the grass has to be cut every week, no clothes out on the line after dark . . ."

"All right, all right." Megan grinned, and any slight constraint that might have been between them was gone. "You might have a point there. Well, as long as you and Jamie are safe and happy."

"We are."

A shadow fell across her lap, and she looked up, startled. A man stood there, and she hadn't heard him approach across the grass. Elderly, English, with white hair and a smile as he watched Jamie empty his bucket.

"He's enjoying himself."

"Yes, he loves the sandbox." Hannah was beginning to get used to the casual friendliness of people here. "He'll carry the sand home with him if I let him."

"Paula wouldn't want sand in the bakery, I guess." He focused on her, holding out his hand. "I'm Phil Russo. And you'd be Hannah Conroy, I'm sure."

"That's right." She stiffened a little, sensing something more than the usual easy greeting of people who knew who she was from seeing her at the bakery.

"I wanted to introduce myself. Our local veterans' group just learned about you being the widow of a serviceman. Sorry to hear about your loss."

She swallowed. "Thank you."

He shook his head. "A sad thing. But you should be proud of him."

"Yes. I am."

Too many reminders were coming at her today—Megan's visit, talking about the past, now this man. She'd told Megan she'd moved on, but that didn't mean remembering wasn't painful.

The man seemed a little disconcerted at her brief responses. "Well, I just wanted you to know that if we can be of help, you can call on us. Wouldn't want you to feel you didn't have support here."

"That's very kind of you. Thank you." She glanced down, realizing that she was turning her wedding ring around and around on her finger.

"Anything you need," he repeated. "We're working on plans for our Veterans Day event right now, and we'd really like to have your participation, you and your little boy."

She pressed her lips together for a moment. "I'm afraid I have my hands full, taking care of my son and helping my aunt with the bakery. I can't take on anything else."

"I see." He obviously hadn't expected to be turned down. "Well, you think about it and let me know. We're in the phone book." He nodded briefly and walked off the way he'd come.

Megan waited until he was out of earshot. "You were kind of eager to get rid of him, weren't you? I'm sure he meant well."

Hannah tried to take a deep breath and discovered that her chest felt too tight for that. She thought about her reaction to the young soldier getting off the bus days ago.

"He meant well," she echoed Megan's words. "But I . . . I'm not ready for the reminders."

Megan didn't say anything else, but Hannah could feel her gaze probing. Pushing. She was just another person who thought she knew what was best for Hannah.

CHAPTER EIGHT

Does your aunt like spaghetti?" Megan stirred the sauce she was making. "Maybe I should have asked that before I offered to cook supper."

"It's not traditional Pennsylvania Dutch food." Hannah stepped over Jamie, who was pushing a car across the floor. "But yes, she likes it. Pizza, too. We've had that a couple of times since I've been here."

"Remember when we used to order in pizza and have supper together? We'd sit and talk for hours at the kitchen table. What was the name of that little Italian place?"

"Luigi's." Hannah had no trouble supplying the name. Those had been happy times, with Travis and Jeff swapping stories or jeering at each other's choice in football teams, while she and Megan talked . . . well, girl talk, she supposed. "I've missed that."

"Me, too." Megan dropped pasta into boiling water. "It's kind of different, the base we're on now. There are lots more social events. And charitable things, too. We've been preparing packages to send to those who've shipped out. And I'm chairing the blood drives now."

Hannah nodded. She could picture those events, could see Megan flitting around, talking to everyone. "You always were comfortable in those mass gatherings. I could never think of anything to say to people." And yet the work day she'd gone to here had been similar, and she'd felt at ease.

"It takes practice, that's all," Megan said.

"So you were always telling me. I'm sure you'll do great, organizing the drive."

"Telling people what to do." Megan grinned. "My favorite thing."

True enough. Megan was a born organizer, and she was always so friendly that nobody seemed to resent her orders.

Busy, busy. Megan always had to be busy, as if three small children and a house weren't enough to keep her occupied. But Hannah knew what was behind that constant busyness. It was Megan's way of dealing with the worry, especially when Jeff was deployed.

She watched Megan's face bent over the steaming kettle. Jeff would ship out again in a few months. Hannah remembered, too well, the mixture of pride and fear that had to be dogging Megan.

If she said something, would it help? Maybe not. Megan had found her own way of coping.

"It smells ser gut in here." Aunt Paula came in, catching Jamie as he ran to meet her. "Hannah, you didn't tell me your friend was such a fine cook."

"Better wait until you taste it," Hannah said lightly. "I remember some of Megan's experiments."

"Like the frosting that curdled," Megan said. "Or the meat loaf that was so hard even the dog wouldn't eat it?"

"Those are the ones," Hannah said. She pried Jamie away from Aunt Paula. "Come on, little man. Let's wash those hands for supper."

By the time she had Jamie settled in his high chair with food in front of him, the meal was on the table. Megan and her aunt seemed to be talking more easily now. Aunt Paula's stiffness wasn't so evident. Either Megan's cheerful friendliness had won her over, or Aunt Paula was being more successful at hiding her discomfort.

Intent on getting more food into Jamie's mouth than on his shirt, Hannah lost the thread of the conversation for a few minutes, only to be startled by a question from Megan.

"Hannah, do you remember? The name of the man who talked to you at the park?"

"Russo, I think," Hannah said. She hadn't intended to mention that meeting to her aunt, but Megan had taken the choice from her.

Since she hadn't asked Megan to keep quiet, she shouldn't be feeling annoyed with her. Still, Megan had surely seen that she didn't want to talk about it.

"Phil Russo." Aunt Paula supplied the name. "It must have been. He comes in for coffee sometimes, and he likes my shoofly pie. What did he want to talk to you about?" Her forehead furrowed.

"I think he just noticed Jamie playing in the sandbox and stopped to say hello," Hannah said. She had no intention of lying to her aunt, but there wasn't any reason—

"He belongs to the local veterans' group." Megan spoke quickly. "He told Hannah that if there was any way they could help her, just to ask."

"That was kind of him." The reserve was back in Paula's voice. "They're nice folks, he and his wife, Nancy. They settled here when he retired from the service, because she has kin here."

"He seemed very pleasant." Hannah shot a look at Megan. *Stop talking about it.*

But Megan chose to ignore the message. "He invited

Hannah to participate in the Veterans Day events, whatever they are."

"A parade," Aunt Paula said. Her gaze, fixed on Hannah, was troubled and questioning. "I know they have a parade. I'm not sure what else."

"Hannah could find out," Megan said.

Hannah felt as if she were being squeezed. "No." Her firmness surprised her.

"But they're only interested in honoring Travis," Megan protested. "I'd think you'd want to be a part of that."

Hannah closed her eyes for a second, trying to find the right words—the words that would stop Megan's pushing and remove the anxiety from her aunt's face. She couldn't. This must be how William felt, trying to express himself and unable to.

"It's too much of a reminder," Aunt Paula said, coming to her rescue. "I think that Hannah is not ready for such a thing yet."

Hannah nodded, the constriction in her throat lessening.

"Oh, Hannah, I'm sorry." Megan put down her fork. "What an idiot I am, pressuring you like that. I didn't mean to."

Hannah managed a smile. "You didn't?"

"Okay, I admit it." Megan's expression turned rueful. "I'm always trying to manage people. I guess I thought it would be good for you to get involved. Forgive me?"

"Of course." Most of Hannah's tension eased away. It would be all right. Their friendship could withstand a disagreement.

But the incident did emphasize the distance between them. They could never go back to the way it had been before Travis died. She and Megan didn't have that common bond any longer.

She had a new life now, and Megan had moved on, too.

Maybe, no matter how much they tried, they wouldn't be able to hold on to their closeness, and she'd have that loss to mourn, as well.

Wednesday afternoon was always quiet in Pleasant Valley, with many of the shops closing early. So far as William knew, nobody was sure how the custom started, but like a lot of things, it was simply what the local people did.

Caleb and Katie would be closing their shops in less than an hour, but that didn't affect him. Caleb wouldn't mind if he stayed here in the workshop, if he wanted.

And William did want that. Working with his hands eased his mind, and he could use that soothing right now. He brushed stain on the rocking chair back he was working on, noticing how it brought up the grain of the wood. He liked to let the rhythm of the work seep into him.

Still, no matter how he tried, he couldn't manage to forget what had happened yesterday. Would Hannah expect to work with him tomorrow? She hadn't said anything. If her guest was still here, she probably didn't, but he wished she'd let him know.

Footsteps on the stairs interrupted a train of thought that wasn't getting him anywhere. He was surprised to see his nine-year-old nephew Joseph, Rachel's son.

"J-Joseph. What are you d-doing here?" He smiled, reaching to the boy.

Joseph hurried to give him a hug. "I went to the dentist. Mammi took me out of school for the whole afternoon."

"How w-was it?"

"No cavities," Joseph said importantly. "Dr. Franklin gave me a new toothbrush. Blue, with a white stripe."

"Gut for you." William leaned against the workbench, relaxing. "S-so what brings you here?"

"Mammi is looking at material for a dress in Katie's shop. She said I could komm up, but not to bother you. I'm not bothering, am I?" Joseph leaned against the bench, too, maybe unconsciously imitating his onkel's pose.

"Never," William said.

"Gut, 'cause I have to tell you something. It's a secret." Joseph whispered the words, even though no one could have heard him.

"If it's a s-secret, m-maybe you shouldn't tell."

"No, it's a secret for you and me and my sisters." He grinned. "Mary will be mad I got to tell you, that's for sure. She's not very gut at keeping secrets."

Mary wasn't even in school yet. She probably didn't understand what her older brother and sister meant about keeping something secret.

"S-so what is it?" Ezra's kinder had been confiding their secrets in Onkel William for a long time. He was glad to see that hadn't stopped.

"Mammi's birthday is next month. We've been saving up for a present for her, and we thought maybe you could make something. We have almost five dollars. Do you think it's enough?" Joseph's small face grew tight with concern.

"Ja, for s-sure." The cost didn't matter. He'd make what the boy wanted, even if he had to cover the difference himself. "What d-do you w-want?"

"We're not sure." Joseph's expression grew very serious. "First we thought a rocking chair, but we don't have enough money for that. So then we thought maybe a bookshelf, except that Gideon made Mammi a whole bookcase for her books last Christmas." Joseph leaned against his arm. "What do you think Mammi would like? You know her really well."

That flicked at his heart, just a bit. Once, he'd known Rachel as well as anyone, he'd have said, but now that she was married to Gideon, he'd cut down on the amount of time he spent there. No matter how generous Gideon was, William didn't want to be a nuisance. He didn't want to

see anything but pleasure in Rachel's face when he came
to her door.

"I'll tell you what your m-mamm would like. A cup
rack." He lifted one down from the shelf above the workbench. "See, l-like this. She c-can keep the cups she uses
out so they're h-handy."

Joseph studied it solemnly. "Could you make it more
curvy?" He made a shape with his hand. "Sort of like
Mammi's flowers?"

"That's a g-gut thought." He ruffled Joseph's hair.
"You're p-pretty s-smart."

Joseph grinned, obviously pleased. "Mammi will like
it, and she'll know you made it special for her. Like when
you made the train for me."

"Y-you r-remember that? You w-were only two then."
He'd nearly forgotten it himself. It had taken him ages,
creating it by trial and error, mostly error. He could do a
better job of it now.

"Ja, for sure. It's on the shelf in my room."

He could make a train like that for Jamie, he realized.
Hannah's boy was just about the right age for such a toy.
It would be a small way of letting Hannah know he ap-
preciated what she'd been doing for him.

"It's s-settled th-then. I'll m-make a cup rack for your
mamm."

"Denke, Onkel William." Joseph leaned against him.
"I knew you would help us."

William put his arm around the boy's shoulders. Joseph couldn't know how much good his visit had done
for William.

He liked knowing someone counted on him and looked
to him for help. To Joseph and his sisters he was someone
special, someone who could be trusted to do what they
couldn't. That attitude was a fine antidote for the way
Hannah's friend had looked at him.

That had been foolishness, letting himself get so upset
by what that woman had said. Childish, and he wasn't a

child, no matter that people seemed to want to treat him that way.

Joseph's innocent faith in him was a reminder he'd needed right now.

Hannah kept an eye out for William at the fire company's barbecue that Wednesday evening, even as she broke up some chicken pieces for Jamie. Aunt Paula held Jamie on her lap at the rough trestle table, managing to keep his hands out of her coleslaw while chatting in Pennsylvania Dutch with the woman next to her.

Megan nudged her elbow. "Do you actually understand them?" she murmured, nodding toward the two women.

Hannah shrugged, trying to grab a bite of her barbecued chicken before Jamie demanded more. "Some of it," she said. "When I was small I heard it all the time, and I'm not sure I even realized whether I was speaking English or dialect. After my family moved away, I lost the language."

"And now it's coming back." Megan glanced at Jamie. "And Jamie will grow up knowing it, I guess."

Hannah shrugged, not sure what Megan was driving at. "It's good to be bilingual, isn't it?"

Megan didn't answer. Instead she glanced around, as if the mixture of Amish, Mennonites, and English gathered around the tables outside the fire hall was strange enough to stare at.

Surely Megan had realized before she came that Hannah's life would be different here, hadn't she? Hannah had thought Megan was getting acclimated, but now she seemed awkward, even uncomfortable, as if she hadn't expected this mix of people.

Hannah scanned a table of Amish men, looking for a familiar face. She wanted to ask William if he would be able to come Friday afternoon, instead of tomorrow, since Megan would be leaving that morning and things would go back to normal.

Not that she wanted Megan's visit to end—of course she didn't think that. But she hadn't expected it to be quite as disruptive as it was turning out to be. She felt as if she had to be constantly alert, explaining Megan to other people as well as helping Megan understand her life here.

"Maybe tomorrow we can take my car and do a little sightseeing," Megan said. "I'll have to make an early start on Friday, so there won't be time then."

"We'll have to work around Jamie's nap. And how busy we are at the bakery."

Aunt Paula, overhearing, waved her hand. "Don't worry about the shop. Naomi will be helping me. You go enjoy yourselves. And maybe Jamie will even sleep in the car for you."

"Great." Megan pounced on that. "Maybe we can make a whole day of it and have lunch out someplace."

"That would be nice." Although Hannah could foresee Jamie having a meltdown if they were out too long.

"I wish I could stay longer," Megan said. "But it's your turn to visit me, don't forget. You can bring Jamie and stay as long as you want."

Hannah caught a look of apprehension in Aunt Paula's face before she had a chance to shake her head.

"That's so nice of you, Megan. But I don't feel quite brave enough to set off on that long trip with Jamie. It was a nightmare just getting here with him. Maybe when he's a little older it will work out."

"Ja, that would be better." Her aunt looked relieved.

Megan seemed about to argue the point, so Hannah got up quickly. "Let's go get some dessert. Aunt Paula, what would you like?"

"Maybe a piece of that chocolate cake with the cara-mel icing, if there's any left. Anna Miller makes that, and it's delicious, for sure. I wish I could get her to make some for the bakery."

"I'll see if there's any left." Hannah scrambled over the bench. "And maybe a cookie for Jamie."

Megan stepped over the bench, too, smoothing down her knit top. "I'm not sure I want anything, but I'll come with you and look anyway."

The crowd hadn't yet gathered around the dessert tables—most were going back to the sizzling grill for seconds. The moment they were out of earshot of her aunt, Megan grabbed Hannah's hand.

"Hannah, don't you see what's going on? The way your aunt reacted at the idea of you coming to visit me? She expects you to stay here for good."

Hannah shook her head, smiling a little. That was Megan, always dramatic. "You're overreacting. My aunt was just agreeing with me about taking Jamie on such a long trip." She gave a mock shudder. "If you'd heard him on the trip here, you wouldn't question it."

"That's not it at all." They'd reached the dessert table, but Megan's mind wasn't on food. "Look, you don't see it because you're too close. I'm telling you, your aunt doesn't want you to ever leave. She probably sees you taking over the bakery, taking care of her in her old age, for that matter."

"That's not so. Really, Megan, you're imagining things. Aunt Paula knew when I came that I'd eventually leave, once Jamie's old enough that I can hold down a full-time job."

"If that's all that keeps you here, don't wait," Megan said promptly. "Listen, you can come to us. Not just for a visit, but to stay. We're going to move off base anyway. I'll watch Jamie so you can work."

"I can't . . ."

"You can. Just forget all this and come back with me. Hannah, you don't belong here."

Megan's voice had risen in her excitement. Hannah tried to hush her, glancing around to see if anyone had heard.

She discovered that William was standing behind her, staring at her, a plate forgotten in his hand. His pleasant, open face seemed to stiffen. Then he turned and walked swiftly away.

"Hannah . . ."

Hannah shook off Megan's arm. She had to fix this, right now. She couldn't have William thinking she intended to leave Pleasant Valley when she'd barely started to help him.

"Please take the dessert to my aunt and Jamie. Tell them I'll be back in a moment."

She hurried off through the crowd, trying to keep William's tall figure in sight. For a moment she lost him when a man lifting a toddler to his shoulder got up from a table in front of her. She stopped, looking around, and then spotted William rounding the end of the cement block fire hall.

She wasn't eager to start anyone gossiping about the two of them, but this misunderstanding had to be set straight now. She walked across the gravel lot, trying to look as if she were just on her way to the restrooms.

Once she reached the building, she slipped around the corner, hoping he hadn't already disappeared elsewhere.

But William was there, leaning against the fender of one of the fire trucks. The trucks had probably been moved back here to make more room for the barbecue dinner.

She approached, her shoes crunching on the gravel, and William looked up. He waited, expressionless, until she stopped next to him.

"Don't look like that." Her words came out involuntarily, startling her as much as they probably did him.

"W-what?" His eyebrows lifted slightly.

"You look as if you're furious and trying to hide it."

He blinked. "Not m-mad." He stopped, shook his head. "Okay. I-I am. You g-gave me h-hope. Now you're leaving." The last words came out on what had to be a wave of anger, and he didn't stammer.

Her throat tightened. Hope. Everyone needed that.

William had let down his guard with her, and now it seemed she was betraying him.

He started to turn away, and she stopped him, grasping his arm.

"I'm not leaving." She said the words firmly. "Get that? I'm not going anywhere."

"Your f-f-friend—"

"My friend doesn't speak for me." She fought down annoyance at Megan. Her fingers tightened on his arm. "You should understand that. People do that to you, too."

William nodded, his face easing. "Ja."

She blew out a relieved breath. He was listening, at least. "Megan is a good friend. She helped me so much when my husband died, and I owe her a lot."

"I know th-that f-feeling."

"I guess you do." She ought to let go of him now. He wasn't going to walk away. But still she held on. It made her feel connected. "Do you feel you owe your family?"

"Ja." He grimaced. "They m-mean w-well. They d-d-don't understand."

"That's Megan, too. She means well. She thinks she knows what's best for me. I don't know . . ." She stopped, because a little piece of truth about herself seemed to be coming clear. "I guess I've let her think that. I've gone along, letting other people make decisions for me."

"Y-you'd just l-lost your husband. That's n-natural."

He covered her hand with his, his palm warm and work-hardened. She seemed to feel his intensity through his touch. And something more than that—a complexity that was normally hidden by his usual pleasant, friendly expression.

"I guess I had an excuse then. But not now." She was almost breathless with the clarity of it. "Jamie needs a grown-up for his mother. I have to decide what's best for him, and for me."

"G-gut," he said, his voice soft.

She tried to smile and had a feeling it wasn't very successful. "I'm finding it kind of scary."

He shook his head, his gaze so intent on her face that it was as if he were touching her. "You are a s-strong w-woman, Hannah. Y-you just d-don't know it."

She looked up into his face, feeling the force of his caring. She wanted to thank him, but when their gazes met, she seemed to lose all track of what she'd intended. And William just stood, hand clasping hers, staring into her eyes.

She didn't know how long they'd have stood there if someone hadn't come out the back door of the fire hall, clattering a couple of pans. She stepped away, sure her cheeks were as red as the engine.

"Will you come on Friday afternoon then, instead of tomorrow?" The words sounded strange in her ears, as if her voice were not her own. "My friend will be leaving Friday morning. All right?"

"Ja." His voice was husky. "F-Friday."

She hurried away, wishing she could find some excuse not to rejoin Megan immediately, afraid of what her face might betray.

CHAPTER NINE

*Y**ou* take it easy on the trip back." Hannah lifted Megan's suitcase into the trunk of her car. "It's such a long way."

Megan checked to be sure she had her keys and closed the trunk lid. "I'll stop at my cousin's on the way home. That'll be a nice break."

They were still being cautiously polite to each other, Hannah realized. Probably Megan felt, as she did, that their friendship was too important to let hasty words spoil it.

Yesterday had been fun, almost like old times. Megan had insisted on taking them all the way to the nearest mall, where she bought Jamie a toy garage. They'd had lunch out, and nothing had happened to remind either of them of their differences.

Well, that wasn't quite true. Just the fact that they were being so cautious was in itself a reminder.

Megan wrapped her in a fierce hug. "You take good care

of yourself and that sweet boy, okay?" She hesitated for a moment. "Look, I don't want to press you. But think about what I suggested. We'd both love to have you, and once Jeff goes on his next tour, I could really use the company."

"I don't think . . ."

"Don't answer now. All I want you to do is promise you'll consider it. Please."

"All right. I will." But Hannah didn't feel it likely that she would change her mind. "Give my love to Jeff, and kiss the children for me."

Megan's eyes glistened with tears, and then she shook her head and smiled. "No crying. I promised myself."

"Call me when you get home, so I know you've arrived safely."

Nodding, Megan got into the car. She gave a final wave, and then she drove off down the street.

Had that hint of tears been because she was leaving? Or because she realized, as Hannah did, that things would never be quite the same between them again?

They'd remain friends, she hoped. But it would be foolish to act as if they were still united by a common bond.

Megan had always been the leader, an experienced army wife when Hannah hadn't known a thing about it. Now Hannah had moved beyond that, and no matter how much Megan thought the difference between them was caused by the life she led now, Hannah recognized the truth. Travis was gone, and with him not only the life they'd shared but also the life she'd shared with the other wives. There was no going back.

She returned to the bakery. It was nearly time to open. Aunt Paula hadn't come down yet, probably wanting to give Hannah space to say good-bye to her friend. Even as she thought that, she heard her aunt's footsteps.

"Megan has gotten off all right?" Aunt Paula asked the question before she'd reached the bottom stair, looking toward the window that faced the street.

"Yes, she—"

It happened too fast for Hannah to get out more than a gasp. One instant Aunt Paula was taking the last step, and the next she went sprawling, giving an involuntary cry.

"Aunt Paula!" Hannah ran to her, heart pounding, as Jamie began to cry, shaking the bars of his play yard as if he knew something was wrong.

"I'm all right. Don't fuss . . ." Aunt Paula had pulled herself up by the time Hannah reached her, but she winced when she put her right foot on the floor.

"You're not all right." Hannah knelt next to her, touching the ankle gingerly. She could already feel the swelling. "It looks as if you've twisted this ankle. Maybe we should take you to the doctor."

"No, no. It'll be fine. I'll put some ice on it after we get through the morning rush."

"You'll do no such thing. You're going right back upstairs and get this elevated. Just let me settle Jamie, and I'll take you up."

Naomi came in the door as she spoke, taking in the scene with a quick glance. "I will get Jamie," she said, going quickly to him. "Is she hurt bad?" She lifted Jamie from the play yard, and he clung to her, his tears waning.

"It is chust a sprain," Aunt Paula declared. "I can work—"

"Hannah is right." Naomi interrupted her with a look at Hannah that conveyed understanding. "We can handle the morning business. Best get off that foot."

Paula looked for a moment as if she'd argue, but then she shook her head. "Ach, what chance do I have, the two of you ganging up on me?"

While her aunt grasped the railing with one hand, Hannah put her arm around Paula's waist, and they made their way slowly up the steps. Obviously the trek was trying enough on her ankle that Paula sat down with a sigh in her favorite chair the instant they reached it.

Hannah shoved the hassock over and lifted the injured

foot, gently removing the shoe. "It's puffing up pretty fast. Are you sure you don't want to go and have it checked?"

Paula shook her head. "I've twisted this same ankle before, and most likely I'll do it again. The right one's always been a bit weak. Chust you go on back downstairs. I'll be fine."

Ignoring the words, Hannah fetched an ice pack from the freezer, wrapped it in a towel, and placed it gently over the swollen ankle. "Do you want anything else? Some aspirin, a cup of coffee, a book?"

"Just push my sewing basket over here where I can reach it, and I'll be fine." She patted Hannah's hand. "You're a gut girl, Hannah. Now you go down and help Naomi."

Knowing her aunt was probably more worried about the bakery than her ankle, Hannah nodded and started back downstairs.

"Call if you need anything. I'll come and check on you in a bit."

When she reached the bakery, she found that Naomi had settled Jamie back in the play yard, where he was busy running cars in and out of his new garage. Naomi stood behind the counter, waiting on the customers who were already showing up for their morning coffee.

"Thanks for taking care of Jamie." Hannah pulled her white apron on, remembering Naomi's reaction the time she'd said something about her making a good mother. "I think my aunt just has a sprained ankle, but still, the fall had to shake her up."

"Ja, for sure. Paula never thinks she can slow down for a minute. It's gut that you're here." Naomi looked up when the bell jangled again and turned to put another pot of coffee on.

For the next hour they dealt with customers, working smoothly side by side, interrupted only when someone asked where Paula was. Hannah suspected that half the valley would know about Paula's fall before lunchtime.

Sure enough, a few minutes later Katie Miller's sister

Rhoda came hurrying in. "We heard about Paula's accident, and my sister sent me along to help out. Can I?"

Hannah almost said they had it under control, but Rhoda looked so eager to help that Hannah didn't want to disappoint her. Besides, learning to help their neighbors was part of Plain life.

"Why don't you take the coffeepot and offer refills to the people at the tables?" she suggested.

"Ja, for sure." Rhoda looked delighted at the prospect, and she carried the pot off quickly.

"She's a gut girl," Naomi said, watching her. "So pert and pretty. I hear the boys all want to bring her home from the singings."

"And I hear there are lots of romances that start at those singings."

Hannah glanced at Naomi, wondering a bit. Probably no one would describe her as beautiful, but Naomi's serene oval face had a charm that surely must have attracted young men. Had Naomi just not found romance? Or had she been too busy for it?

"Ja, that's true. Singings are a chance for teenagers to start pairing off." For a moment it seemed Naomi would stop there. But the line had dwindled down, and Rhoda was tending to the customers at the tables. "I didn't go to them much, myself. My mammi died when my youngest sister was a baby, so I was busy taking care of my brothers and sister."

Hannah wasn't sure how to respond. Naomi didn't seem bitter, but surely she must have some regrets. "It sounds as if you had your hands full, but it's a shame you had to miss . . ."

What? Romance? Marriage? Aunt Paula's comments had made it sound as if Naomi's father had been selfish, or at least that's how Hannah had interpreted the remark.

"I didn't think so much about it then," Naomi said slowly, as if she were looking back at the girl she'd been. "But now that all my friends are married and have growing families of their own, it can get lonesome sometimes, ain't so?"

Hannah nodded. "I know. It's good to have women friends who are going through the things you are. It makes for strong bonds."

"Your friend was here for a visit, ja? You were close with her."

"We were." Again Hannah hesitated, not sure how much to say. But the impulse was strong to confide in someone who didn't claim to know what Hannah should be doing. "After my husband died, my friend Megan helped me out a lot. But now . . ."

She let that trail off, shrugging.

"You don't have so much to talk about anymore, ain't so?"

Hannah nodded. Naomi understood. In her own way, she was isolated, too, so she saw it in other people.

"I'll go up and check on Aunt Paula, now that things here have quieted down a bit, if you can handle the shop."

"For sure. And if Rhoda stays, we could manage the lunch rush wonderful easy," Naomi said.

Hannah stopped at the end of the counter, remembering. William was supposed to come this afternoon. She'd hate to put him off again.

"Hannah? Was ist letz? I mean—"

"What's wrong, I know." Words and phrases in dialect kept popping back into her mind. "Just that William is supposed to come this afternoon. Maybe I should change the arrangements."

"No need for that," Naomi said. "I'm certain-sure we can manage. No reason to disappoint him."

Hannah nodded, but as she hurried up the steps, she found she was thinking of those moments behind the fire hall. Would William be disappointed if they didn't meet today? Or would he be just as happy to avoid her?

The feelings of attraction she'd felt had taken her by surprise, and she still didn't know what to make of them. One thing she did know—William had felt them, too.

When Hannah reached the living room, her aunt was hand sewing a quilt patch. She started to get up, the ice bag sliding off to land on the floor.

"Do you need me? I can come down."

"No, we don't, and you're staying right here." Hannah pushed her gently back in the chair and picked up the ice pack. "I'll get some fresh ice for that ankle, and you keep it elevated. Rhoda Miller has come to help, and she's doing very well. With her here, Naomi and I feel sure we can handle everything right through. You just rest."

"I should help." Her aunt's jaw had a stubborn set to it.

Hannah patted her shoulder. "If I were the one hurting, you'd insist that I sit still and let that swelling go down, ain't so?"

Her aunt smiled at Hannah's use of the Pennsylvania Dutch phrase. "All right. Ja, I will rest."

Fetching another ice pack from the freezer, Hannah reflected that luckily it was one of those items any mother of a toddler had on hand. Then she detoured to the refrigerator and poured a glass of juice, adding a few cookies on a small plate and carrying them all in to her aunt.

"Here you are." She put the ice bag in place, set the snack on the side table, and tucked a knitted afghan over Paula's knees. "Don't even think about coming down those stairs."

Aunt Paula reached up to pat her cheek, and Hannah realized there were tears in her eyes.

Her heart clutched. "Are you in pain? What's wrong?"

"Nothing, nothing." Paula blinked the tears away. "I'm being foolish, is all. But you're taking such gut care of me."

"No more than you've done for us," she said.

"That is a pleasure, and you know it." Her aunt hesitated, eyes serious. "You know, don't you, that the bakery will go to you when I'm gone."

"No, I . . ." Hannah's head spun, and she shook it. "Don't talk that way. You've only sprained your ankle, not had a heart attack. You have plenty of time to think about that."

"There's no thinking to do," she said. "We planned it that way long ago, your uncle and I did, when we made out our wills. It is what both of us wanted."

"I don't know what to say." Hannah couldn't quite comprehend it. Why would they choose her?

"Don't say anything." Aunt Paula's voice had regained its usual briskness. "There's no need to. But I was just thinking that since you're here now, maybe we shouldn't wait. You're taking on so much responsibility already. Maybe you should come in as a partner to me, right away."

The shock of it left Hannah staring. "Aunt Paula, you don't mean it. It's your bakery. You're the one who built it up. You shouldn't—"

"Ja, it is mine, so it's my decision what happens to it. You are already taking on so much, noticing what stock we need, making gut suggestions." Her voice gentled. "I want you to feel a part of it, Hannah. All right?"

The offered gift was taking her breath away. Aunt Paula was showing her love in the most practical way she could.

But . . . for some reason she seemed to hear Megan's voice in the back of her mind. *She'll do anything to keep you here. Anything.*

That was foolish. But she couldn't quite get it out of her head. And her aunt was waiting for a response.

She sucked in a deep breath. "I'm honored, Aunt Paula. Is it all right if I have some time to think about it?"

Disappointment showed for a moment in her aunt's face before she masked it with a smile. "For sure. Take all the time you need. I won't change my mind."

She wouldn't, Hannah felt sure of that. She just wished she felt as sure of her own mind.

William approached the bakery right on time, but he doubted he'd be staying. According to Katie, Hannah's aunt had injured herself, so Hannah would have her hands full.

Maybe that was just as well. Hannah might be taking what had happened between them in her stride, but he wasn't.

He had to be on his guard. Friendship was one thing, but anything more would cause problems. If people even suspected he had feelings for Hannah, the gossip would fly.

Hannah probably didn't understand the power of talk in a community like this one. It was the downside of living in a place where people cared so much for one another. They also knew too much.

Well, whether Hannah understood or not, it was his duty to protect her against careless talk. He pushed open the door.

Naomi was refilling the bakery case after the lunch rush, and Katie's sister Rhoda looked cheerful to be wiping off tables. He nodded to her.

"K-K-Katie said y-you were h-helping."

"Ja." Rhoda's eyes sparkled and she smiled, showing the dimples in her cheeks. "It was wonderful-gut fun, waiting on the tables. I could do it every day."

"You would soon get tired of it," Naomi said, smiling at her enthusiasm.

"H-how is P-Paula?" He approached the counter, preparing to be told Hannah didn't have time for him today.

"Hannah had to threaten to close the bakery if she didn't stay in her chair for today." Naomi smiled to show that she was joking. "I think Paula is doing some better, but Hannah wants her to stay off her feet a bit longer."

"I-if Hannah is b-busy, I c-can—"

"Ach, no, Hannah is expecting you." Naomi waved her hand toward the kitchen door. "Go in, go in. She's waiting for you."

So. It looked like he'd have to figure out how to face Hannah already. He crossed the room and pushed the swinging door into the kitchen.

Hannah was putting the baby monitor on the counter, but she turned when she heard him. "Good, you're here."

Her smile looked almost natural, but her gaze slid away from his face.

"Ja. B-but if y-you are b-busy . . ." He let that trail off, leaving the decision to her.

"No, it's fine." She carried a notebook to the table and waved to him to sit down. "You heard about my aunt, I guess."

He nodded, taking his usual seat.

"I think she'll be fine if she doesn't rush to get back on her feet. But you know how Paula is."

"D-doesn't like to s-slow down." He concentrated on taking easy, relaxed breaths, the way Hannah had showed him.

Hannah flipped open the notebook. "Have you practiced speaking slowly and stretching the vowel sounds?"

"Ja. S-sounds funny, though. I-I practiced in th-the barn. N-nobody but the c-cows can hear."

"Good idea." She smiled, some of the tension in her face easing. "The cows aren't very critical, either."

"N-no." At first it had felt really odd, speaking that way. For sure he wouldn't want anybody to hear him. But Hannah had said that was only for practice, to retrain his speech muscles.

"We're going to practice that again today," Hannah said, "but there's something else I'd like to try first." She frowned a little, glancing down at her notebook and making him wonder what was written there. "You know how you don't stutter as much when you talk to Jamie?"

He nodded. "Other k-kids, too. Like m-my nieces and n-nephews."

"That's what I thought. And what about animals, like when you're driving your horse?"

"N-no, for sure I d-don't stutter then." He smiled at the absurdity of it.

"Well, then, there are plenty of times when you don't stutter. What about when you sing?"

"Sing?" he repeated doubtfully.

"Yes, like in church or wherever you might sing."

He grinned. "I d-don't go around singing."

"Maybe you should," she said, and smiled back at him.

He felt the feather-light touch of awareness, the same awareness that had stunned both of them the other night. Just smiling together was dangerous, it seemed.

If Hannah noticed, she didn't let on. "Try something for me," she said. "Put your fingertips here." She started to reach out to him, but seemed to change her mind. She put her fingers against her own throat.

He copied her, placing his hand against his neck, and found he was thinking about how it would have felt if she'd touched him there.

He shook off the thought. "Ja?"

"Now I want you to breathe out and hum. Just hum a note. It doesn't have to be a song."

He did as she said, feeling foolish. This was another thing he'd have to hide in the barn to practice, he suspected. The hum was a little uncertain.

"There, do you feel the vibration when you hum? Feel how it stops when you stop humming?"

He nodded, not sure how this related to his speech.

"When you speak, if you can take an easy, relaxed breath in, then let out a little air and ease into the word, you'll find it comes out more smoothly."

Hannah demonstrated on herself, putting one hand on her middle and one on her throat. Unfortunately that made him notice how slim her waist was, and how smooth her skin.

Concentrate, he ordered himself.

"You see?" she asked.

"Ja."

"Okay, we'll practice it some more later, but right now I want us to sing something together."

Again with the singing. Did she realize that the Amish didn't listen to popular music? Singing was a big part of worship, but he doubted she knew the songs from the Ausband.

"There must be something we both know," she said, obviously following his thoughts. "What about children's songs? Or old folk songs?"

"At singings, s-sometimes w-we'd s-sing those. Bishop M-Mose agreed." Some Amish congregations were stricter than that, but Bishop Mose always said there was no harm in the old songs.

"Good. What do you know?"

He shrugged. "'Row, R-Row, Row Your B-Boat'?"

"Okay, let's sing that. Together." She began singing, her voice mellow and light, and after a moment's hesitation he joined in.

They reached the end and sat grinning at each other, as if they'd won a race.

Hannah seemed to recall herself. "Did you hear what happened when you sang? Not a single stutter."

He hadn't stuttered, had he? He'd never actually realized that. "I c-can't sing everything."

"No, but you can notice how your throat and your mouth feel when you're singing, and try to do the same, even when you're not. Let's try again, something faster. Do you know 'She'll Be Coming Round the Mountain'?"

He nodded, somewhat reluctantly. "Some, I g-guess."

Hannah began to sing, nudging him when he didn't start with her. He had to join in, and Hannah was determined. Not content with one verse, she plunged on, and he tried to follow.

First he mixed up the verses, and then she did. She started to giggle, hardly able to mouth the words, and the song collapsed into laughter.

And somewhere in the midst of the laughing, he realized it was already too late to guard against feeling anything for her. He already had feelings, and he didn't know what he was going to do with them.

The session with William had gone better than she'd expected, Hannah told herself as she tidied the bakery that evening. Any embarrassment that might have existed had slipped away in the laughter. Singing with him had been a good idea.

Aunt Paula had attempted to come downstairs after supper, but Hannah had managed to forestall it. Staying off that ankle as much as possible was the only sensible thing to do.

Once she'd finished in here, she'd have to start the bread for tomorrow. Little though Aunt Paula would like it, they'd have to get along with fewer varieties of pastries than usual. Hannah was learning, but she hadn't mastered everything by a long shot.

Someone knocked at the bakery door, and she looked up, startled. A man stood on the other side of the glass. Didn't he see the Closed sign?

She went to the door, shaking her head. "We're closed." She said it loudly, reluctant to open the door when she was alone here. And then she realized the man was Isaac Brand, William's older brother.

"I must talk with you." He said the words firmly, his voice coming to her through the closed door. "I know the bakery is not open, but I have something to say to you."

That didn't sound like much of an incentive to open up. She doubted that Isaac had anything helpful to share.

Maybe she was misjudging him, but she'd formed an opinion when she'd heard him speak to William. He hadn't just been rude. He had shown contempt, as if he thought William was negligible, not smart enough to have an opinion.

She'd been the recipient of that contempt herself, as a child going to a city school for the first time, wearing traditional Mennonite clothing, hardly able to understand the other children.

So she didn't want to hear what Isaac had to say. But she could hardly walk away and leave him standing there. She unlocked the door, pulling it open and holding it ajar.

"What is it? The bakery is closed, and I have work to

be done." Maybe he'd deliver his message and be on his way.

"I must come in." He glanced over his shoulder. "This is not something to talk about on the street."

No, that would have been too much to hope for. She opened the door wider, letting him in and feeling her apprehension deepen with each step.

Isaac stood for a moment, stocky and determined, staring at her. She could understand a little of how he intimidated William and the rest of his family. The force of his personality seemed to demand that people pay attention to him.

She looked away from him, moving toward the counter where she'd been working. "How can I help you?"

Now that he was in, Isaac didn't seem to know where to start. His gaze wandered around the room, not landing anywhere.

"This is a nice little business of your aunt's," he said finally.

"Yes. It is." Clearly he hadn't come to tell her that.

"I understand she was hurt today."

"It's just a sprain. She's resting now. It's amazing how quickly word spreads in the valley."

"Ja. Everyone hears, sooner or later." He faced her then, his gaze hard. "They hear, they talk."

He obviously meant something in particular, but she had no idea what. "I suppose that's natural in a small community."

"Some things I do not want to get around and be talked about. Like you meeting my brother behind the fire hall."

For an instant she couldn't breathe. "But . . . I was just talking to him." *Was that all?* A voice whispered in the back of her mind. "About when we'd meet to work on his speech."

"It does not matter why you were there. People will talk. I don't want gossip about my family."

Hannah felt herself cringing inside and longing to run

away from a fight as she always did. But little though she liked confronting people, she couldn't accept Isaac's skewed version of events.

"It was perfectly innocent," she said, trying to keep her voice cool and firm. "And it was between me and William."

Not you, she almost said, but thought better of it.

"You do not know how things are here." Isaac looked at her with open dislike. "This business of trying to master his stuttering—my brother doesn't need your help. We love William as he is, and we'll take care of him."

"Maybe he wants to take care of himself."

Isaac's gaze narrowed. "William will listen to me. Nothing but trouble can come of this. He can only be hurt by spending time alone with an Englisch woman."

Isaac's mouth shut like a trap. He stalked to the door, walked out, and slammed it shut.

CHAPTER TEN

Saturday morning was always a little different in the bakery. The early-morning coffee-drinkers were less likely to visit, but more people stopped in while out shopping, or they came by for lunch.

By midmorning, Hannah was satisfied that all was running smoothly with the help of Naomi and Rhoda. But Jamie wasn't used to being left alone with his toys for so long, and he began to fuss. Hannah's thoughts bounced from Aunt Paula, alone upstairs, to Jamie.

She touched Naomi's arm as she wrapped bread for the sole person waiting. "I'm going to take Jamie upstairs for a few minutes and check on my aunt. Will you be all right without me?"

"Ja, for sure." Naomi's face showed her concern. "How is Paula?"

Hannah paused, not sure how to answer. "Her ankle looks better. Very bruised, of course. But she seemed so down this morning, and I'm not sure why."

"Maybe the accident upset her, like you said yesterday," Naomi suggested. "Paula is always so strong. Getting hurt might have reminded her that none of us can go on forever. Life changes when we least expect it, ain't so?"

It was an unexpected insight, and it unsettled Hannah.

"You're a wise woman, Naomi," she murmured.

Naomi shook her head, smiling, and turned to the customer.

"Mama, Mama!" Jamie shouted, loud enough to turn everyone's head.

Rhoda started toward him, saying something soothing.

"Thanks, Rhoda, I'll take him. I'm going upstairs for a bit. I think he needs a snack and a change of scenery, don't you, little boy?"

Hannah lifted him, and his pout turned quickly to giggles. "Mama," he said again. "Up."

"For a man of few words, you make your wishes known, don't you?" She snuggled him, planting a kiss on his cheek. "Let's go see Aunt Paula."

She headed upstairs, carrying him on her hip, and he clung to her like a little monkey.

Naomi had a good point, she suspected. Aunt Paula had done everything on her own for years, but what did she see now when she looked to the future?

Well, Hannah knew that, didn't she? Aunt Paula had offered her a partnership, a share in the business that would assure the future for Hannah and for Jamie.

Hannah still hadn't given her an answer, although she felt as if she'd thought of little else. Accepting would calm all her worries and would ensure security for Jamie—the most important thing in the world to her.

And she was tempted for other reasons, as well. This short experience of actually running the bakery on her own had been a pleasure, in spite of her worries about her aunt. She'd liked dealing with customers, working with Naomi and Rhoda, even making the decisions about what baked goods she could offer. She'd found herself thinking about what she might do if she really were in charge.

She could be, thanks to Aunt Paula's offer. But could it cost her child in the future? She'd be committing to live her life here in Pleasant Valley. Was that the life Travis would have wanted for his son?

She pinned a smile to her face as she reached the living room, and found her aunt cautiously trying to put her weight on her foot.

"Are you sure that's a good idea?" Hannah fastened the gate at the top of the stairs and went toward her. "You don't want to set yourself back by doing too much too soon."

"I'll certain-sure drive myself crazy if I sit around up here." Aunt Paula sounded fretful, but then she looked at Jamie and smiled. "Ach, I'm sure a complainer. Komm, Jamie." She sat down and patted her lap. "Let me see you."

Hannah set Jamie on his feet, and he went across the floor in his usual rush, flinging himself at Paula's knees. "Watch your foot," Hannah exclaimed, afraid he'd land right on it, but her aunt had already picked him up.

"He's all right." Paula bounced him a little, smiling. "He wants to play peek-a-boo, I think."

Jamie, understanding, clapped both hands over his eyes, making them laugh.

"Why don't you leave him up here with me? We'll have fun together."

Hannah hesitated. "But if you had to get up . . ."

"I was thinking about that. There's an old cane up in the attic that my daad used. If you'd get that for me, I think I could get around pretty well. It's right on top of the chest of drawers by the window."

"I'll get it if you promise not to do too much," she said.

"Ach, ja, I promise. Go on with you."

As Hannah started up the attic stairs, she heard her aunt singing something to Jamie in Pennsylvania Dutch, and the sound followed her, stirring memories. Had someone sung that song to her a long time ago?

Some daylight filtered into the attic from the windows at either end of the building, but the contents were shrouded in shadow. She pulled the tangling chain of the overhead bulb, flooding the attic with light.

Hannah turned slowly, looking for the chest of drawers her aunt had mentioned. There it was, and she could see a long object swathed in plastic on top of it. She crossed the rough wooden planks to the chest and unwrapped the cane. It was a sturdy one with a smooth, rounded handle, just the thing for Aunt Paula.

Hannah left the plastic on the chest to use when she put the cane away again. It didn't surprise her that the cane had been carefully wrapped. Aunt Paula's attic was as neat as the rest of her domain. Most things seemed to be stored in plastic bins or cardboard boxes, all carefully labeled. At a guess, Paula would know where to lay her hand on anything up here.

Smiling a little, Hannah started back toward the stairs. And then she stopped, feeling as if she'd taken a blow that left her breathless. Several boxes, stacked atop a trunk, were neatly labeled in Aunt Paula's printing. *Elizabeth's things*.

Hannah let a breath out slowly. Drawn to the label by an urge she didn't quite understand, she went closer, putting out a hand to touch the topmost box. She ran her fingertips over the lettering. *Elizabeth's things*.

The things Elizabeth had left behind, in other words. The remnants of their life here, not just left behind, but unwanted.

Hannah reached toward the flap of the box, secured by tape. It would be easy enough to pull the tape off and see what was inside.

She snatched her hand back, her stomach churning. She didn't want to look. Didn't want to know what was inside, didn't want to be reminded. She spun, yanked the light chain, and hurried down the stairs.

By the time she reached the living room, she'd managed

to regain her composure. "Here it is; it was right where you said." She held the cane out to her aunt, and Jamie made a grab for it. "Not for you," she said.

Jamie stuck out his lower lip for an instant. When that didn't get any result, he trotted over to the toy basket and pulled out a stuffed bear, carrying it back to Aunt Paula.

"Bear story," he announced, shoving the bear onto her apron.

"You are the smartest boy." Her aunt lifted him to her lap. "Ja, I will tell you the bear story. Once upon a time . . ."

The telephone rang, and Hannah went to answer it, the story of the three bears unwinding behind her. Jamie's favorite, especially with the voices Aunt Paula gave to the bears.

"Hello?"

"Is that Hannah?" A male voice, brusque. It took her a moment to pin it down.

And then she knew. Robert Conroy, Travis's father. How could she forget his voice? She just hadn't expected a call from him.

"Yes, it's Hannah. It's nice to hear from you, Robert. Is anything wrong?" She glanced at Aunt Paula and saw from her expression that she understood who the caller was.

"I'm fine." The curt voice reminded her of what Travis had said about his father—that he was better at giving orders than relating to people. "Did you get the photo I sent?"

Her throat tightened. "Yes, I did. That was kind of you. I did write you a note, thanking you, but you probably haven't received it yet. I put some recent pictures of Jamie in the envelope, too."

"Good. Is the boy okay?"

The boy. She suppressed annoyance that he didn't use Jamie's name. "Jamie's fine. He's growing like a weed and trying to learn new words all the time."

As if he knew she was talking about him, Jamie looked

up from his bear and gave her the smile that was uncannily like Travis's.

Aunt Paula, probably thinking to offer her some privacy, struggled to her feet with the aid of the cane. "Komm, Jamie. Snack time."

She started for the kitchen, and Jamie raced ahead of her.

"Good." Robert repeated himself as if he had trouble finding something to say to her.

Well, was that so surprising? She and Travis had visited him once after their marriage, and it hadn't exactly been a success. Travis and his father had gotten into a quarrel over something so trivial that Hannah didn't remember what it had been. She just remembered that they'd left a day earlier than they'd planned, and she'd felt helpless to make things better between them.

The next time she'd seen Robert had been at Travis's funeral.

Robert cleared his throat. "You're still staying with your aunt, I guess."

"Yes, we are. It's working out very well. I help her with the bakery, and she helps me with Jamie."

"This aunt of yours." He paused. "She's Mennonite, I understand."

A slight trickle of apprehension touched her, as if a draft had tickled the back of her neck. There'd been an odd undertone to his words.

But that was silly.

"Yes, that's right." She hesitated, wondering what he wanted to know. "Well, I am, too, of course. We attend worship with her."

Silence greeted her words. And then—

"You think that's what Travis wanted for his son, being raised by people who are against everything he stood for?"

She was so stunned that for a moment she couldn't speak. What on earth did he mean? For an instant she wanted to hang up the receiver, as if that would allow her to avoid the entire subject.

But she could hardly do that. She had to try to get along with Jamie's grandfather. It wasn't right to let Travis's troubles with Robert spill over into another generation.

"I'm not sure what you mean." She kept her voice calm with an effort. "It's true that Mennonites and Amish believe in nonresistance, but that doesn't mean anyone would say anything derogatory about Jamie's father or his service in the military."

He made a sound that was close to a grunt. "I've been asking around, and I don't like what I'm hearing. People living like they did a hundred years ago, keeping to themselves—who knows what goes on there. You know what it sounds like? It sounds like a cult."

"It's not a cult." Dismayed, she realized her voice was shaking a little. "The Mennonite church is a perfectly legitimate one."

"Wearing strange clothes, using horses and buggies . . . You call that normal?"

Hannah closed her eyes for a moment, praying for calm. And wisdom, lots of wisdom.

"My aunt has a car. We use electricity and the telephone. There are just some things we choose to live without."

You couldn't be with your own son for more than a day without starting a quarrel with him. And I'm beginning to understand why.

"Why do you have to stay there?" Robert's question was so intense that she suspected that was where this conversation had been headed from the beginning. "Why didn't you accept your friend's offer?"

The questions seemed to batter her, and for an instant Hannah couldn't think. Then she realized what he'd said, and it was like a cold hand on the back of her neck.

"My friend? Do you mean Megan Townsend? What do you know about her offer?" He'd obviously been in touch with Megan. Was he spying on her?

"She called me. She's worried about you. She told me what it's like where you're living, with people wearing old-fashioned clothes and driving horses. Doing without stuff everybody in this country takes for granted. You're no kind of a mother to that boy if you expect him to live that way."

Megan. Megan had done this. Her friend had brought it on her. Hannah felt as if she couldn't breathe.

The line was silent, and it seemed to her that wariness was present in that silence. Maybe Robert was already regretting his harsh words, but he probably wouldn't say so.

She took a deep breath, saying another quick prayer. Then she spoke.

"I will be glad to talk to you anytime about how Jamie is doing. But I think right now we should hang up before we say something we will regret."

Suiting the action to the word, Hannah hung up the receiver. She stood for a moment, hand on the phone, half-expecting Robert to call her again immediately, furious with her for hanging up on him.

He didn't. But she couldn't imagine that this disagreement between them was over.

The setting sun touched the plumed tops of the sumac in the hedgerow, making them look like so many torches. William leaned against the fence. September was a fine month on a farm, and it was good to have a moment to enjoy it.

If circumstances had been different, most likely he'd have been the son taking over Daadi's farm, as usually happened in Amish farm families. The younger son was most often of an age to take over when the father decided to retire, while the older ones would have moved on to their own farms or businesses.

But Daad's ill health had changed that for all of them. Isaac had been pushed into running the farm at an early age, and he'd done it well. Ezra, when he was old enough, married Rachel, taking over the farm next door. It was the sensible solution, but now . . . well, it had somehow left no place for William.

Still, maybe that had worked out for the best. He loved working with wood, and Caleb seemed to think he had a gift for it. He could be happy doing that for his life's work.

He heard a step behind him, and then Isaac came to lean on the fence next to him.

"A gut day, ja? Soon enough it will start getting colder."

William nodded. "S-sumacs are t-turning." Relaxed breath, take it easy going into the word, he reminded himself.

"We'll maybe get one more cutting off that south field," Isaac said. "I'll need you here the first part of the week, ja?" Isaac turned, as if he'd said all he'd come for.

William's jaw tensed. They both knew full well that Isaac had plenty of help for that job from his sons. And if William was ever going to speak up, this would be a good time.

"I-I-I'm b-b-busy." He tried to remind himself again of how to approach the words, but it seemed to do no good when his jaw was clenched tight.

Isaac wheeled toward him. "What?"

"B-b-busy." He took a breath, trying to ease his throat muscles. "Caleb h-has t-t-to go s-s-someplace Monday. I-I'm watching the shop."

Better, that was better. All he had to do was remember what he'd been practicing.

Isaac frowned for a moment. "Well, I guess you can't let him down, if he's counting on you. But Tuesday for sure."

"I h-have my m-meeting w-with Hannah."

Isaac reddened under his tan, and he looked as if he controlled himself with an effort. "It's time you gave up on that foolishness. You don't need to change yourself."

"I-I-I . . ." He seemed to choke on the words he wanted to say. Now was not the time for his lessons to desert him.

"I knew you'd understand." Isaac clapped him on the shoulder. "You'll see. This is for the best, and that is what I told Hannah Conroy."

"You d-did what?"

"I went to see that . . . Hannah Conroy last night. I explained that these lessons weren't gut for you. I'm sure she understood."

"How could you d-do that?" It seemed anger worked even better in helping him get the words out. Isaac had gone to Hannah behind his back, as if he were a child.

Isaac took a step back, his hand dropping from William's shoulder. The slanting sunlight made his face even ruddier.

"You are my little bruder. I must take care of you, ain't so? I can't let you—"

William turned away, not wanting to hear any more. Not wanting to hear Isaac compare his friendship with Hannah to his mistaken infatuation for Rachel. Worse, if he tried to tell Isaac what he thought, he'd end up a stammering, incoherent mess.

He strode quickly toward the stable, praying that Isaac wouldn't attempt to follow him. He could hitch up the buggy and be in town in fifteen minutes or so.

It wasn't until he was on the road that doubts began to creep into his mind. What if Isaac was right, and these sessions didn't help at all? What if he was kidding himself that he'd ever be able to speak well? He certainly had failed at this effort to speak his mind. Maybe it would always be that way.

Worse, what if Hannah had accepted Isaac's demands? Isaac could be intimidating, and Hannah might just want to keep peace in the community.

He was on the outskirts of town, and he slowed the pace at which he'd been driving the animal. His first thought had been that he had to see Hannah, to tell her not to heed whatever nonsense Isaac had told her.

Now that he was nearly there, it wondered him what

exactly he could say. The mare seemed to sense his inde-
cision, turning her head to look at him. Well, he was here
now, and he wouldn't go away without setting this straight.
"Step up, Bess."

In a few minutes he was pulling into the alley beside
the bakery. He slid down and tied the mare to the hitching
rail. It was well past closing time, so they were probably
upstairs. He went to the back door that opened onto the
kitchen stairway and rang the bell.

He heard someone coming. Hannah, he realized, rec-
ognizing her footsteps. She opened the door and stood
looking at him.

"We h-have t-to talk."

She nodded as if she'd been expecting him. "Come
into the bakery kitchen. It's quiet there. My aunt is playing a game with Jamie."

It must be a tickling game, judging from the squeals
and giggles coming from upstairs. He followed Hannah
into the room where they usually met, and she gestured
for him to close the door.

It was warm in the kitchen, heat still radiating from the
big gas ovens. Hannah faced him, strain evident in her
face.

Had Isaac upset her that much? A fresh surge of anger
went through him, and he tried to conquer it.

"I kn-kn-know I-Isaac came and talked to you. I'm
s-sorry."

Hannah blinked, as if she had to refocus her thoughts.
"Yes. He did." She put her hand up to her cheek, as if she
needed comforting. "Did he tell you what it was about?"

William felt a frown wrinkle his forehead. "A-about
our l-lessons, ja?"

"That." She took a breath, pressing her lips together as
if she didn't want to say anything more. "And the fact that
we met privately behind the fire hall Wednesday night. He
made it sound as if we . . ." She let that trail off.

His hands clenched into fists, but for Hannah's sake, he

must take it lightly. "That's f-foolishness. If h-he saw us or s-someone else t-told him, it's s-still silly."

"That's what I thought. I told him it was perfectly innocent. I don't know if he believed me." But there was still a question in her eyes.

"D-doesn't matter," he said, forcing the words out. "I am a g-grown man. I d-decide for myself."

She smiled, her expression lightening a little. "I told him that, too."

"Gut." The anger slid away, and he smiled at her. As long as Hannah knew how to take it, he didn't care what Isaac said.

But the worry wasn't gone from her face. The skin around her eyes seemed to be stretched tight. She'd already been upset when she came to the door. But if not because of Isaac, then what?

"Hannah?" He reached out, wanting to touch her to ease the strain, but drew back. "Was ist letz?"

"Nothing." She stopped, looking uncertain. "Well, that's not quite true. I had a call that upset me. From Travis's father."

"Is h-he all r-right?" She hadn't mentioned her husband's family. He'd had the idea they weren't in the picture.

"Oh, he's fine. Just angry." Her hands twisted together. "He's angry because I'm living here. Can you believe it? He has the idea that because Mennonites believe in nonviolence, they will condemn Jamie's father for being a soldier." Her lips trembled, and she put her hand up to hide them.

"That's n-not so. No one w-would."

"I know. That's what I told him, but he wouldn't listen. He said . . . he said I wasn't a good mother if I brought Jamie up here."

She wrapped her arms around herself, unconsciously moving as if she held her babe in her arms. William felt as if he'd been punched in the heart by her pain.

"You are ser gut as a m-mammi. Everyone kn-knows

th-that." Unable to hold back any longer, he took her twisting hands, and wrapped them in his. "D-does Paula know about this?"

Paula Schatz was a strong woman who understood the world better than most. She'd do anything to protect Hannah and Jamie.

"I . . . I tried to keep her from hearing the worst of it. I didn't want her to worry." Hannah shook her head, but tears spilled over onto her cheeks anyway. "It was Megan who told him that nonsense. My friend, reporting to him behind my back."

A sob caught in her words. He seemed to feel her pain and disappointment, as if the betrayal had hurt him, too.

"Don't, Hannah. D-don't hurt so." He couldn't stand it. He drew her into his arms, wrapping them around her so that she was enclosed in his embrace.

She buried her face in his chest, and he felt the tears soaking into his shirt. Sobs shook her body, and all he could do was pat her and whisper soothing words, his cheek against her hair.

Hannah wept helplessly, clinging to him, for several moments. Then the sobs lessened and she straightened, as if becoming aware of who she was holding on to.

"I'm sorry," she murmured, sniffling a little. "I shouldn't let myself cry." She drew back, looking into his face.

They were very close—so close he could feel her breath on his skin. Her eyes seemed to widen in a question, and then to grow darker, the golden brown turning to chocolate.

"William?" It was soft, questioning, and it touched his heart.

He couldn't stop. He leaned forward, closing the distance between them, and found her lips with his.

Her arms were already around him, but now they tightened as she held him as tightly as he held her. Her lips were soft, sweet, and kissing her was like coming home, home to a place he'd never known.

He didn't want to end it, ever. But he had to. Slowly he

pulled back from her. Hannah's expression was bemused, as if she didn't quite know what had happened, but a trace of a smile lingered on her lips, and she lifted her fingers to touch them.

The enormity of what he'd done hit him with nearly enough force to knock him off his feet. "I-I-I am s-sorry," he stammered. He blundered toward the door and came close to running outside.

He'd been wrong. He didn't just care what happened to Hannah. He was falling in love with her. And that could lead to nothing but heartbreak.

CHAPTER ELEVEN

From where she sat in the churchhouse, Hannah could see Aunt Paula seated on the left, closer to the front. There was logic, as well as tradition, in the seating arrangements in the plain, simple churchhouse. Older men sat on the right front, facing the ministers' bench, while older women sat on the left. The rest of the community filled in the benches in the center, women and girls on one side, men and boys on the other.

Hannah sat with other young mothers, and they were quick to help each other. Warm smiles and comforting pats soothed fretful little ones, and for the most part, the babies and toddlers were quiet throughout the two-hour service.

Hannah snuggled Jamie against her. He was nearly asleep, and she watched his eyes drift shut.

The bishop was giving the long sermon today, and she focused on his face, weathered and kindly. At first she'd come to worship because Aunt Paula just assumed that she would. She'd gradually grown to value the peace she found in this plain, simple space, to find herself turning to God more and more often, like a child turned to a parent. Unfortunately that peace she usually felt was eluding her today.

Concentrate on the sermon, she ordered herself. Shut out other thoughts and worries—things like Robert's attitude, Megan's betrayal, William's kiss. Her breath caught, and she prayed her cheeks weren't red at the very thought of it.

It didn't mean anything. It couldn't. William was attracted to her, maybe, and maybe she felt the same. He was strong and kind and she'd selfishly leaned on that strength in a weak moment when she felt bombarded on all sides.

But it wouldn't be fair to William to let him imagine there could be a romantic relationship between them. Somehow, she'd have to find a way of being sure he understood that.

The bishop's wise, reasoned sermon on the love of God drew to a close. Two other ministers spoke briefly from their seats on the ministers' bench, endorsing the bishop's views. And then they all slid from the benches to their knees for a prayer.

As if realizing Hannah might not be as practiced at kneeling while holding a sleeping toddler, the woman next to her took her elbow and helped her. Hannah gave her a smile of thanks as they bowed their heads.

A few minutes later, they were all on their way out of the churchhouse, cheerful voices raised in greeting and conversation. Hannah had the feeling that no one would think to leave until they'd greeted everyone, even a relative outsider like herself.

Jamie, of course, woke up the minute she'd walked outside, and he clamored to get down. She set him on the grass but kept a careful grip on his hand as she scanned the crowd for Aunt Paula.

"Ach, this little boy wants to run off some energy, ain't so?"

The bishop, Ephraim Zimmerman, bent to ruffle Jamie's hair. As he straightened, he beckoned to several teenage girls who were talking, heads together, probably about boys to judge by the way their glances drifted in the direction of a cluster of youths not far away.

The girls came quickly in answer to the bishop's summons, faces apprehensive, as if Bishop Ephraim had seen their interest.

"Mary and Anna, you will take little Jamie to play in the grass for a bit, ja? Give his mammi a chance to visit."

"Ja, sure." They looked relieved, nodding quickly. The older of the two gave Hannah a shy smile, while the other knelt, speaking to Jamie and holding out her hands.

With a babbled response that might have meant anything, Jamie lunged toward her. Then, chortling, he trotted across the grass as fast as his chubby legs would carry him, with the two girls in hot pursuit.

"Denke," Hannah said, using the Pennsylvania Dutch word for thanks. "That was thoughtful of you."

"My wife has taught me the value of a little break for our young mothers," he said, his gaze searching her face. "And you were looking troubled in worship this morning, Hannah."

She started to say that she was fine, but the words died on her lips. He was looking at her as if he saw into her heart, and she suspected he would know in an instant if she didn't tell the truth.

"I'm sorry," she said. "I should be able to leave my worries behind when I come to worship."

He considered. "True, but if they won't be left behind, it's best to bring them to the Lord. Is there something that I can do? Or my wife?" He smiled, his gaze seeming automatically to search out his wife, a dumpling of a woman with white hair and rosy cheeks who reminded Hannah of Mrs. Claus, although she certainly wouldn't say so.

"I don't think so, but I'm grateful for the offer. It's hard, sometimes, to know what is best to do. Especially when you feel pulled in opposite directions, as I am." She hoped the oblique answer would satisfy him.

"Ja, I can see that. This life must be much different from what you've been used to." Again that searching look touched her face.

That was certainly true, but it wasn't the surface differences that troubled her. "It's certainly brought back the memories of my childhood here."

"Ja, it would." He smiled slightly. "I married your mammi and daadi, did you know that?"

She was startled, but it wasn't so surprising, was it? Thirty years wasn't long in a community like this one. "No, I didn't know. After we left here, my mother didn't talk about the past."

"It grieved me when they left us." He shook his head, lines deepening in his face. "I feared we had failed them."

"They weren't happy." The words were out before she could censor them. "They thought they wanted a different place, but it didn't bring happiness."

"For you most of all," Bishop Ephraim said quietly. "And now you are stuck between the two worlds, not sure where you belong."

"Yes."

That was exactly right. Where was the belonging and the security that she was looking for? Or was she destined to be eternally dissatisfied, as her parents had been?

"Your aunt wants you to stay, ja? To become part of our lives here and mend the place that was broken when her sister went away."

Hannah couldn't tell him about Travis's father, with his prejudiced reaction to Mennonites. And she certainly couldn't tell him about William. But the bishop had put his finger on exactly what troubled her about her relationship with Aunt Paula.

"I'm not sure I can be what she wants."

Her eyes followed Jamie. One of the girls was swinging him around, and he was giggling, looking happy, content, as if he belonged. That was what she wanted for him. But was that unfair to Travis's memory?

"Your aunt is a strong woman. She will accept whatever you decide." The bishop paused. "You are part of our community by birth, Hannah. You will always be welcome here, whatever you choose."

"Denke," she said again. "Thank you."

He smiled, nodded, and took a step away, and someone else came to greet him. She realized that people had tacitly accepted his conversation with her, careful not to interrupt until he'd signaled he was finished.

Bishop Ephraim was a wise man, and a kind one. Even though she hadn't felt able to tell him everything that troubled her, he'd helped her toward a measure of understanding.

It wasn't fair to keep Aunt Paula hanging. She had to give her an answer about the partnership. She just wasn't sure what that answer should be.

William glanced toward the bakery as he drove the buggy down Main Street on Monday morning. Then, as quickly, he looked away, afraid he might see Hannah. Or maybe afraid she might see him.

He had to deal with the situation. He should have told Hannah how sorry he was after their kiss, not walked off like a dumb lump. What did she think of him now? He didn't even want to guess.

He'd failed with Isaac. There were no two ways about that. His confidence in his ability to speak had vanished, blown away like a leaf in the wind.

And he'd failed with Hannah. She'd been hurting. She'd needed comfort from a friend, not . . .

He pushed the thought away vigorously and turned the horse into the alley that led to the stable behind Caleb's shop. It was time to put that mistake behind him and get on with the business at hand. There was something he'd been wanting to talk to Caleb about, and today was as good a time as any.

In a few minutes he'd unharnessed the horse and turned it into the small paddock where both Caleb's and Katie's buggy horses stood side by side. They whickered a welcome, for all the world as if they were greeting an old friend.

William went in the back, as he usually did when he came to work, just as glad that he didn't have to go out on the street again.

Caleb stood at the counter, showing something to young Becky Brand, his niece, who sometimes minded the shop.

"William, it is gut that you are here. I was just telling Becky to call you if anyone has a question she can't answer. She'll stay and take care of the shop while you are working."

"S-ser g-gut." He nodded to Becky, relieved that she'd be there to wait on any customers. Becky was a sweet girl, just sixteen and best friend to Katie's sister.

Becky dived behind the counter and came up with a dust cloth. "I will start with cleaning the display. If you want me to go for coffee later, Cousin William, just let me know."

He nodded, not sure how to reply. Everyone was used to him going for coffee in midmorning. What would Hannah think if he didn't come? Maybe she'd be relieved.

"Let's go up to the workshop, and I'll show you what's ready to work on." Caleb started up the stairs, with William following.

When they reached the workshop, William put the letter he'd been carrying onto the workbench in front of Caleb, along with the list he'd made.

Caleb, giving him a puzzled glance, picked it up. "Is this for me?"

"Not e-exactly." William reminded himself to keep his breathing easy. He'd rehearsed what he would say. "You w-were saying that t-trade falls off i-in the winter. I thought m-maybe you'd want to see if s-some stores in the bigger towns w-w-would take pieces on c-consignment."

Caleb studied the list William had made, including all the furniture stores in the county. The letter describing what Caleb and William had to offer had taken more time to compose, but he'd enjoyed writing it. It was so much easier to express himself that way than with speech.

Caleb didn't respond right away, but William hadn't expected him to. Caleb was one who thought before making a decision. Finally he looked up.

"You did all this on your own?" He gestured with the papers.

"Ja. I-if you th-think I shouldn't h-have—"

"No, no. I'm impressed." He grinned. "I think it's a fine idea, William. You're right. We do need more outlets for our work. And we won't lose anything by trying, ja?"

Relief swept through William, making him realize how tense he'd been about presenting his idea. "Ja," he said.

Caleb clapped him on the shoulder. "Gut. We will do it." He paused, giving William a long, steady look. "Was ist letz? You look like something else is on your mind."

William shrugged. He couldn't say anything to anyone about what had happened with Hannah. That was private, and he'd have to reveal too much that wasn't his to tell. But Caleb already knew about the situation with his brother, and in a way, he was already involved.

"Isaac. L-like always."

"What is it now?" Frowning, Caleb moved to the work-bench where a rocking chair was in progress. "He's not happy with you working here?"

"N-not exactly." William picked up one of the spindles for the rocking chair, turning it over in his hand. "He j-just wants m-me to be there when he w-wants me."

And he wanted William to give up on working with

Hannah on his speech. Why? What did it matter to him? Just his natural tendency to dislike anything he hadn't thought of? Or was it something else?

Caleb's frown deepened. "I'm sorry he's taking your working here this way."

Maybe it was time William asked the question that had been lingering in the back of his mind. "You r-really n-need me, ain't so?"

Caleb understood almost at once what he was really asking. "I didn't offer you the job just to put a spoke in Isaac's wheel. Or because I don't always like the way he treats you." He gestured at the workbenches, the projects in various stages of completion. "You do gut work, William. This is your gift, I think."

Rachel had said something similar, but it meant a lot, coming from Caleb. "Denke."

"Ja." Caleb's expression grew serious. "It's certain-sure I need you. But is this really what you want? You can tell me the truth. If you're missing the farm and you'd rather be there . . ." He let that fade off, studying William's face as if he could read the answer there.

William leaned against the bench, trying to think how to respond. "I-if the f-farm had komm to me, I w-would not have thought of a-anything else."

An Amish person would not say that one job was better than another, so long as both were done to the glory of God, but most folks felt in their hearts that farming was best.

Caleb nodded his understanding. "If your father had lived longer it would be different."

"Ja. B-but now I can do what c-calls to me." He ran his fingers along the curve of the spindle. "That i-is the wood."

"That's what I thought." Caleb nodded, seeming satisfied. He paused. Then he cleared his throat. "Do you want me to talk to Isaac? I will, if you want."

The temptation was strong to say yes. So strong.

But if he let Caleb speak for him, he wasn't behaving like a man.

"Denke, Caleb. But I w-will s-speak to him myself."

Aunt Paula sank into her chair with a sigh she probably wished she could hide. Monday had been a long day, and as much as Hannah and the others tried to keep Paula off her feet, she evaded them.

Hannah shoved the footstool over to her. "Your ankle is paining you. I can see that. Please, prop it up for a while, and I'll get some ice."

She was prepared for an argument, but it didn't come. Aunt Paula meekly put her ankle up, shaking her head a little.

"I am too stubborn, ja? I should have listened to you and Naomi."

"I'll remind you of that tomorrow."

Hannah hurried into the kitchen and retrieved an ice bag and a towel to wrap it in. When she returned, Aunt Paula was leaning back in the chair, eyes closed. The lines in her face seemed deeper, her usual rosy complexion pale.

"Is it very bad?" She put the ice bag gently over the puffy ankle.

"I'm chust tired." Aunt Paula managed a smile. "I must be getting old, to be so tired out by a simple twisted ankle."

Hannah remembered what Naomi had said—that for older people, sometimes the smallest accident could be an unwelcome reminder that they couldn't do what they used to.

"You can still bake rings around anyone in the valley," she said, hoping for a bit more of a genuine smile. "You just need to take it a little easier."

Paula patted her hand. "Denke, my Hannah. It means so much to have you here."

Unspoken was the question—will you accept my offer?

Hannah hesitated. Her aunt, perhaps thinking that she'd pushed too hard, spoke again before Hannah had to say anything.

"I saw that Bishop Ephraim was talking to you yesterday. It is always a special day when he is with us."

"He's so kind." Hannah pulled her chair a bit closer and sat down. "And wise. I had the feeling he understood all the things I didn't say." Such as her complicated feelings about her mother and Aunt Paula.

Your aunt is a strong woman. The bishop's words seemed to ring in her ears. If he were here, she suspected he'd be telling her to be open with Aunt Paula. It was the right thing to do.

"Ja, he is wise. A great comfort in times of trouble, and I think you are troubled. I did not mean to make you unhappy with my offer, Hannah."

"You didn't," she said quickly. This was what came of not being open, it seemed. "I am worried, yes, but about Travis's father, not about your offer."

Paula leaned forward, clasping Hannah's hands in both of hers. "But . . . what has happened? I thought he chust called to ask about Jamie. Is something wrong?"

Hannah took a deep breath. This would probably hurt her aunt, but she didn't see any way out of telling her.

"It seems Megan called him and told him some garbled story about our lives here. He was angry." Her voice dragged, and she had to force the rest of the words out. "He said I wasn't being a good mother, to bring up Travis's son among people who hated everything he stood for."

"The military?" Her aunt seemed to grapple with the problem. "But why? Ja, we do not believe that violence is the answer to a problem, and we do not take up arms to fight. But no one would make the mistake of hating a soldier for following a different belief. Or teach Jamie anything but respect for his daadi." She glanced at the door to Jamie's room, as if to assure herself that he was safe in his crib. "Didn't you tell him that?"

"He caught me so much by surprise, and I was so shocked by what Megan had done." Her lips tightened. The anger with Megan was still there, but behind it was pain and grief. "I probably didn't handle Robert Conroy as well as I should have."

"You must talk to him again. Explain," Paula urged. "He will understand if you explain it to him."

Hannah felt herself begin to tremble inside at the thought of another angry encounter with Robert. She couldn't. She was no good at confronting people.

"I don't know." She took a steadying breath. "Travis always said his father could be unreasonable. And the two of them could never be together without ending up shouting at each other. I won't be able to make him listen to me."

Hide. That was what she wanted to do. Like the little girl she'd been who'd hidden in the closet when Mammi was having a bad spell and wouldn't stop crying.

"You must." Her aunt's hands tightened on hers. "He has to understand that you and Jamie have a gut future here. You have people who love you, a home, a business if you want it."

"Aunt Paula . . ."

"Ja, ja, I said I would give you time. But maybe it would help with Mr. Conroy. He would see that you have security here."

Security. The thing she'd always longed for and never found.

Would that help with Robert? Or was he so wrapped up in his own views that it would seem like even more of a threat?

"I don't know. Really, I don't. He's Travis's father, but I don't understand him. I never have. If he decides to cause trouble . . ." She couldn't finish that sentence, not wanting to go there.

"What trouble could he cause?" Paula asked, her tone rational. "You are the boy's mother. Where he lives is up to you." She hesitated, seeming to struggle with something in her mind. "After all, you could live here and still be Englisch. Send Jamie to the Englisch school, go to an Englisch church."

"You couldn't be happy with that," Hannah said, her voice gentle. "Admit it."

Aunt Paula sighed, shaking her head a little. She looked down at their clasped hands, and with her head bent, Hannah could see the way her hair, thinning a little from years of pulling it back in a bun, was turning completely white. The sight gave an odd, vulnerable tug to her heart.

"No, I wouldn't be." Paula looked up, and there were tears in her eyes. "I want to see you a true part of the community, as you would have been if my sister hadn't gone away. But I would settle for less if it kept you and Jamie here."

Hannah leaned forward and kissed her cheek, struggling to control her own tears. It was impossible for Aunt Paula to see her in any way that didn't involve her mother, it seemed.

"I know," she said softly. "But if I am to bring Jamie up the way his father would want, can I do that here?"

"Travis is gone." Aunt Paula's voice was filled with sympathy, but there was steel in her voice, too. "I have thought that way, too, sometimes in the years since your uncle passed. Wondering if he would approve of all the decisions I've made about the business. But he's not here, and I have to decide as best I can. Just as you must."

Travis is gone. The words echoed in Hannah's mind. She'd said them herself, often enough, but had she ever really accepted what they meant?

"How would it be," she said slowly, feeling her way, "if we try out the partnership for a few months before we make a final agreement? That way, if either of us feels it's not going to work, we can say so."

Paula studied her face for a long moment. Then she

nodded. "Ja. All right. We will do that." She smiled. "But I will not change my mind."

One burden seemed to lift from Hannah's shoulders, at least temporarily, and she felt relief. But there were others.

William. Robert Conroy. And Megan. Those she would have to deal with on her own.

Chapter Twelve

Would William show up or wouldn't he? Hannah went down the back stairs to the bakery kitchen, carrying the baby monitor. Jamie had been talking himself to sleep, his voice drowsy and slurred. Fortunately he didn't seem to have picked up on his mother's anxiety.

Maybe she shouldn't have waited until today. Maybe she should have tried to talk to William sooner about what had happened between them on Saturday. She could at least have made it clear that he wasn't to blame.

She didn't want to lose the opportunity to help him. And she certainly didn't want to hurt him. If he didn't show up today—

Hannah walked into the kitchen. William was there already, waiting for her. He'd taken off his straw hat, and his hair was the pale gold of ripe wheat under the overhead light. His expression was so serious that her breath caught. Had he come to tell her he was giving up? If so, he wasn't the only one who'd be hurt.

"I'm glad you . . ."

"H-Hannah . . ."

They both started to speak at the same time, and both stopped at the same time. Hannah took a few quick steps toward him, until only the width of the table separated them.

"Let me go first," she said, rushing the words and then hesitating, not sure what to say. "I'm sorry," she said finally. Simply. "What happened between us was my fault."

"No." William gave a quick shake of his head. "M-mine."

A spasm of pain in his face hurt her heart. She had to make this clear to him, and she didn't dare lose control of herself again.

"I was upset." She managed a rueful smile. "I guess that was obvious. My father-in-law . . . well, he intimidates me at the best of times, and his call left me so shattered."

She pressed her lips together, trying not to think about Megan's betrayal or about the threatening tone of Robert's voice.

"Anyway, I shouldn't have cried on your shoulder like that."

"Because I-I am n-not c-capable?" William's jaw tightened and hurt mixed with anger in his blue eyes.

She had done exactly what she hadn't wanted to do. She'd sent him the message that she didn't take him seriously, and she had to fix that, even if it took her onto dangerous ground.

"No." Hannah's fingers tingled with the urge to reach out and touch him. She knew how his arm would feel if she did, his muscles taut, his skin warm. She shook off the image. "It's exactly the opposite. I leaned on you because you are strong and kind and dependable. But I shouldn't have. I'm ashamed."

The anger and hurt faded from his face. "Not y-you. I-I'm the o-one to feel sh-shame. I k-kissed you."

"But I kissed you back." She felt her cheeks grow warm, hardly able to believe they were talking this way. "I know better. I'm older . . ."

The words were out before it occurred to her that he'd probably heard them before, from Rachel.

"Ja."

He turned away, but not before she'd seen the hurt—hurt she seemed destined to cause whatever she said to him.

"I didn't mean it that way." She bit her lip, appalled at how inept she was with him.

William looked back at her, his gaze probing. "You are thinking about R-Rachel."

"Yes. But our situation is not like that one was." She wasn't his sister-in-law, for one thing, though that didn't make it any easier. "I just meant that I should know better how many barriers there are between us. And I'm the one who crossed the line."

She surely didn't need to enumerate the barriers for him. She was Englisch, she'd been married to a soldier, she had a child, and she had trouble with Travis's father looming over her.

"My future is too uncertain for me even to think about a relationship with anyone."

William studied her face, eyes serious, as if measuring her feelings. "Ja, but even s-so it c-can't be wrong to have a friend. Or t-to c-comfort a friend."

She closed her eyes for a second, reliving how it had felt to let go, to depend on William and borrow some of his strength. It had felt good, dangerously so.

"I'm glad to have you for a friend, William. But we have to be careful. If people started gossiping about us, it would be . . . unbearable." She looked at him, seeing his instinctive need to reject that. "You know it's true," she said.

He nodded, his jaw tensing until a muscle twitched there. "You w-want to quit helping m-me, ain't so?"

"No, I didn't mean that." It was nearly a cry, she felt so strongly about it. "You're making progress already. We can't quit now. You won't, will you?" Until this moment she hadn't known how much her sessions with William meant to her.

"N-no. N-not as long as it's okay w-with you."

Relief washed through her. "That's good. We'll go on, then."

In answer, William pulled out the chair he sat in when they worked together. Then he paused, one hand braced against the table.

"J-just remember. If y-you need a friend, I am always h-here."

She smiled, nodded. And tried not to think about just how much she'd like to lean on him.

By the next Friday, Hannah's emotions had settled down to something approaching normal. As she sat in the rocking chair with Jamie, singing softly to him as he finished his pre-nap cup of milk, she wondered if she'd overreacted all along the line.

She hadn't heard anything more from Robert Conroy. He wasn't likely to admit he was wrong about anything, but she'd write to him over the weekend, a newsy letter about Jamie, avoiding any mention of their conversation. And life would go back to the way it had been.

The sessions with William were rewarding beyond anything she could have hoped. Of course, she couldn't know how well he did when talking with his family, but around her, he'd come a long way. More important, he seemed to be overcoming that instant embarrassment when a word wouldn't cooperate.

The cup slipped from Jamie's grasp as his hand relaxed. She caught it, setting it on the dresser next to her. Jamie wouldn't object when she put him in his crib, as close to sleep as he was, but she treasured this moment, cradling his warm body against hers. Too soon he'd rebel at that, probably, pushing forward to being a big boy even as she clung to his babyhood.

Already he took steps away from his dependence on her. Of course now he had others he could trust and rely on. Aunt Paula, for one, who loved him like her own grandchild. And Naomi, who was part of his daily life, always patient and loving.

He'd developed a relationship with Rhoda, as well, laughing each time he saw her. Even though Aunt Paula was well enough to get back to her usual work, Rhoda popped in most days, lending a hand when they were busy, playing with Jamie when they weren't.

And there was Myra, the unexpected cousin she'd found. Myra stopped by the bakery each time she was in town, giving Jamie a chance to play with his little cousins.

Jamie had the home and family Hannah had longed for. It was a family of women, though, and that did trouble her sometimes. A boy needed a man in his life to model himself on. Maybe that was why Jamie seemed to turn to William almost instinctively, running to him the moment William appeared.

She dropped a kiss on Jamie's damp curls as she rose and carried him to the crib.

"Sleep tight, little lamb," she whispered.

Without opening his eyes, he reached for his teddy bear, pulling it close and rubbing his cheek against it in his sleep routine. Smiling, she walked softly out of the room.

As she pulled the door shut, she took one more look back. The blue curtains at the windows moved in the breeze, sending shadows dancing in fanciful patterns on the white walls. Aunt Paula had hung an illustrated Bible verse between the windows—Jesus blessing the children. The room was peaceful, quiet, safe, and her son was asleep already.

Hannah walked down the hall to the living room. She'd take the monitor downstairs and give Aunt Paula a hand. She'd need it, with all the extra baking she'd been doing.

Everyone in the valley had been busy this week, it seemed, getting ready for the charity auction tomorrow. Katie's quilt shop had been a hive of activity as women sorted out quilts to go to auction. Caleb was donating some wooden furniture pieces, and William had been working with him as well as helping to set up stands and canopies at the fire hall.

As for Aunt Paula . . . well, every other minute it seemed she was thinking of something else she should bake for the stand. Naomi, carrying in jars of honey from her bees that morning, had suggested that she and Hannah might have to take away her wooden spoon if she didn't stop soon.

Smiling at the memory, Hannah headed for the stairs, only to stop when the telephone rang. She snatched the receiver up quickly, not wanting the phone to wake Jamie when he'd just gotten off to sleep.

"Hannah? It's Megan."

The familiar voice made her throat tighten. She wasn't sure she was ready to talk to Megan yet. But apparently she didn't have a choice.

"I . . ." A slight hesitation, unusual for Megan. "I wanted to thank you again for the nice visit."

Megan was feeling her out, it seemed. Maybe she was wondering if Robert Conroy had contacted her yet, or if he'd given away the fact that Megan had talked to him.

Anger flickered in Hannah despite her effort to stay calm. "At least your visit gave you plenty of things to report to Travis's father."

"He's talked to you, then." Megan didn't sound remotely sorry.

"Yes. Something you should have done instead of spying on me for him."

"Come on, Hannah. It wasn't spying. And I did try to talk to you, if you'll recall. I told you just what I thought about your current situation. But you wouldn't listen."

Hannah gripped the receiver so hard that her fingers

cramped. "I listened, Megan. I just didn't agree with you. So you turned around and complained to Robert Conroy."

"For goodness' sake, Hannah, don't dramatize this!" Megan was crisp, scolding, as she so often was when people didn't see things her way. "Don't forget, I even offered to have you move in with me. I care about what happens to you, and I thought maybe Travis's father would help."

Any softening she'd done when Megan spoke of caring for her vanished at the mention of Robert, and she fought to contain herself. "Help? Robert didn't offer to help. He called me a bad mother for daring to bring his grandson up in a place he doesn't approve of."

Silence for a moment. "I'm sorry. I had no idea he'd do that. I was just trying to help you see things more clearly."

Hannah took a deep breath and let it out slowly. Megan was motivated by concern. But she was also so sure she was right that she didn't consider any other possibility.

"Hannah? Are you still there?"

"I'm here. Megan, you're my friend. I know you mean well, but this is my life and my responsibility. Jamie and I are safe and happy here. Isn't that the most important thing?"

Megan was silent. Maybe that silence meant agreement. Surely Megan could understand—

"That's what your aunt wants you to think," Megan said flatly. "Don't you even know when you're being manipulated? She wants you to stay, wants you to take your mother's place. And you feel so guilty about your mother's death that you're letting her."

Hannah sucked in a breath, feeling as if she'd been hit in the stomach. She'd told Megan about her mother's overdose because Megan was the closest friend she'd ever had. She'd never expected that knowledge to be turned against her.

Hannah held the receiver for another moment, her hand frozen as she tried to think of something to say. She couldn't. Then, very gently, she hung up.

She turned to go downstairs. Stopped. And went up the steps to the attic instead.

Light slanted across the wide floorboards from the windows. Without hesitation, Hannah moved to the boxes marked with her mother's name.

She had been so happy the day she'd learned that the financial aid had gone through—the money that would allow her to attend college. Putting the financing together had been a struggle that seemed impossible at times. If not for the help of some sympathetic teachers and the Davis family she babysat for, she'd never have succeeded in getting that far.

She'd expected her mother to be happy for her. Mammi had tried to respond in the way she should. But watching her effort to manufacture joy and show pride had been painful to Hannah.

She sank down onto the floor and pulled one of the boxes into her lap. She worked the lid off and folded back the worn sheet that someone, probably Aunt Paula, had put around the contents.

A little girl's dresses and matching aprons. A hand-knit child's sweater. They were things Hannah had outgrown before they'd left, probably. Aunt Paula had carefully put them away.

Hannah touched the fabric of a print dress, the pattern so tiny, blue and white. She remembered the day Mammi had finished it, sliding it over her head, laughing at how much taller she had gotten. She remembered herself spinning around, making the skirt swing out.

She held the dress against her cheek for a moment, imagining she felt her mother's touch.

Beneath the dresses were a few toys. A soft faceless doll with dresses made to match Hannah's. A set of tiny doll dishes. A well-worn toy dog. Hannah picked him up, smiling through the tears that dripped on her cheeks.

Spot, she'd called him, without much originality but with much love. Jamie might not appreciate the doll, but he'd like Spot. She laid the dog aside and put the other things back into the box, folding the sheet over them, tucking them in.

Beneath the box was a trunk. Hannah lifted the lid, and then nearly closed it again when she saw what it contained. More clothes . . . her mother's this time.

She pushed the lid all the way back, letting the memories wash over her. Childhood memories, from before they went away.

They'd been happy here, hadn't they? A child doesn't understand the decisions parents make. Doesn't have a say in them. But a child hears, even when she doesn't understand.

Her father, insisting they would be happier out there, somewhere, in some rosy place where life would be different. He'd been all energy and enthusiasm, sweeping away every objection.

And Mammi? What had Mammi wanted? She had been happy here. But she had gone along with what Daadi wanted, always, even when it ended in sorrow. If she'd stood up for what she wanted . . .

Hannah shook her head, her throat tight with unshed tears. That had been Mammi's weakness, maybe, that way she had of putting Daadi's wishes ahead of anything else. She'd given up who she was for him.

But Hannah didn't have to do the same. And she didn't have to wonder who she was or where she belonged.

She picked up the topmost dress, one she remembered her mother wearing. She stood, holding it against her. Then she unbuttoned her jumper, let it slide to the floor, and pulled the Plain dress over her head.

William hammered another nail into the frame of the stand he and Caleb were setting up on the fire hall grounds. Grasping the upright, he gave it a pull, satisfying himself that it sat evenly.

"We'd best put a shelf along the opening," Caleb said. "I know most vendors will need one."

William nodded, picking up a board to use. "This sh-should w-work. I guess w-we are l-looking for a gut c-crowd tomorrow."

"Ja, Katie says the organizers expect the biggest crowd ever this year for the auction." Caleb measured the shelf. "Glad we have a gut turnout of folks to help set up."

"For s-sure. All that f-flooding d-down south w-was bad. Lots of help n-needed if w-we are to r-raise enough money."

He glanced around. The grounds swarmed with folks working. Amish, Mennonite, Englisch—it didn't matter who, everyone was pitching in. Tomorrow morning, visitors would start arriving bright and early, and Pleasant Valley must be ready for them.

Folks had been making an effort all week. It was warm for late September, with mums and asters blooming in pots along the street. Rachel would be selling plenty of those tomorrow, he'd guess.

"Seems like Brother Isaac is staying far away from you today, ain't so?" Caleb snapped his tape measure closed and glanced at him. "Did you and Isaac quarrel?"

William glanced toward the bench where water jugs were lined up. Isaac stood there, his face ruddy as he drained a cup of water.

"Isaac d-didn't like it when I w-went my own w-way this week." He paused, tipping the straw hat back to wipe his forehead with the back of his arm. "I-I didn't d-do so gut a job explaining t-to him."

Just thinking about that made him hot with humiliation. He should have been able to tell Isaac what he wanted.

"I would not want to be the cause of a breach between you and your brother." Caleb's clear blue eyes were troubled. "If you change your mind about me talking to him . . ."

William shook his head. "No. I m-must do this my-self." He shrugged, spreading his hands. "Isaac has bbeen staying clear of m-me for a time. Saying s-something about w-waiting until I komm to my s-senses."

Caleb grinned. "Reminds me of Ezra. Remember how he dealt with Isaac's bossiness? Ezra always listened politely to Isaac's advice. Then he'd go ahead and do what he'd planned all along."

William nodded, a lump in his throat when he thought of his middle brother. Ezra had been gone for several years now, but William still missed him.

"Of course, Ezra was living on his own by that time," Caleb said, his voice casual. "That made a difference."

"Ja. It did." Was Caleb suggesting he should move away from the farm? It was a tempting thought, but it would cause trouble for sure.

Still, he might do better to adopt Ezra's method. Since he didn't seem able to get anywhere by trying to explain his feelings to his brother, silence might be the answer.

It rankled that he hadn't been able to speak his mind to Isaac. His speech was improving; he knew it. Except when it counted.

A flutter of movement on the sidewalk caught his eye. Hannah came toward him, pushing Jamie in the stroller. Not an unusual sight except for one thing—she was wearing Plain dress.

Caleb nudged him. "There's Hannah. When did she start dressing Mennonite?"

"I-I don't know." Not long ago, that was sure.

As she neared, William realized Hannah's cheeks were flushed. She must be aware that people were taking note of what she had on.

The stroller slowed. Was she regretting letting so many people see her at once? Without stopping to think about it, he walked quickly toward her, leaving Caleb standing there staring after him.

"Hannah. Jamie." William bent to respond to the boy's shouted greeting and straightened, regarding her seriously. "You are dressing Plain, ain't so?"

She nodded, the pink in her cheeks deepening. "I'm attracting attention. I didn't do it for that. Maybe I should go home."

"Folks w-will get used to it soon, for sure. Just g-give them time."

The dress was a soft shade of blue, not so very different from the denim jumper she often wore. But dressing Plain was like an announcement for Hannah, saying she belonged here.

"I hope so." She brushed the skirt with her palm. "This was my mother's."

Jamie, maybe tired of being left out, grabbed hold of William's pant leg and tugged. "Will, up. Up."

He smiled, bending as Jamie held up his arms. In a moment he'd lifted him, holding the boy high in his arms. "There. Now are y-you happy?"

Jamie patted his face, grinning. "Will," he declared again.

"Good talking, Jamie." Hannah smiled at her son. "But you're working, William. We shouldn't take you away from that."

"It's t-time I had a b-break." He nodded toward the dress. "P-Paula must be p-pleased. What made you decide?"

She hesitated, as if not sure how to answer that, her hand stroking the material of her skirt. "Megan called me," she said finally. "I . . . I confronted her about what she'd done, talking to Robert Conroy that way. She wasn't even sorry. She thinks she knows what's best for me better than I do."

That didn't really explain why it had made her want to dress Plain. He suspected there were things she wasn't telling him, but that was her right.

Her gaze darted to his face and slid away again. "Aunt Paula had saved everything my mother left behind. I think she felt one day we'd come back and want it."

"A-and you d-do," he said.

"Yes. I was looking at the dresses, thinking about why

my mother left and how she let other people decide things for her." She smiled, and her voice was stronger, more definite. "And I knew I should decide for myself. So I did."

"That i-is g-gut." He bounced Jamie in his arms, and Jamie giggled. Gut, he thought. Hannah was making a commitment to life here. And even though she didn't want more from him than friendship, he was glad that she would be around.

"Y-you will be h-here tomorrow, ja?"

From the corner of his eye he noted a car moving slowly along the street near the curb. The driver craned his neck, probably intrigued at the sight of so many Plain people.

Hannah nodded. "We'll set up our stand early. Aunt Paula says people will be wanting their coffee and sweet roll the minute they get here."

She glanced back across the street as she spoke, toward the bakery. The car William had noticed pulled to the curb and parked. The door swung open, and the driver got out.

Next to him, William felt Hannah stiffen. She grasped his arm, her fingers digging into his skin. Her creamy skin lost its color, and her brown eyes looked stricken.

"Hannah? Was ist letz?" His heart thudded uncomfortably.

"I can't believe it." Her voice sounded strangled. "That man . . . it's Travis's father. Robert Conroy."

CHAPTER THIRTEEN

Hannah absorbed the shock, vaguely aware that she was clutching William's arm. She let go, realizing through the chaos in her thoughts that seeing her with William would give Travis's father the worst possible impression.

Robert stood by the car, dark glasses hiding his expression. She sensed that he was taking in the scene, and was perhaps not in a hurry to confront her.

She forced herself to take a deep breath as she murmured a silent prayer. *Please, give me the right words.*

Maybe she should have prayed that before she'd hung up on Robert after that disastrous conversation. That must have been what brought him here.

Robert had come east for his son's funeral. Not for their wedding, not even for Jamie's birth. But he was here now, walking toward her with rigid military posture.

Hannah tried to manage a smile of welcome, imagining the scene as he must see it. What an ironic twist of timing, that she had chosen today to dress Plain. And William stood beside her, Jamie on his shoulder, waiting with her as if they belonged together.

Robert stopped a few feet from her and greeted her with a crisp nod as he took off the sunglasses. Short-cropped gray hair, steely gray eyes, still muscular at sixty but with a slight paunch that emphasized his barrel chest . . .

Travis hadn't looked much like his father. He'd had his late mother's curly brown hair and quick smile.

"Robert. It's nice to see you." She debated whether to kiss his cheek, but nothing about his attitude suggested that would be welcome. "We didn't expect your visit."

"I thought I'd surprise you." His gaze swept William, and it annoyed her that he didn't immediately focus on his grandson.

"This is my friend William Brand."

William ducked his head in the slight nod that passed for a greeting with him. With a slight jolt, she realized that he was assessing Robert just as Robert was sizing him up.

"And this is Jamie, of course." She gestured toward her son, and William set Jamie on the ground, his big hand lingering reassuringly on Jamie's shoulder for a moment.

"Jamie, say hi to Grandpa." She stumbled over the word. She'd shown Jamie photos, but at his age, he wasn't likely to remember anyone from a picture.

Robert stared at him for a moment, his face seeming to soften a little. "Hi, Jamie."

"Hi." Jamie's vocabulary was limited, but he could usually be trusted to greet people. Then he promptly hid his face in her skirt.

Hannah touched his curls. "He doesn't talk a lot yet."

Robert cleared his throat. "Good-looking boy. Looks like his daddy."

"Yes, I think so," Hannah said softly, and for a moment there seemed to be a bridge between them.

Robert put his glasses back on, maybe wanting to hide his feelings. He glanced around. "What's going on here?"

"We're getting ready for tomorrow's auction." Talking about anything other than Travis seemed desirable. "Twice a year the community has a big fundraiser. Everybody pitches in."

Robert nodded, seeming to make an effort to express interest. "Got some community project to raise money for?"

"N-no," William answered, startling Hannah. "F-for others."

"The money goes to disaster relief," she said. "This year it will be mainly for flooding and tornado victims down south."

Robert nodded, but she suspected he really didn't care what the people of Pleasant Valley were doing. He'd come to see her.

She caught a look of support from William. Comforting as it was, there was nothing William could do to help her. She'd have to deal with Robert on her own, and that was considerably harder now that there wasn't a continent between them.

"My aunt's place is across the street and down a little way."

Her mind raced. Where were they going to put a male visitor? Maybe she could set up a cot for herself in Jamie's room.

"I'd like to see it. I got a room at a motel in Mifflinburg. Seems to be the closest."

"You're welcome to stay with us." She bent to put Jamie in his stroller, just as glad to hide her face for a moment, so he wouldn't see her relief that he didn't intend to do that.

"I'll be better at the motel."

There didn't seem to be anything to do but to spring him on Aunt Paula. She glanced at William. "Good luck with the building. We'll be over early in the morning to set up."

"Ja." He gave Robert another fleeting glance and headed off to where Caleb was working.

"This way." She started back the way she'd come. "You can leave your car here, if you like."

Robert walked beside her. "That friend of yours." He said the words as if he didn't like the taste. "Doesn't he speak English?"

"William is Amish. He speaks both English and Pennsylvania Dutch. That's a form of German that's common around here."

She almost said something about William's speech problems, but stopped. That wasn't any concern of Robert's, and it might sound as if she were trying to explain away their friendship, which also wasn't Robert's concern.

"So the costumes . . ."

She winced at the word. "Not costumes. The Amish and some Mennonites wear Plain dress. It's part of their beliefs."

Our beliefs. Was she denying that already?

"I don't get it," he said bluntly. "Why would you want to be part of a church that makes you dress that way?" He gestured toward her outfit.

She sought for a way of explaining that he'd understand without getting into four centuries of history. People here in rural Pennsylvania had grown up with the differences, and for the most part accepted them as the way things were.

But for someone like Robert, everything that was so comforting to her was alien. Odd, she supposed he'd say.

"When you wore a uniform, you showed where you belonged," she said. "And that you obeyed the army's rules in regard to dress. We dress Plain for the same reason."

His face seemed to harden, even though he didn't say anything. Obviously he didn't understand. Or he understood, but was confirmed in his opposition.

"Here's my aunt's bakery." She turned toward the door, not sure whether to be relieved or even more nervous at the thought of bringing Robert and Aunt Paula together.

"We're having a busy day getting ready for tomorrow. We'll have a stand at the auction, you see, and we have to be there early."

She was babbling. That meant she was more nervous than relieved.

She reached for the door, and Jamie tried to stand in the stroller, knowing they were home. Robert reached for the door, holding it closed.

She glanced at him, startled.

"You're wondering why I'm here."

"Yes, I suppose I am." She could hardly deny that or pretend his visit wasn't a shock.

"I'm a reasonable man," he said.

She nodded, although from everything Travis had said about his father, *reasonable* wasn't a word she'd have chosen.

"I decided I shouldn't take someone else's word on something this important. So I've come to see for myself how you're raising my grandchild."

She should be relieved at that. The words were reasonable. So why did she sense an implied threat in them?

The bakery stand had been busy from the moment they'd opened at eight this morning. Hannah had been thankful—she'd needed that respite from worrying about the meaning of Robert's visit.

Now, though, the midmorning lull had set in, and they weren't busy enough to keep her thoughts from circling. She kept replaying, again and again, everything that had happened after Robert appeared in Pleasant Valley.

Not that there'd been any open warfare after his unexpected arrival, but she'd had the feeling, through what was left of the day, that he was watching her every move critically.

It hadn't helped that Aunt Paula hadn't tried very hard to hide her unhappiness with Robert's visit. She hadn't

been openly hostile, but she'd seemed intent on emphasiz-
ing the closeness of her bond with Jamie, in contrast with
the nonexistent one between Jamie and Robert, and how
different Jamie's life was here.

A mug of tea appeared on the counter in front of Hannah. "You are worrying. That's not good for you." Aunt
Paula shoved a stool toward her. "Sit, relax for a little. Do
you want a sticky bun?"

Hannah accepted the stool, glad to be off her feet for a
moment, but she shook her head at the sticky bun. Sugar
wasn't going to help her think this situation through.

"How can I help but worry? I don't understand why
Robert would come all this way."

Aunt Paula's forehead wrinkled. "You said he told you
why he is here. That he just wants to make sure Jamie is
all right."

"That's not exactly what he said."

She sipped at the tea . . . Irish Breakfast sweetened
with some of Naomi's honey. Hannah needed the warmth,
as the sun hadn't yet reached their booth to take the morning chill off. It was a gentle reminder that despite the
warm days, autumn was settling in.

"You think he wants to cause trouble?" Aunt Paula
shook her head in disagreement. "I can't see it myself. In
all this time since you met Travis, Robert has barely
shown an interest in you. Or in Jamie, his own grandson.
Why should he all of a sudden care where you live?"

"I don't know why, but I know he does." Hannah struggled with an explanation. As wise and capable as her aunt
was, she'd had little experience of the world outside Pleasant Valley. "You have to understand that Robert doesn't
know a thing about Amish and Mennonites. His whole
life has been the army. I guess he's concerned that I might
not be bringing up Jamie the way his father would want."

"From what you've said, he wasn't that wonderful gut
a father to his own son." Aunt Paula hesitated, with a
sense of weighing both sides. "Although I suppose he

might feel guilty about that now that Travis is gone. Folks feel that way, sometimes, regretting the things they said and didn't say once it's too late. Maybe Robert has some thought of making amends."

Hannah realized she had done Aunt Paula a disservice by thinking she couldn't understand Robert. Her aunt understood people, and at heart, people were the same, whatever their background.

"You might be right. And if that's the case, it's all the more important that we show him that Pleasant Valley is a good place to bring up Jamie. Don't you see? Robert is Jamie's link to Travis. I must keep peace with him."

Her aunt seemed to absorb that. "Ja, I see," she said slowly. "I have not been a gut example of a peacemaker, have I? The bishop would be sore disappointed in me." She smiled ruefully, wrinkles deepening around her eyes. "I am sorry, Hannah. I made this situation harder for you."

Hannah couldn't deny that, but she clasped her aunt's hand. "Just try to be nice to him. For Jamie's sake."

Aunt Paula nodded. "Still, I wish—"

Whatever that wish was, Hannah wasn't destined to hear it. Paula dropped the thought when Naomi hurried to the counter laden down with another box of baked goods.

"Ach, so many people are here already," Naomi said. "I could hardly get the box through the crowd." She spoke in dialect.

Without conscious thought, Hannah answered in the same tongue. "We were ready for more baked goods, that's certain-sure."

And then she stopped, realizing that Robert Conroy had stepped up to the counter beside Naomi. He had heard her speak, and he was looking at her as if she'd just sprouted another head.

"Good morning, Robert." *English,* she reminded herself.

"Morning."

Naomi took a quick look at his face and scurried behind the counter, busying herself with unpacking the carton.

"Can I get you a coffee?" Aunt Paula smiled at him, and Hannah hoped he didn't notice the tension around her eyes. "And maybe a donut?"

He shook his head, his gaze sweeping the stand. "Where's Jamie?" His tone was sharp.

Hannah had to remind herself to follow her own advice: Answer peacefully, no matter how brusque he seemed.

"Some of the teenagers are watching the young children, safely out of the way of the crowd." She slipped from the booth. "Come, I'll show you where he is. You can stay and play with him, if you want."

Robert looked at her as if the word *play* wasn't in his vocabulary. He walked beside her when she headed for the children's section, his shoulders stiff as they maneuvered through the congested area.

But it was a friendly crowd, surely he saw that. People were intent on getting good buys, but they also knew every penny was going to charity, and they were in a happy, generous mood.

"I didn't know you spoke that dialect . . . Pennsylvania Dutch," he said abruptly, skirting around a woman clutching a quilted wall-hanging. "Travis never mentioned it."

"Maybe the subject never came up. Pennsylvania Dutch was the language of my childhood. I suppose I never really forgot it, and since I hear it all the time now, the words have come back to me."

Robert didn't respond, and she wasn't sure what else to say. They rounded the auction tent and circled to the back of the fire hall, where several teenagers, Rhoda and her friend Becky among them, were watching the children. They had gathered at a shady spot on the grass next to several picnic tables and benches. It didn't surprise Hannah to see that Rhoda was playing with Jamie, talking away to him in Pennsylvania Dutch as he ran his toy truck through the grass.

As they crossed the lawn Jamie looked up and saw them. "Mammi, Mammi," he shouted, running to her with Rhoda following close behind.

Hannah swept him up in her arms and planted a kiss on his cheek. "Are you being a good boy for Rhoda?"

He nodded solemnly, and Rhoda laughed, showing her dimples. "He always is."

"Look, Jamie, here's Grandpa." She pointed to Robert.

Jamie leaned his head against her collar bone, affecting shyness, and then wiggled his fingers at Robert.

Robert touched the small hand, not seeming to know what to say.

"Rhoda, this is Jamie's grandfather, Robert Conroy, come to visit." She turned to Robert. "Rhoda is one of Jamie's favorite people."

Rhoda nodded to Robert, still smiling. Either her naturally outgoing personality or her work in the quilt shop had given her an easy confidence when she was around English people, and Hannah was thankful for that.

"He is such a sweet boy. I love to watch him." Rhoda glanced at Hannah. "Were you wanting to take Jamie with you now?"

"No, I'm afraid you're stuck with him until nap time. We're still very busy at the stand, but I'll come get him then." Hannah passed Jamie back to Rhoda. She thought perhaps Robert would suggest that he watch Jamie, but it didn't seem to occur to him.

Jamie showed a tendency to pout, but Rhoda distracted him with his truck, averting any tears as they left him.

Robert was frowning again as they walked away, and Hannah was beginning to feel that he'd been frowning ever since he'd arrived. "She was talking to him in Pennsylvania Dutch." Obviously he didn't approve.

"Rhoda speaks to him in both languages," Hannah said, keeping her voice pleasant with an effort. "As you heard, she's fluent in both."

"Fine." He ground out the word. "But I want my grandson to understand me when I talk to him."

Those words touched her heart. Did Robert fear his relationship with his grandson was at risk? "English is Jamie's first language." She hurried to assure him. "Of course he'll understand you. But it's usually considered an advantage to be able to speak another language."

He didn't pursue the subject, and she could only hope he accepted what she said. But she feared the issue might be another small stone in the wall between them.

"I really have to get back to the stand. We'll be busy over lunch. Would you like to come with me? Or stay and watch Jamie playing?"

Robert shook his head, his expression giving nothing away. "I think I'll just look around for a while." He walked off toward the auction tent.

William concentrated on the small wooden train he was putting together, trying to ignore the people watching. Caleb had suggested that William work on a project in the booth to draw attention.

That was fine with him, as long as Caleb did all the talking. At the moment six or eight people had stopped to watch, and there was a good chance they'd buy something before they left.

The booth next to theirs was Katie's quilt stand. Her cousin Molly was helping her at the moment, since Rhoda had offered to watch the young children this morning.

By the look of things and the lilt he could hear in Molly's voice, she was enjoying the outing, smiling and chatting with anyone who came near the booth.

Some people just seemed naturally suited to that, and Molly had always been outgoing, while Katie, although very self-confident, was quieter.

Though not as quiet as he was, that was certain-sure.

He glanced across the open space between the rows of stands. Rachel's garden stand was opposite them. She'd been doing a brisk business, too, with her older daughter helping. Joseph scurried past, carrying a jug of lemonade. He grinned at William, giving him a thumbs-up sign, and William smiled in return. The children had picked up the cup rack he'd made for them to give to their mother, and they would be giving it to her tonight, when they celebrated.

It was turning out to be a grand day for the auction. Everyone seemed to agree on that fact. The lively tones of the auctioneer, rumbling through the speaker, formed a backdrop for all the chatter, reminding people of why they were there.

A father and young son stopped in front of him, the father lifting the boy up so he could see. The boy's eyes went round with amazement as William fastened a wheel in place. Maybe he'd never realized that someone actually made the things he played with.

"Can he touch it?" The father grinned at his son's expression.

"For s-sure." William put the locomotive in the boy's hands and found he was thinking of Hannah and Jamie again instead of the customer.

He couldn't see Paula's stand from where he stood, but that fact wasn't enough to keep his mind off Hannah. She'd been upset at her father-in-law's arrival. No wonder, after what she'd told him about the man's phone call.

He'd wanted to do something to show his support. But all he'd done was stand there like a block and hope she felt his caring.

The man handed back the locomotive, over the little boy's protests, and moved to join the line in front of Caleb.

"I'll get you one, I promise," he said. "But we have to wait our turn."

People in line shifted a little, and William realized that

Robert Conroy stood at the rear of the small crowd, staring at him. What was the man thinking?

And what would he say if he knew that the train William was making was destined for Jamie?

He focused on the train, trying not to stare back at Conroy. The next time he looked up, Conroy was walking away, but Gideon, Rachel's husband, hurried toward him, frowning.

"Gideon? Was ist letz?" William asked.

Gideon leaned over the counter, as if to make sure that no one else heard what he was about to say. "That Englischer, the older man in the green shirt, do you know who he is?"

William tensed, affected by Gideon's obvious concern. "Ja. It's Hannah Conroy's f-father-in-law. He sh-showed up y-yesterday, surprising her."

Gideon shot another glance at Conroy's back. "So that's it. I wondered. The thing is, he's been going around asking people about Hannah. About you, also."

William felt the jolt of that right down to his shoes. "Asking what? What k-kind of questions?"

Gideon shrugged. "He started talking to me, not realizing I knew you, I guess. He's been asking people if they know Hannah, what she's been doing since she came to Pleasant Valley, and does she see a lot of you. He wasn't as blunt as that, but that's what it amounted to, anyway."

"W-what d-did you say?" He thought he knew, but he had to ask.

"I did my best imitation of a dumb Dutchman, of course." Gideon's eyes twinkled for an instant, but then he grew sober again. "Ach, you know he won't get anything from us, but you know also there's plenty of people who can't keep their mouths shut when it comes to other folks' business."

"Ja. I know." Pleasant Valley had its share of blabbermauls, most of them not intending to be mean, just not able, like Gideon said, to keep their mouths shut when it came to gossip.

"It wonders me the man would act like that," Gideon said. "But I thought you should know what he was doing. It's not right, her own father-in-law asking those questions of just anyone. It will make folks start thinking there is something wrong. Someone needs to tell Hannah about it."

"Ja. I-I will." William nodded toward Caleb, who was busy with a customer. "Tell C-Caleb where I am going, w-will you?"

Not waiting for an answer, he slipped out of the booth and walked along the back of the rows of stands. It was quieter here, with the stands blocking the crowd from his view and nothing on the other side of him but a hedge of overgrown lilac bushes.

He needed a quiet moment to think this situation through, that was for sure. Still, Gideon was right. Hannah had to know what her father-in-law was up to, even if knowing hurt her.

William reached the bakery stand too quickly to figure out how exactly he was going to tell her. All three women were behind the counter, and fortunately Hannah was closest to him.

He leaned across, touching her arm lightly. "K-komm. I need t-to t-tell you something."

Hannah's initial smile turned to a puzzled look. "We're awfully busy right now. Can this wait until later?"

He resisted the urge to grasp her arm and urge her out. "N-no. It's important."

Hannah's gaze searched his face before she nodded. She leaned over and whispered something to Naomi, then lifted the flap and came out to join him.

Catching her arm, William guided her around the stand to the quiet space he'd found. But once there, looking at her, he didn't know how to begin.

"What is it?" Hannah put her hand over his. "You can tell me."

"G-Gideon Z-Zook came to me."

He could see her mentally trying to place Gideon. Then she nodded.

"Rachel's husband. The windmill maker."

"Ja." He had to push the next words out. "H-he thought I ought t-to know. And you, also. He says Robert i-is asking f-folks about you. And a-about me."

Shock. Pain. There could be no doubt about Hannah's reaction. She struggled with the emotions in silence for a moment, and then she sighed, shaking her head.

"I didn't think he'd go that far," she said. "But he seems determined to find out for himself if I'm making a good home for Jamie."

"E-everyone knows that you are." The words burst out of William on a wave of anger.

"Denke, William." Her voice was soft, and her eyes misted. "I appreciate that. But I'm afraid Robert isn't convinced. Everything here is so strange to him, you see. He just doesn't understand."

"Then he should t-try." He had to force down the anger, knowing that it wasn't of any use to Hannah now. "How c-can he act this w-way toward his own g-grandbaby's mammi?"

She pressed her lips together for an instant. "I don't know, but I can't stop him from asking questions. I'm just sorry he involved you." Distress was clear in her eyes. "If only he hadn't seen us together yesterday, he wouldn't be involving you." She put her hand on his wrist, looking up at him. "William, I'm so sorry. I don't want you to be hurt by what's between me and Robert."

"I a-am not important. But y-you and Jamie are. What if h-he is not satisfied w-with what he learns?"

"I don't know." Her brown eyes darkened with pain, and she turned away as if to shield that pain from him. "I just don't know."

CHAPTER FOURTEEN

Robert held open the door to the Plain and Fancy Restaurant so Hannah could wheel the stroller through. "Here we are." He seemed to be making an effort to be jovial. "I've heard this is a great place for Sunday brunch."

"I'm looking forward to it," Hannah responded politely.

Actually, she'd been surprised by Robert's invitation to take her and Jamie out for a meal. Given that he'd apparently been conducting his own investigation of her yesterday, she'd expected a confrontation rather than a meal out.

When he'd mentioned it, she'd still been so tensed up that she'd nearly refused, but then she'd thought better of her answer. Maybe this invitation meant that the answers to his questions had satisfied him. If Robert was ready to make peace, she couldn't ask for more.

The restaurant was a popular one out on the highway. The Pennsylvania Dutch theme was evident in everything from the murals on the walls to the distelfink rhyme on the menus.

Several families sat on leatherette benches in the entryway, apparently waiting for a table, and the large room echoed with voices and the clink of china.

"It's very busy," she said. "We may have a wait."

Not too long, she hoped, or Jamie would be protesting. Hannah doubted that Robert understood all that was involved in going out to eat with a toddler. The diaper bag dragged at her shoulder with all the items she'd felt it necessary to bring.

"I made a reservation," Robert said confidently, and his confidence was well-founded. In a moment the grandmotherly-looking hostess was clucking over Jamie and then leading them to a table for four, already set up with a high chair at the end.

Hannah took the precaution of putting some of Jamie's favorite crackers on the tray before lifting him in. His incipient cry stopped when he saw the crackers, and she settled him quickly.

"Very clever," Robert said, holding her chair for her. "You distracted him."

"I had to, or he'd have been crying to get d-o-w-n so he could run all over the place. You probably did the same with Travis when he was this age."

Robert sat across from her, giving her what seemed the first real smile she'd seen since he'd arrived. "I'm afraid I don't remember that far back. I just remember that Travis looked a lot like Jamie does now."

As if feeling they'd be better off not talking about Travis, he glanced around, seeming to search for a change of topic. "This looks like a nice place. I hope the guy who recommended it was right. He said the food's good."

That gave Hannah something else to worry about. Who would have told him about the restaurant? One of the people he'd asked about her? She shoved that question to the back of her mind.

"It's very popular, I know. I'm sure I was in here ages ago, but not since I've been back in Pleasant Valley this time."

"Does your aunt keep you that busy with the bakery?" Robert was glancing at the menu, and she couldn't be sure if the question was critical or not.

"The bakery is a popular place," she said carefully, thinking she heard an echo of Megan's comments in his question. "And usually on Sundays we have lunch or supper with some of my aunt's relatives. Aunt Paula doesn't have children, but she claims to have more cousins than anyone in the township, and they're always inviting us for meals."

"Yeah, your aunt said she was going to a cousin's house today."

Robert had invited Paula to join them, but she'd begged off, saying she already had plans, and he hadn't tried to change her mind. Maybe he felt more comfortable with just Hannah and Jamie. Certainly it was easier for Hannah not to have to be on guard between her aunt and her father-in-law.

"So, your aunt pays you a salary, I suppose?" Robert put the question casually.

It was too bad she couldn't take it the same way. Given that he'd never offered to help her himself, it was an awfully personal question.

Fortunately the server appeared to take their orders just then, giving Hannah breathing space.

Once the young woman had departed with their orders, Hannah busied herself breaking up a muffin from the basket for Jamie.

"You were asking about my arrangements with Aunt Paula." She tried not to let annoyance show in her voice. After all, Robert was expressing concern for his grandson, which was surely a good thing. "I share her living space and meals, and she also pays me a salary."

A small one, but the value of being part of the family was immeasurable.

Maybe Robert heard some criticism in her tone, because he frowned slightly. "I just want to be sure you and Jamie are being treated fairly. Someone could take advantage of you."

She took a breath, calming herself. Here was her opportunity to say something to him she should have said before.

"There's no question of taking advantage where my aunt is concerned. I needed help, and she offered me a home. Here I don't have to rely on babysitters I know virtually nothing about, or be away from Jamie for hours every day working. I can be with him all the time, and I know that he's surrounded by family . . . people who love him."

Robert was watching her face. He seemed to be listening, but she suspected there was something else on his mind.

Jamie pounded his tray, sending a cracker flying, and pointed toward the bread basket.

"More?" She held up the other half of his muffin.

Jamie nodded vigorously, and she put it on his tray, smiling when he tried to cram it all into his mouth.

Seeing Robert's somber look, she said, "I'm afraid toddlers don't have very good table manners."

Robert shook his head. "It's not that. I'm just wondering if you really think you'll be satisfied with this life for yourself and Jamie in the future. What about when he goes to school?"

Genuine concern threaded his voice, and Hannah liked him better in that moment than she had yet.

"I don't know," she said, trying to be honest. "I love it here. Jamie is safer and more secure than he has ever been. As for the future . . . there are good schools here, too."

Robert lifted an eyebrow. "I thought the Amish and

Mennonites sent their kids to little one-room school-houses."

She flashed back, just for an instant, to the one-room school where she'd gone as a child. She hadn't been aware of missing anything. But now, with computers in every classroom and small children with cell phones . . . could she really say that Jamie wouldn't be missing anything if she made that choice?

Robert must have sensed her hesitation, because he leaned across the table toward her. "Jamie's education is important. Isn't it?"

"It's not the only important thing. Anyway, I don't have to send Jamie to a Mennonite school, even if we stay here. He can attend the public elementary school, which has a very good reputation."

The server brought their food then, and Hannah felt a relief at the interruption. She didn't want to be thinking of her future with Robert's eyes on her, weighing her every word, her every expression. Seeing doubts . . . or maybe sowing doubts. Perhaps that was what he intended.

But even if Robert had a point, could she possibly walk away as easily as she'd come?

She was concentrating on convincing Jamie to have some scrambled egg when she realized Robert was waving to someone, half-rising from his seat. Who did he know in Pleasant Valley to wave to?

She sucked in a breath. She couldn't imagine how Robert would have met him, but she knew the older man coming toward them, a woman who was probably his wife in tow. It was Phil Russo, the veteran who'd introduced himself to her at the park.

"Hey, it's nice to see you again." Robert stood, shaking hands. "As you can see, I followed your advice about the restaurant." He gestured to her. "This is my daughter-in-law, Hannah Conroy. And my grandson, Jamie Conroy."

Phil smiled, looking cherubic and not at all as if this meeting had been set up. "I already know Hannah and

Jamie. Hey, buddy, it's good to see you." He patted Jamie's head.

Jamie grabbed for his hand, and Hannah shook her head at him. "Better not let him get too close, or you'll be wearing his lunch on your shirt."

"I don't mind that. We've got grandkids of our own, don't we, Nancy? This is my wife, Nancy. Honey, this is the young woman I told you about. The one who—"

"Works with her aunt at the bakery," his wife finished for him, smiling and perhaps changing what he'd intended to say. Nancy's mop of gray curls and the bright blue eyes in a tanned face seemed familiar. "I know Hannah from the bakery. And little Jamie."

"Yes, of course," Hannah replied. "I'm sorry I didn't remember your name."

"Don't think a thing about it," Nancy said. "You can't be expected to know everyone who comes into the bakery."

"Join us, please." Robert pulled out the chair next to him. "We'd love to have you."

Hannah could hardly object, even though she felt quite certain this wasn't the accidental encounter Robert wanted her to believe. In a few minutes the two of them were settled at the table, and the server appeared to take their orders.

"How did you two happen to meet?" Hannah looked from Robert to Phil.

"I dropped by the local veterans' post last evening," Robert said, his gaze sliding away from hers. "Ran into Phil, and we just started talking. You know how it is."

She thought she could imagine. Whatever he'd managed to hear about her at the auction hadn't been enough for him, and he'd hoped to learn more. Trying to persuade Jamie to take a few more bites of egg was as good a way as any to hide what she was thinking. Jamie, uncooperative, turned his face away.

Nancy chuckled in what seemed to be genuine amusement.

"Oh, my, that brings back memories. Isn't it amazing how little ones can make their wishes known, even before they're talking much?"

Hannah was prepared to be on her guard with these people who'd been foisted on her, but the warm interest in Nancy's face was hard to resist. "How old are your grand-children?"

"The youngest is five, so we're past the toddler stage, at least for the moment. Maybe our younger daughter will come through with a couple more grandchildren." She appeared hopeful. "After all, she's only been married a year."

Hannah couldn't help but smile. "Maybe you shouldn't suggest that yet, then."

"Oh, dear, I try not to." Nancy shook her head ruefully. "But I suspect she knows what I'm thinking. Mothers and daughters usually do know each other too well, don't you agree?"

There was no point in mentioning her mother. "You're probably right. You were in the bakery late this week, as I remember."

"Yes, I can't resist Paula's homemade rye loaf. Or her rhubarb crumb cake, for that matter, even though I try." Nancy patted her middle. "I'm not much of a baker myself."

The conversation stayed general throughout the meal, and Hannah felt her initial suspicion ebb away. If Robert had some special reason for bringing her together with these people, it wasn't apparent. Nancy was pleasant company, and they talked recipes, and quilting, and the results of the charity auction while the men had their own conversation.

Jamie was intent on some game of his own, which seemed to involve pretending a piece of roll was a car, and Hannah was glad to take the respite that offered. Soon enough she assumed he'd start to fuss, ready for his nap.

And then she realized the men had gone from talking about retirement to talking about their service in Viet-nam. They seemed intent on topping the other's stories, chuckling now and then as if enjoying the look back at what must have been a difficult experience.

She didn't begrudge them their memories, and if they could find something to smile about, she was glad. But she didn't want to hear it: It reminded her too much of Travis and the roadside bomb that had ended his life too soon. Her stomach tightened until she wished she hadn't eaten the scrambled eggs and hash browns.

Nancy touched her arm. "Did you know the restaurant has a nice little spot in the side lawn where you can sit? I was thinking we might take Jamie out there and let him stretch his legs. I'm sure he's stayed in that high chair as long as any reasonable person could expect of a toddler."

"I don't want to interrupt your meal . . ." Hannah began.

But Nancy pushed her plate away. "It's fine. I'm finished." She shoved her seat back. "Phil, Hannah and I are going outside with the baby. You'll find us in the side yard when you finish winning the war."

That seemed to be that. Hannah suspected that no one, least of all Nancy's husband, argued with her when she took that tone. So Hannah lifted Jamie from the high chair, grabbed the diaper bag, and followed the older woman between the tables to a side door.

The instant they stepped outside, Hannah's remaining tension began to slip away. Jamie squealed at the sight of the lawn, squirming in her arms.

Nancy led the way to a bench in the shade of an oak tree. Hannah sat down, letting Jamie slide onto the grass. She pulled a couple of toys from the diaper bag, but she suspected he'd be happier running around for a bit.

Sure enough, he ran as far as the sidewalk that meandered around the back of the building and then stopped, looking at her as if for permission.

"Stay here on the grass, okay?" She was never sure just how much he understood, but it was probably more than she sometimes thought.

Taking his yellow ball, she tossed it onto the grass. Jamie went hurrying to find it. He picked it up, lifted his arm above his head to throw it, and dropped it behind him. He swung around with such a puzzled look that she had to laugh.

Nancy was chuckling as well. "He is such a little sweetheart," she said.

"He won't be sweet for much longer, I'm afraid. He'll be wanting his nap, and he can get cranky. I don't want his grandfather to think—" She stopped, because that gave away too much about her strained relationship with Robert.

"Men," Nancy said, on a note of loving exasperation. "They don't understand half what they should. Look at those two in there, reliving those days in Nam without thinking about the pain of it."

"Maybe they've reached a point in their lives when they have to remember it that way," Hannah suggested, although Nancy had voiced what she thought.

"Probably so. Don't get me wrong—I am proud of my husband for his service. But I remember only too well what it was like when Phil came home. He was a long time getting back to being the man I'd married."

Hannah nodded, looking down at her hands linked together in her lap. "I worried about that. About what it would be like when Travis came home."

"And the reality was much worse than you'd anticipated," Nancy said softly. She put her hand over Hannah's. "Those two men hatched this meeting up, you know. They wanted me to try to convince you to get involved with the veterans' group. Maybe take part in the parade."

Hannah's gaze went, startled, to Nancy's face. "I couldn't."

"Well, I know that, believe me." Nancy patted her. "You're not ready, and I certainly won't try to persuade you. And I'll make an effort to explain so that your father-in-law will understand." She smiled ruefully. "Although I can't guarantee I'll be successful."

Relief flowed through Hannah, and thankfulness. "Travis always said how stubborn his father was. But I didn't know Robert well at all. I've only seen him twice, before this visit."

"It's difficult." Nancy's voice was warm with sympathy and understanding. "I just want you to know that anytime you need to talk to someone, you can come to me. Anytime."

"Thank you." Hannah's voice was husky. Maybe she hadn't reached any better understanding with Travis's father today, but it seemed she had found an ally who did understand.

It was later than his usual time when William turned the horse into the lane that led to the stable behind Caleb's shop on Tuesday. Isaac had asked for his help with the milking that morning.

Asked was the surprising word, William decided. After more than a week of silent disapproval emanating from his older brother, William had gotten used to the state of affairs, and when Isaac had actually requested his help instead of assuming it, William had been unaccountably moved. Maybe Isaac was beginning to see him as an adult at last. That was progress he hadn't anticipated.

The mare stopped automatically at her usual spot, whickering a greeting to the horses already out in the paddock. William slid down, his thoughts running through the day ahead and coming to an abrupt halt at the afternoon, when he'd see Hannah.

There'd been no opportunity to see or speak with her since Saturday, but that didn't mean he hadn't thought about her. And he'd worried about her situation with her father-in-law.

It wondered him that any man would behave that way toward his own kin. Asking questions about Hannah as if she'd done something wrong—well, William couldn't wrap his mind around it.

If Robert Conroy had thought his questions would go unnoticed, he didn't know much about places like Pleasant Valley. Murmurs had been drifting through the community like smoke, enough so that the back of William's neck prickled when he drove through town. Hannah probably felt it even more.

His hands paused on the harness buckle when he caught a glimpse of movement. Hannah, coming toward him along the lane between the buildings, was a graceful figure in her green dress, apron fluttering a bit in the breeze that sent a few leaves slipping down from the maple next to the fence.

She looked as if she belonged here now. The thought stuck in his heart. She belonged here.

But then he saw her face and knew something was wrong.

He moved to meet her, but she waved him back.

"Don't stop what you're doing," she said. "I just happened to see you go past the bakery, and I wanted . . ." She looked up at him and seemed to lose the thread of what she was saying.

He wasn't doing very well in that area himself. He couldn't look at her without remembering the touch of her lips, the softness of her body in that moment when she had clung to him.

He shook the thought away, focusing on her face. "You w-wanted . . . ?" he prompted. Was it his imagination, or did the pink in her cheeks deepen?

"I wanted to thank you again. For Saturday." She took a step back, then turned and stroked the mare's neck as if hiding her face from him.

"Knowing about y-your father-in-law h-hurt you. I am sorry."

"You thought I needed to know, and you were right." She straightened. "I'm sure half the township knows about it by now." She gave him a fleeting glance. "Be honest with me, William. You've heard people talking about it, haven't you?"

He nodded, reluctant to upset her more. "B-but most p-people feel for you, not him. I know it."

No need to mention the few who considered that Hannah was an outsider and what happened to her was no concern of theirs.

Still, something in her quiet brown eyes suggested that she probably knew that well. Did she know, too, how he had wanted to protest when he'd heard people say those things? But his habit of silence was too ingrained, and he hadn't managed to speak out.

Hannah stood silent, caught in some sad imaginings of her own. He had to say something.

"H-has your father-in-law said anything to y-you about it?"

"About his asking questions about me? No, but then, he wouldn't, would he?" A worry line appeared between her eyebrows. "I wish I understood what he wants."

"H-he wants you t-to leave, ain't so?" That seemed clear. It was the why that eluded William.

"He hasn't said that to me again." Her frown deepened, and she rubbed her forehead as if she could erase the thought. "But I feel all the time as if he's judging me. Us. This whole place. As if there's some special behavior he expects from his son's widow, and I'm disappointing him. Letting him down. More important, letting Travis down."

"Ach, th-that is foolishness. You w-wouldn't."

"How can I be sure?" Pain filled her voice suddenly. Maybe it had been there all along, and William just hadn't heard it. "Whatever I do, it seems I'm failing someone, just like I—"

She stopped, as short as if she'd shut off a tap. But he felt sure that whatever she'd been about to say was important. To her, and so to him, as well.

"Just l-like you what, Hannah?" He asked the question softly, afraid she'd push him away. "Who d-do you think you f-failed?"

Hannah drew in a long breath. She was staring at the

horse, but he didn't think she even saw the mare standing there patiently while they talked.

"My mother." Her voice seemed to choke on the words. "I went off to school, not even noticing how down she was that day."

He was silent, mind busy, trying to fill in the blanks of what she was saying. Hannah's mother had suffered from depression; he knew that from something Paula had let slip to Katie. And Hannah's father had run off, leaving her to cope with the situation.

"What happened?" he murmured when it seemed she wouldn't go on.

"She took an overdose." Hannah's voice was thick with unshed tears. "If I'd been there, if I'd found her sooner, they might have saved her. But they couldn't." She closed her eyes, as if to shut something out. "They couldn't."

His heart seemed to be ripping into pieces. He longed to touch her, but he feared comforting might turn to more, and Hannah didn't need that now.

"It w-was her choice. Not y-yours."

"But if I'd been there—"

He couldn't help it. His hand closed around her wrist, and he felt her pulse thud against his palm. "And the n-next time? And the time a-after that?" He hurt so much for her, but he was afraid nothing he said was going to help. "You c-couldn't be there all the t-time."

"I don't know." She lifted her hand, and he let go at once. She brushed her palm across her forehead, as if to push the bad memories away. "What you say is true, and I've said it to myself." She tried to smile, but it was a failure. "Still, I can't help feeling that I let her down when she needed me. And now Robert is making me feel that I'm letting Travis down."

Clearly she didn't want to talk about her mother any further, so he had to respect her wishes, but even that small amount had shown him a great deal about Hannah.

He tried to speak more lightly, but he'd been mulling

over what he knew about Robert, trying to make sense of his actions. "We are n-not what Robert is used to, ja? He finds everything here s-strange, and h-he is still g-grieving for his s-son. G-give him some t-time. Let h-him see that you h-have not forgotten Travis. Robert w-will come around."

"I hope so." Her hand moved toward him, as if she would touch him, and then she drew it back. "In the meantime . . ." The words trickled off, but he thought he knew what she would ask him.

"You think it w-would be best if I d-don't come today."

Pressing her lips together, she nodded. "I think it's best. I'm sorry."

"It's all r-right." It wasn't, not really, but he couldn't add to her burdens right now. "Wait." He turned, reaching under the seat for the object he'd intended to take to Jamie this afternoon.

"Here." He put it in her hands. "This is f-for Jamie."

Her breath went out in a soft exhale as she held the toy locomotive in her cupped hands. "It-it's beautiful." She blinked, as if to chase away tears. "You made this for him?"

"Ja." He closed her fingers around it. "No n-need for R-Robert to know. This is between us."

They stood for a moment, looking at each other, and William knew that it might as well be his heart that she held in her hands.

CHAPTER FIFTEEN

I see you can't walk very far in this town without running out of sidewalk."

Robert was pushing the stroller, having said he'd like to go for a walk with Hannah and Jamie. It was one of the few times he'd taken any initiative where Jamie was concerned, and Hannah decided it was best to ignore any implied criticism in his comment.

Besides, Pleasant Valley *was* small. There was no denying that, but it was part of what she loved about the place. She waved to Cliff Wainwright, who was sweeping the sidewalk in front of his bookstore.

"That's okay. Jamie likes it when the stroller bounces along in the grass. It's just a little hard on the person pushing." Hannah nodded, smiling at Rachel Zook and her daughter, going in the other direction.

Rachel greeted them warmly, but didn't stop to invite conversation. Because Robert was with her? That was possible.

"You seem to know everyone in town," Robert commented.

"Not everyone, but it's hard to stay a stranger here. Especially when you're related to a good number of them in one way or another."

Robert shot her a glance, eyes narrowing. "You have relatives here besides your aunt? You didn't tell me that."

"My extended family has lived in Pleasant Valley for a long time." Robert, with a career that had sent him all over the world, probably couldn't imagine that. "Most of the Amish and Mennonite families here are related if you go back far enough. It's been nice to get re-acquainted with family I'd almost forgotten."

Robert nodded, indicating that he understood, but the realization seemed to annoy him for some reason she didn't understand. Hannah sought for another subject that might interest him.

"Across the street is our churchhouse." She nodded toward the white frame structure, plain and square, surrounded by grass and trees. The cemetery beyond had rows of identical markers, showing that humility extended beyond life.

"Churchhouse?" he echoed the word. "Why not just church?"

She shrugged, afraid her ignorance was showing. "I don't know. That's just the traditional expression. The Amish worship in homes, but Mennonites worship in churchhouses."

Robert shaded his eyes against the sun, low in the sky this late in the afternoon. "Can we go inside?"

"Of course, if you want. It won't be locked." Hannah wasn't sure whether to be pleased that he was taking an interest or concerned that he was gearing up for another assault on her choices.

They crossed the street, and Robert parked the stroller near the door. Hannah lifted Jamie from his seat, ignoring his obvious desire to get down in the grass. She automatically led the way through the women's door, then thought how odd Robert would find that if she told him.

Inside it was cool and quiet, a shaft of sunlight coming through the west window setting dust motes dancing. With the backless benches empty, the room seemed larger.

"No padded pews," Robert said, smiling a little. He sat on the closest bench and looked around.

Hannah put Jamie down, knowing there was nothing here he could get into, and smiled as he ran along the row of benches. Robert watched him, too, and she couldn't quite make out his expression.

"You know, I got to thinking last night when I was at the motel. I was in Japan when Travis was the age Jamie is now. His mother handled things on her own. We were apart more than we were together." He shrugged. "Guess I didn't get to know Travis as well as I should have."

His honesty startled her. So far as she could remember, he had never admitted any wrongdoing in the raising of his son.

"I'm sure they both missed you a lot." What else could she say?

"His mother took care of things. That's how it was when you were in the military." He sounded defensive.

"I know." She did. She'd lived the life, too, although he seemed to have forgotten that.

"His mother did a good job. Travis turned out to be a pretty good man, anyway."

"Yes. He did." Tears stung her eyes. Jamie ran to her and leaned against her legs, as if he'd sensed her distress. She ruffled his curls, remembering what William had said—that Robert was still grieving, maybe afraid she was forgetting Travis.

Robert watched for a moment, making no move to touch Jamie. "If Travis had lived, you wouldn't be thinking of staying here."

"I suppose not." Though she might always have felt

something was missing, even if she hadn't known what it was. "But he didn't come back. I miss him every day, but I have to do the best I can on my own." They kept returning to that hard, simple truth.

Sitting next to Robert in the quiet churchhouse, she prayed he could understand. Prayed that she knew what to say that would make him understand.

"Is something wrong?" He seemed more keyed in to her feelings than he had been in the past, and she didn't know whether to be pleased or upset.

She couldn't tell him what she was really thinking. Instead, she patted the bench. "It seems a bit strange, sitting here with you. Men and women don't sit next to each other in worship."

"Why not?" Robert would probably ask that same question about everything here.

"It's considered less distracting for the sexes to be separated, so that they're concentrating on worship." She pointed. "Men and boys sit on that side, women and girls on the other. This is the singers' table. The song leaders sit here. And that is the ministers' bench."

He nodded. "It's not very fancy, that's for sure. Not that I'm much of a churchgoer."

"The interior of the churchhouse is meant to emphasize our beliefs. Especially our belief in showing humility, not competing with others or trying to have something that looks better or fancier. That goes for clothes, houses, and churchhouses."

When she'd lived on base, it had been easy to judge the rank of the husband by the size of the house. Amish and Mennonites didn't operate on those standards.

"Humility, huh." Robert didn't sound very impressed. "I can't say I ever thought much about it."

She couldn't argue with him. Humility wasn't a popular virtue for many people.

"Look." He turned on the bench so he was facing her, face intent, and she knew they were getting to the real reason for this walk together. "Your religion is your own business. But my son was a soldier. You knew that when you married him. How can you belong to a group that looks down on the service he died for?"

"We don't look down on the service. That's not it at all."

Hannah had an overwhelming sense of inadequacy. How could she explain Anabaptist beliefs in a way someone like Robert would understand?

Still, at least he seemed willing to listen. That was more than he'd done before.

"What is it then?" His face twisted, and she heard the frustration in his voice. "Back when I was in Nam getting shot at for my country, you people were draft evaders."

If she were as educated as she should be, she'd know her own history better. "We don't believe in meeting violence with violence. We try to bring peace. Mennonites didn't run away to avoid the draft. They went into other kinds of service, for the most part. Some of them even went to jail for their beliefs. Can't you understand that kind of devotion?"

"No." His reaction was blunt. "My son gave his life for his country. I want my grandson brought up to respect and honor that."

Her head was starting to throb. "Of course I'll bring him up that way."

"You can't," he said flatly. "Not here, surrounded by all this." His gesture took in more than just the churchhouse. He meant all of Pleasant Valley, it seemed. Hannah suspected he'd planned this conversation, determined not to lose his temper this time. "I just don't see why you don't take your friend Megan up on her offer. If it's a question of money, maybe I can help out."

There was a time when that offer might have made all the difference. Not any longer.

"I appreciate that. But I couldn't go back to living like . . . like an army wife, and that's what it would be if I moved in with Megan. I'm not an army wife any longer. I'm a widow."

Robert just stared at her, looking baffled and angry.

She'd thought they understood each other a little better now. But it seemed even understanding didn't really help when there was no room in the middle for compromise.

The sun was barely above the hills when William arrived for the barn raising. Not that he wouldn't have come anyway, but this new building for Caleb and Katie was special. They'd bought a house at the edge of town, and Caleb wanted everything to be ready for them to move in as soon as they were married.

Most newlywed couples spent time visiting relatives on a wedding trip after their marriage, but since they both had businesses to run, they'd decided to wait until after Christmas for that.

William surveyed the scene as he turned the horse and buggy over to one of the boys appointed to care for the animals. The preliminary planning had been done already. Ammon Esh, who'd supervised the building of more barns than even he could probably count, had laid out the design several weeks ago, and the lumber was piled next to the site. All that was required now was willing hands, and they were arriving every minute.

William crossed still-wet grass to where Caleb stood, nodding respectfully at something Ammon was saying. William waited until they'd finished, then grinned at Caleb.

"This is one s-step closer to your w-wedding," he said.

"Ja, for sure." Caleb's answering smile was warm. "I can't believe the number of people who are here already. More than we expected on a Thursday."

Barn raisings were usually on Saturdays, but that was such a busy day in the shops that they'd decided on a weekday. There'd be some who couldn't get off to help, but Caleb was right. Plenty of folks were here to accomplish the work. Most of the church, of course, and since Caleb and Katie were friends with so many of the shopkeepers in town, there were Mennonites and even a few Englisch present as well.

Ammon glanced over the site and gave a short nod, indicating he was satisfied that all was as it should be. Without a word of direction, the work began.

Well, no one needed direction when it came to something so familiar. There was no room for pride in a community like theirs. Everyone knew the extent of your talents, and you'd automatically go to the work you were suited for.

It was a satisfying way of life, William thought as he fastened his tool belt. How could he ever give it up?

The thought gave him pause. Where had that idea come from? There was no question of him giving up this life.

Hannah . . . well, he loved Hannah, he couldn't deny those feelings. But she'd given no sign that she felt the same way about him. She'd merely leaned on him in a time of trouble, and for now, that was enough.

Gideon, working next to him, nudged him. "Are you dreaming, then, William? I asked you for a handful of nails, and you stared at that upright like you'd never seen one before." Gideon's tone was teasing, but there was an undercurrent of concern in it, as well.

"Ach, I'm half-asleep yet." William handed over the nails.

Gideon nodded, but it seemed to William that he didn't quite buy that explanation.

"I see Paula Schatz and her niece are here," Gideon said, nodding toward the driveway.

"W-where?" William turned, narrowly missing his thumb with the hammer.

"Just there, by the house. By the size of those boxes, I'd say Paula brought enough baked goods to feed half the township."

"Ja, th-that's Paula." He caught a quick glimpse of Hannah, a box in one hand and Jamie clinging to the other, heading into the kitchen.

Gideon was silent for a moment, maybe remembering the issue with Hannah's father-in-law. "Hannah seems like a gut woman, from all I've heard. Settling down here. I hope her father-in-law isn't going to cause any problems."

"Ja. Me, also." He didn't think he needed to say more. He'd best be careful not to give folks anything to buzz about. He drove a nail with concentrated care. Focus on the work. That was the best way.

He did pretty well at that through the morning. He continued working beside Gideon, talking now and again, but for the most part letting the echo of hammers and the whine of saws do the talking.

By the time they took a break in midmorning, most of the framing had been done. William snagged a wedge of shoofly pie from the picnic table and accepted a mug of coffee from one of his many nieces. The Brands were out in full force today, of course. He was probably related to more than half the people here.

Looking for a spot to sit, he rounded the corner of the porch and nearly ran into Hannah, bearing a tray heaped with donuts. A flash of pleasure, quickly masked, lit her eyes at the sight of him.

But he had seen it, and he wouldn't forget.

"You've had a busy morning," she said. "I was watching the work for a while. The barn is going up so fast."

"Ja. We w-will finish today." He gazed at her, longing to say the words he couldn't.

Hannah belongs here, some part of his mind argued. If she had never left, never lived another life, surely no one would think a thing about a relationship between them.

Well, that wasn't quite true. But it happened. Amish fell in love with people from other Plain groups. It would be accepted, in the end—even the fact that Hannah was a couple of years older than he was and a widow.

The need to speak pressed against his lips. He had to tell her—

"My father-in-law is here," Hannah said quickly, almost as if she guessed at his thoughts. "He wanted to see a barn raising, so Aunt Paula told him he'd be welcome." She gave a shrug that had something rueful in it. "She is trying hard to be hospitable to him. For my sake."

"N-not easy for her, I know. Paula s-says what she thinks."

He smiled, to show he accepted what Hannah was doing. She was reminding him of the barriers that stood between them. And maybe also trying to erase what she might see as weakness in confiding so much in him.

"She does. I . . . I should get these donuts to the table." But she didn't move. "On Tuesday, I think you should come as usual."

"Is h-he leaving, then?" No need to spell out who they were talking about.

"I don't know." Her voice firmed. "But I want to get back to normal. All right?"

Whether she was right or not, William didn't know, but he nodded.

Hannah went on toward the picnic table, her slim back straight. William stood where he was, taking a sip of his coffee. But it had gotten cold while they'd talked, and he poured it out.

Come to think of it, he wasn't really all that hungry. He swallowed a couple bites of the shoofly pie and tossed the paper plate in the trash. He might as well get back to work.

He headed over toward the supply area. He'd be working fairly high for the next few hours, and he wouldn't want to be coming back down for anything he could take up to begin with.

No one else was there, which was maybe just as well. He didn't feel much like talking at the moment. If Hannah—

"It's William, right?"

The sound of the Englisch voice behind him had William spinning around, grasping a handful of nails. "J-ja."

It was Robert Conroy, and at the sight of him William's tongue seemed to tie itself in knots. His fingers tightened until the nails bit into his palms. Stupid, to let the man affect him this way.

"I saw the little toy train you made for Jamie." Conroy didn't seem to notice or care whether he spoke or not. "Nice work."

William ducked his head in the characteristic Amish response to a compliment. He didn't deserve praise for what had been a labor of love, and he didn't want it.

"I'd never seen a barn raising before." Conroy glanced up at the structure that loomed above them—the bare ribs of what would be a barn before the day was over. "It's like watching something from the past."

If he thought William would be bothered by the implication that he was old-fashioned, he didn't understand the Amish.

William reached for a post that would be needed, grasping one end. To his surprise, Conroy took the other. He hefted it easily, obviously fit for his age.

"Where to?"

"By the l-ladder." Together they put it in place.

"I understand my daughter-in-law has been helping you with your speech problems." There was a question in Conroy's eyes. Was he asking if there was more to their relationship? Maybe not satisfied with the answers he was getting from everyone else?

"J-j-ja. Sh-she h-has." His stammer seemed to worsen at the mention of the lessons.

Conroy nodded. "Well, it gives her something to do here besides working in a bakery. A chance to keep her hand in her career."

William didn't even attempt a response to that comment.

"It's a shame she wasn't able to complete her education before she and my son got married."

Conroy's face tightened, whether at the reminder of his son's loss, or disapproval of that marriage, William wasn't sure.

"Anyway, once Jamie is a little older, Hannah will be able to go back to college. She'll finish her education and have the career she always wanted, right?"

Apparently satisfied that he'd made his point, Conroy walked away.

"*Now* what do you suppose those two have found to talk about?"

Startled, Hannah turned to the person who'd spoken and found that Rachel Zook was standing next to her. Obviously Rachel had been watching the conversation between William and Robert Conroy as intently as Hannah had.

Rachel caught Hannah's eye and flushed a little. "Ach, I'm sorry. I shouldn't have spoken—"

"It's fine." Hannah touched her arm lightly. "You and William are family. I understand that you care for him."

And she'd love to know, too, what Robert had found it necessary to say to William. It had been obvious that Robert had initiated the conversation. Obvious, too, in his expression when he walked away that he thought he'd achieved something. But what?

"We just don't want William to be hurt," Rachel said, her voice soft so that none of the others, busy serving the midmorning food, would hear her. "He's . . . well, he's special."

"He is." But maybe by *special*, Rachel meant William's stammer.

If so, she'd be wrong. William was special because of the warmth of his heart and the strength of his character.

Each time she saw him, Hannah was more aware of those qualities.

Rachel studied her face for a moment. Then she smiled. "I believe you do understand."

"I don't want him to be hurt, either, believe me, especially not because of me. My father-in-law has some ideas that are . . . troublesome."

"He wants you to leave here, doesn't he?" Rachel's quick understanding seemed to leap ahead of explanations. "Why? Because of your faith?"

"I suppose in a way that's at the heart of it." She spoke slowly, feeling her way. She'd been so busy worrying that she hadn't really been able to see Robert's attitudes clearly. "He seems to feel that if I bring Jamie up here, he will forget his father. Or maybe be ashamed of his father's military service." She shook her head ruefully. "I tried to explain about nonviolence, but I probably didn't do a very good job of it. I've been away too long."

"No." Rachel patted her hand. "You were nine when you left. You'd already been raised in faith, and even though you left for a while, that wasn't lost."

"I've begun to feel that I was the one who was lost during those years." Strange, that it was Rachel who was helping her understand. "Now, with Robert pressuring me, I see how much my faith and my family mean to me." She shook her head. "I shouldn't burden you with my troubles. I'm sorry."

"Don't be sorry. I understand, maybe better than you know. My brother, my twin, jumped the fence to the outside world, and I know now that he won't ever come back." Sorrow touched her expression. "It's ser hard to accept that, but I have managed to. But you can come back, Hannah, if that's what you want, no matter what other people say. Just listen to your heart."

Tears pricked her eyes at Rachel's unexpected kindness. "Denke," she whispered.

Rachel nodded. "Think how embarrassed William would be if he knew we were talking about him." She glanced toward the construction site. "Look, Gideon and William are going up to the top to work."

Hannah picked William's figure out easily. And what did that say about her feelings, that she could identify his back in an instant among a whole crowd of similarly dressed men? She hadn't recognized at first that the man with him was Rachel's husband.

The two men had reached the top, and they walked easily along a beam that looked as thin as a tightrope from where Hannah stood.

"It scares me, to see them working way up there without a safety harness," she said.

"I know. When Gideon works on installing windmills now, he does wear one, since he's often working alone up there. He talked to the bishop about it, though."

The two men seemed to be talking as they worked, and once, Hannah saw William throw his head back and laugh, exposing the strong column of his throat.

"It's wonderful that they get along so well. I mean . . ." She stopped. Maybe Rachel wouldn't like that she knew about William's feelings for her.

"Because William proposed to me once?" Rachel smiled. "That was William being kind, wanting to take care of us. He confused that with love. I told him that one day he'd find the right woman for him, and when he did find her, his stammer wouldn't matter at all."

Hannah wasn't sure how to respond. It was true that William's stammer didn't matter to her, except that it had brought them together. But was Rachel implying—

Rachel gasped, her hand going to her lips. Hannah followed her gaze to the top of the barn, and her heart seemed to stop. One of the men . . . Gideon, it was Gideon . . . had slipped. He dangled from the beam, legs swinging as he held on with one arm.

For an instant the scene froze, then it broke as suddenly. All over the structure, men swarmed toward Gideon.

But William was already there. As smoothly as if he were flat on the ground, he dropped full-length on the beam, reaching down to grab Gideon's other arm, drawing it up so that Gideon could grasp the beam.

"It's all right. William has him." Hannah clasped Rachel's hand, not realizing until she'd done it that she'd spoken in dialect. "He's safe. William won't let him fall."

He wouldn't. He wouldn't let Gideon fall, and he wouldn't fall himself trying to help him. He wouldn't.

But she couldn't pull her gaze away, as if by the sheer force of her stare she could keep him there, keep him safe.

Please, Father. Please. Hold them in Your hands.

The other men were closer now, and Hannah was startled to realize that Robert had started up the ladder, as if to help. William wasn't waiting. Straddling the beam, he helped Gideon inch himself upward. The movement was so slow, so painful she could feel the strain on his muscles, sense his single-minded determination.

And then Gideon was high enough to get his leg over the beam, and William hauled him the rest of the way. A relieved murmur went through the crowd, and Hannah realized she could breathe again. He was safe. They were both safe.

In fact, they were slapping each other's shoulders as if it had all been a game of some sort.

"Men," Rachel murmured, and the word expressed Hannah's feelings perfectly.

But those tense moments had shown Hannah something very clearly. She loved William. And she didn't know what she was going to do about it.

Her cheeks went hot with the realization, and she pressed her palms against them, hoping no one had noticed. Most of the women were still focused on what was

going on atop the building site. Rachel had turned away
to say something to a friend.

And then she realized that one person was staring right
at her. Robert Conroy, still on the ladder, had turned toward her, and judging by his expression, he didn't like
what he was seeing.

CHAPTER SIXTEEN

Hannah expected a reaction from her father-in-law, and she assumed it wouldn't be long in coming. Fortunately he'd kept silent while her aunt was around, saying only that he'd stop back to see Hannah once Jamie was in bed.

Jamie slapped his hand on the bathwater, sending up a spray that narrowly missed her, and chortled.

"I think you're getting more wound up instead of more relaxed."

Hannah handed him his yellow ducky to divert him while she rinsed his hair. Cupping her hand across his forehead, she poured a cupful of warm water over his head, getting the shampoo out before he had time to protest.

"There we go, all done, and you didn't cry, did you?"

"No cry." Jamie shook his head solemnly. He lifted his arms with a sudden change of mood. "Out."

"Put your toys in their net first. Who can catch the big

fish?" She swooped the duck across the water, chasing the other toys.

Giggling, Jamie corralled the plastic boat and whale, and together they put the toys in the mesh bag that hung from the faucet.

"Now we're ready." She held out the bath towel, wrapping the wet, wiggly little body as she lifted him out. "That's my boy."

In a matter of moments the bath-time routine was completed, and she sat with Jamie on her lap in the rocking chair. Already drowsy, he leaned against her while she said his nighttime prayers.

"Now I lay me down to sleep, I pray the Lord my soul to keep. Let angels watch me through the night, and wake me with the morning light."

It was the prayer Travis wanted his son taught, the one his mother had taught him.

Kissing Jamie's damp curls, she added a prayer of her own. *Please, Father, help me to be the mother I should be. To make the right decisions for this precious boy.* She sighed, her mind straying to Robert, then to William. *Give me wisdom, Father, because I don't see the way forward.*

She lingered, rocking Jamie, wanting to prolong this peaceful time. Unfortunately, her thoughts were anything but peaceful. They kept reliving those moments when William had been in danger. Those moments when she'd realized she loved him.

It was no wonder she hadn't recognized what was happening. Her feelings for William had developed so differently from her love for Travis.

She looked back at the girl she'd been then and was hardly able to recognize herself. She'd been standing at the cash register in the convenience store near campus, and she'd come up a dollar short to pay for her items. With the clerk staring at her suspiciously, and her cheeks red with embarrassment, Hannah had tried to decide which item to put back.

Then a hand came into view, holding out a dollar. "Let me."

She'd looked up into warm, smiling brown eyes, barely registering the uniform he wore, and her legs had turned to water. She'd tumbled hard and fast into love, dizzyingly so. On their second date Travis had asked her to marry him, and she'd said yes without a moment's hesitation.

With William, every step of their relationship had been different. She'd been sorry for him at first, watching him struggle and knowing so well what he was going through. And then she'd seen him as a student, someone she could help.

But the teacher-student balance had shifted when she began to depend on him as a friend. She'd grown to respect his strength of character, to rely on his calm, steady presence. If Robert realized it was the threat he'd posed that had pushed her into William's arms, what would he think?

And then, all in an instant when William was in danger, the blinders fell from her eyes, and she'd known that what she felt was love.

She rose, carrying Jamie across to the crib. Half-asleep, he went willingly, snuggling his favorite blanket close. Hannah stroked his back.

"Nighty-night, my sweetheart. Sleep tight. Mammi loves you."

She walked slowly from the room, her thoughts still centered on William. He cared for her—she knew that. But was it love on his part, or just sympathy for her situation? And if it was love, how could it ever work out between them? William was secure in his Amish faith, and she could never ask him to change.

And her first duty would always be to Jamie. She wouldn't change that, but how could she bring up Travis's son as Amish?

Hannah was just closing the door to Jamie's room when she heard the doorbell. Her stomach clenched. It would be Robert. She had to face him, and she didn't have any answers.

The stairs seemed steeper than usual as she went down. Robert's face, seen through the glass in the back door, was set in harsh lines. Since it was dusk, he didn't wear those sunglasses that turned his face into a mask, but she almost wished he had. She wasn't sure she wanted to read the expression in his eyes.

Her hand closed on the knob, and she swung the door open. "Robert. Won't you come in?"

He gestured toward the porch swing. "Why don't we sit here and talk? We'll have more privacy."

Not sure she wanted privacy, Hannah had to nod anyway. She went out, closing the door. The porch light, which she had turned on earlier to welcome him, cast a yellow glow over the weathered floorboards of the porch, and the pot of mums by the steps made a bright splotch of color in the fading light.

Hannah sat down on the porch swing, drawing her skirt close so that there was room for him to sit next to her. Instead, Robert pulled the wicker rocking chair to face her and sat, hands planted on his knees.

"I've decided that I'm leaving on Monday morning."

The blunt announcement took her by surprise, even though she hadn't expected him to stay as long as he had. "I see. You're welcome to stay longer, you know."

A muscle twitched in his jaw. "It's time I got back to Arizona, but I want things settled between us before I go. What I want to hear from you is that you're leaving, too."

She could only stare at him. "I don't—"

He cut her off with a sharp chop of his hand. "I know. I've heard all the reasons you have for staying. Maybe I even understand some of them. This is a nice place to live, but Jamie's future is more important than all that."

She took a breath, hoping she could say what needed to be said without sounding confrontational. "I don't understand why you feel so strongly about this, Robert. You never . . ."

"What? I never expressed much interest in Jamie before?" He looked a little shamefaced at that for an instant, but he rallied. "I never got along with my own son? Is that what you're saying?"

It took all her courage. "Yes."

"Fair enough. After his mother died, Travis and I didn't have much in common, but that doesn't mean I didn't care." His gaze seemed to bore through her. "I know you have to leave here to give Jamie the life he'd have had if Travis had come home."

That went straight to her heart, taking her breath away for an instant. When she thought she could keep her voice steady, she spoke.

"Travis didn't come home. That's the whole point. He's gone, and I have to do the best job I can on my own." How many times had she said that, but he didn't seem to hear?

"And you think that best job is raising Travis's son among people who deny themselves modern conveniences, who believe in raising their kids to be ignorant of progress? What do you think Jamie would grow up to do in a place like this? Be a farmer? You'll take away all his chances of making something of himself."

Her head had begun to pound, her stomach to ache. She hated confrontation. Loud voices and arguments made her want to hide in the closet and put her hands over her ears.

But she had to try to make him understand. "I would never take away Jamie's choices. He'll always have the right to decide for himself. Once he's old enough to understand, if he doesn't want to live Plain, I'll do everything I can to help him create another life."

"After he's been brainwashed by people who hate everything his father stood for? People who turn their backs on Travis's sacrifice?" His voice had risen, sharp against her ears, and he stood, looming over her.

"Robert, you don't understand." Her voice sounded weak in her own ears. "That's my fault. I didn't explain it well enough. Amish and Mennonites don't belittle what Travis did. It's just that they've chosen another road. The way of nonviolence."

"Words." He dismissed them with a strong sweep of his arm. "You don't even believe that yourself. I know the truth. I've seen it. You want to stay here, deny my grandson his rightful future, because of that Amish man."

William. Robert had seen, and he knew she loved William.

She should have been prepared for his anger, and she hadn't been. She'd muddled everything about dealing with Robert.

"That's not so. There's nothing between me and William . . ."

"Don't bother. I know what I saw with my own eyes." He ground out the words. "You'd better think this over carefully, Hannah. Very carefully. Because, believe me, the wrong decision is going to cost you."

Robert spun and stalked off, anger radiating from him as he went.

Hannah huddled on the swing, her arms crossed over her stomach as if to protect herself. This was worse, far worse, than she'd feared.

"*What* can he do?" Nancy Russo's voice was calm. She carried a teapot to her round kitchen table and poured the fragrant brew into Hannah's cup. "I'm sure Robert is as upset as you say, but really, what can he do about it?"

"Denke." Hannah replied absently in Pennsylvania Dutch, and then realized what she'd done. "Thank you."

Nancy smiled, sitting down across from her. "It's all right. I don't know much dialect, but I understand a few words."

Hannah sipped, the warmth and aroma seeping through

her, soothing her. Or perhaps the serenity was emanating from Nancy. She was a comforting person, with her soft gray curls and a face that seemed made for smiling.

Maybe that was why Nancy had popped up in Hannah's mind during a mostly sleepless night. She'd known she needed to talk to someone about Robert, someone who might understand the man better than she did. And she'd remembered Nancy.

Hannah put the cup down. "You know, I had no intention of blurting the whole story out like that the minute I walked through your door. I was going to lead up to it gradually, but when you looked at me with so much sympathy, it just poured out. Does that often happen to you?"

Nancy smiled. "Sometimes. Anyway, I'm glad you did. I meant it when I said I'd like to help."

"You said that before I realized I was going to need it."

Hannah leaned against the spindle-back of the chair, surprised at how comfortable it was, and wondered if the piece was Amish-made. Nancy's house was a modern ranch, but the kitchen had a comfortable country air, with one wall of faded brick and cast-iron skillets hanging from a rack.

"Yes, well, I had a feeling from Robert's attitude that there might be trouble," Nancy said. "I've seen his type of man before. He's the kind who's intent on getting his own way."

"I think he means well." Hannah rubbed her forehead, where a headache lingered, made even worse by her sleepless night. "He just won't listen to any other point of view but his own."

"No. Well, you see that sometimes with people who've spent their entire careers in the military. Not often, maybe, but it happens. They're used to a world where there's only one right way to do things."

"Maybe so," Hannah said slowly, trying to adjust her view of Robert. "I have to admit, I don't understand him. Travis . . ." She let that trail off, not sure she wanted to talk about Travis.

"Are you afraid Travis would have turned out like his father?" Nancy said, her voice gentle.

"No, no. In fact, he was determined not to be like his dad. Travis was proud of his service, of course, but he wasn't going to re-up. He'd decided that when we found out I was pregnant." She smiled, remembering his joy, and his immediate response. "He said he didn't want his child to grow up with an absentee father, the way he had. He said the cost was too great."

She stopped, the words echoing in her mind. That was very nearly the threat Robert had leveled at her.

"What is it?" Nancy was quick to read the change in Hannah's feelings.

"Nothing." She rubbed her arms, suddenly chilled. "It's just—that was what Robert said to me. That if I stayed, the cost might be too high."

Nancy patted her hand. "I wouldn't let him intimidate you. Robert doesn't understand Plain people, and what he doesn't understand threatens him."

"You're Englisch, and you don't feel that way, do you?"

"I've lived around Plain people all my life," Nancy said. "Pleasant Valley was my home, and that's why we retired here. There's not much I don't understand. And admire, for that matter. It's different for someone like Robert, who has never been exposed to it."

"I tried to explain our beliefs about nonviolence, but I obviously failed." Hannah looked at Nancy hopefully. "Maybe if you talked to him, he'd listen."

"I'll be glad to do what I can, but I'm not sure he'll hear me. He said something to my husband about you taking his grandson into a cult, if you can believe that. Phil tried to explain, but . . ." She shrugged her shoulders. "You can see it didn't do much good."

No, it hadn't. "Well, please thank him for trying. And thank you. Whatever you can do, I'll appreciate."

"That's all right, my dear." Nancy patted her hand. "I know it's worrisome, but when it comes right down to it,

HANNAH'S JOY   217

you're doing the best you can for that little boy. If your father-in-law doesn't approve—well, in-laws don't, sometimes." She paused. "I guess the only thing to ask yourself is whether you're sure. After all, you've lived in the outside world for a long time."

"I was Plain for nine years. That's a good big chunk of my life." She tried to think how best to explain what she hadn't really articulated to anyone else. "When we moved away, I was devastated. I didn't understand what was happening to us. I adjusted, eventually. Accepted. But there was always a hole in me." She put her hand on her chest. She could almost feel the remembered pain. "When I came back here, I didn't really intend it to be for good. But I began to see that my faith had always been here, underneath. This is my place."

"Then listen to your heart, and you'll be all right."

The words, coming from Nancy and echoing what Rachel had said, gave Hannah comfort. Still, there was that edge of fear. "I wish Robert could understand that as well as you do."

"I do, too, my dear. But if he refuses, well, there's still nothing he can do about it. I feel sure he'll come around in time. You just have to stand your ground."

Hannah nodded, hoping Nancy was right. Unfortunately, she knew that standing her ground was not one of her gifts.

William had a feeling something was going on that he didn't know about around the supper table that evening. His married sister, Emma, and her husband, John Eicher, were there. Not that it was so unusual to see them. With their children grown now, they often came over for a meal.

Isaac and Emma had been the two oldest of the family, the ones who'd taken over when Mamm and Daad were both doing poorly at the same time. William and Ezra, being a good bit younger, had generally been left out of any decisions to be made.

William scooped up the last bite of Ruth's excellent apple crumb pie. One thing about having Emma and John here—it put Ruth on her mettle to produce the finest meal possible, even though she'd never have admitted to any competitive feelings.

But tonight . . . well, he wasn't sure why he felt uneasy. Isaac and Emma were doing most of the talking, as they usually did. His earliest memories were of the two of them fighting, but then instantly supporting each other if anyone else criticized.

Ruth moved back and forth between stove and table, making sure everyone had plenty, her mind clearly focused on the meal to the exclusion of everything else. And John, aside from a few comments about the fall harvest and the quality of the pumpkins he was raising, concentrated on eating. But each time his gaze met William's, he looked quickly away.

Isaac and Ruth's three teenage boys were their usual selves, eating heartily and teasing each other about what girls they'd see at the singing on Sunday night.

John had barely taken the last bite of his pie when Isaac collected everyone's attention and bowed his head for the prayer after meals. When the silent prayer had ended, he glanced at his sons.

"You get on with the evening chores now. It's getting late."

It wasn't, but no one argued. They rose quickly, and William started to go with them.

Isaac gestured to him. "Sit down, William. Stay. We can talk a bit now with those boys out of here."

"Would anyone like some more pie?" Ruth poised her knife above the pastry. "John? I'm sure you can manage another piece."

"Ach, not a whole piece, that's for sure. Maybe chust a sliver, ja?"

Nodding, Ruth cut the pie and flipped it deftly onto John's plate. Catching her husband's eye, she seemed to flush. She slid back onto her chair.

Isaac cleared his throat, as if he was about to say something of importance. He looked around the table, making sure everyone was looking at him.

"William, it is time we talked to you seriously. We are all agreed on that."

Emma nodded. Ruth looked down at her lap in what might be considered a nod. John made a movement of his heavy shoulders that seemed to indicate he'd rather be somewhere else.

William's stomach tightened. Isaac seemed to be waiting for a response from him.

"J-ja?" William made it a question, but he didn't doubt he knew what Isaac wanted to talk about.

"Stories are going around," Isaac said. "Stories about you and that Englisch woman, Paula's niece."

William fought to control his temper. "N-not Englisch. H-Hannah is M-Mennonite."

"Well, that's as may be. Just because she's dressing Plain, that doesn't mean she's living Plain. Or that she'll stay."

William couldn't help glaring at his brother. "Are y-you the j-judge of th-that?"

Isaac dismissed his question with a gesture. "It is not what I say. It is what everyone says. People know that her father-in-law is here. That he has been trying to make her leave. That he has been asking questions about you."

John put his fork on his plate. "William cannot control what that man says." At a look from his wife, he shrugged. "It is true."

"That is not the point," Isaac said firmly. "The point is that William has been linked by talk to this woman . . . to Hannah," he corrected himself. "I am not saying that she is not a gut woman, William. I am saying that I don't want my brother the subject of gossip."

"I-I have d-done n-n-nothing against the Ordnung." Nothing but fall in love with a woman who probably didn't love him. He wasn't in danger of having people talk about him. He was in danger of having his heart broken.

"Sometimes just the appearance of wrongdoing is enough," Emma said tartly. "You should do nothing that would embarrass your family."

He was not going to be cowed by his older siblings. He frowned back at Emma. "I h-have d-done nothing. H-Hannah has d-done nothing. She i-is a g-gut p-person. I d-did not think you w-were a b-blabber-m-maul, E-Emma."

Emma looked surprised, either at his attack or at his stringing so many words together.

"This isn't about whether or not Emma is repeating gossip," Isaac said.

Emma switched her glare to Isaac. "I am not a blabbermaul."

"Ach, we are getting off track." Isaac's face had reddened. "William, we are your family. We have a right to know. Are you involved with Hannah or not?"

He might argue that Isaac didn't have the right to ask that, but it would just prolong this discussion. If he could not protect Hannah in any other way, he could at least do this.

"W-we are f-friends. Th-that's all."

Isaac's tension visibly eased. "Gut. That's gut."

"We are not saying there's anything wrong with her," Emma put in, ready to be conciliatory now that they'd had the answer they wanted from him. "It's wonderful brave of Hannah to come here with her little boy, starting over like that. But she is not for you, William."

"No, she's not." Isaac didn't seem to relish having Emma take over. "However gut a person, Hannah is not of our faith. She is a widow, and of a soldier, besides. She is older. She has a child. It is all unsuitable. Everyone in the family agrees."

That shook William. They'd all been talking about him. His control began to slip.

"E-everyone?"

Isaac looked surprised. "Everyone, ja. Even Caleb. What is wrong? You said there was nothing between you but friendship."

"There i-i-isn't." He stood, the chair scraping back. "Y-you d-d-didn't ask i-if I w-wanted there t-to be."

Isaac stood as well, his ruddiness deepening. "This is foolishness. I am telling you—"

William started toward the door. "J-ja. Y-you h-have s-said. I-I h-heard." He stalked out the door and closed it firmly behind him.

It would be satisfying to follow that declaration by going to Hannah and telling her his feelings, but he wasn't that foolish. Hannah liked him, maybe was even attracted to him. But that didn't mean she'd welcome hearing that he loved her, and telling her could put an end to their friendship.

Still, he'd finally made his feelings known to his brother. He suspected he owed Hannah for that. Let Isaac make of that what he would. He had heard enough advice for one day.

Or maybe not quite enough. If Caleb was against him, too . . . well, he had to find out.

He tried not to think at all during the drive to town. Caleb had said he was having supper next door with Katie and Rhoda at Katie's apartment. He should still be there.

The route to the quilt shop led past the bakery. William couldn't help glancing at the windows on the second floor. Lights were on in the living room, and the longing to stop was like an ache in his chest.

Halting the mare at the hitching rail behind Katie's and Caleb's shops, William jumped down from the buggy. He had to know.

He leaned on the doorbell at the back door, wondering what he'd say if Katie or Rhoda came to answer. But it was Caleb who came down the stairs and opened the door.

"William?" Surprise widened his eyes. "Was ist letz? Has something happened?"

"We h-have to t-talk." Only after he'd said it did he realize that it was the same thing Isaac had said to him.

"Ja, sure, komm up. I bet there's some cake left." He grinned. "Rhoda baked it, but it's gut."

He shook his head. "This w-won't take long." It was as if something inside him pushed him forward with his need to know. "Isaac a-and Emma d-decided to lecture me at s-supper. About Hannah."

"I'm sorry." Caleb stepped out onto the porch, closing the door behind him as if to give them privacy. "That was foolish of them."

Foolish, not wrong. Wrong was what he'd wanted to hear.

"They w-want me to stay away f-from Hannah." That was what it had amounted to, no matter how they tried to dress it up.

"I'm sorry," Caleb said again. "I know Isaac means well, but he doesn't often see other people's point of view."

"Ja." It struck him suddenly. "Like Hannah's f-father-in-law."

Caleb seemed surprised, but then he nodded. "You are right. Both of them think they know what's best for other people. They don't see the harm they are doing."

William was comforted that Caleb saw the truth, but there was another question he had to ask.

"Isaac s-said that the f-family agreed with him. All th-the family. Including you."

Caleb hesitated for a long moment. William's heart sank. He'd thought Caleb was one person he could depend upon.

"You, t-too, then." His voice was tight.

"I didn't talk to Isaac about you," Caleb said quickly. He put his hand on William's shoulder. "Believe me on that. Isaac tried, but I told him what you did was nobody's business but your own. But . . ."

"But what? Y-you agree w-with him?"

"No. But I am worried about you." His grip tightened. "I like Hannah. You know that. But there are problems involved in loving her. I wouldn't want you to get hurt."

William took a long breath. So. It seemed he was on his own. Well, maybe that was for the best.

He took a step away, and Caleb's hand fell from his shoulder.

"Y-you are right," he said. "It is n-nobody's b-business but mine."

CHAPTER SEVENTEEN

*K*neading bread dough was a good outlet for the frustration Hannah was feeling. She could twist and pummel the dough all she wanted, letting the worry work itself out. Even the unbaked dough had an aroma of its own, which seemed to release as she worked the dough.

She glanced at Aunt Paula, wondering if she noticed her aggression and guessed at the cause. But her aunt was bent over the rye loaf she was shaping, her face serene, her hands strong and skilled.

"I will never be as fast as you are with the bread." Hannah plopped the dough into the earthenware bowl, turning it so that all sides were greased. "You are miles ahead of me."

"I have been doing this for thirty or forty years, don't forget." Her aunt gave the finished loaf a satisfied pat. "It's gut, working with the dough. Satisfying, ja?"

So she had noticed. "Ja, it is. I wish . . ."

The phone rang upstairs. Surely not loud enough to wake Jamie, was it? She headed for the steps. "I'll get it."

She ran lightly up the stairs, crossed the room, and snatched up the receiver. "Hello?"

"Hannah, is that you? You don't sound like yourself." Megan didn't sound like herself, either. Her voice was tentative, almost timid, as if she feared Hannah's reaction.

"I just ran up the stairs. I'm out of breath." She pressed the receiver against her ear, waiting. Megan would have to go first. Neither of them could pretend she'd just called to chat.

"We . . . haven't talked lately. I just wanted to ask how you're doing."

All of Hannah's worry came surging to the fore. "How do you think I'm doing? Thanks to you, my father-in-law has been here for a week."

"Well, he does have a right to get to know his grandson, doesn't he?" Defensiveness slid through the words.

"He does, but that's not what he's been doing. He's been snooping and prying and making my life miserable."

Thanks to you, she thought but didn't say. Forgiveness was a basic tenet of her faith, but at the moment, it was the one she had the most trouble with.

"What? Why would he be doing that? I told him . . ."

"You told him that I was planning to raise his grandson in some kind of cult. What did you think was going to happen when you did that, Megan?" For someone who cringed from confrontation, she seemed to be doing surprisingly well when her son's future was at stake. "Robert is trying to force me to move away from here. He wants me to give up my family, my home, and my faith because they don't suit his ideas."

"Hannah, I never expected that." Megan rushed into speech. "I thought that if he knew, maybe he'd come through with some financial support that would let you live independently. That's all I wanted. You have to believe that."

The pain in Megan's voice sounded real enough. Hannah's anger began to seep away. That was Megan, after all. She'd act before she thought, and then try to clean up afterward. But this was more serious than her usual mis-understandings.

"Hannah? Please say you forgive me. Tell me what I can do to help."

Hannah rubbed the back of her neck, where tension had started to build. "There's nothing you can do. It's too late for that. I forgive you." Saying it was the first step toward making it so, wasn't it?

"There must be something I can do. Maybe if I talked to Conroy, I could convince him that I was mistaken."

"It's too late for that," she repeated, knowing it was true. "I thought surely he'd see what a good life this is for Jamie, surrounded by people who love him, able to be with me all the time instead of shipped off to day care. But he refuses to understand. This life isn't his idea of normal, and that's all he can see."

"I'm so sorry, Hannah. I'd give anything if I could take it back. Honestly. I love you and Jamie. I don't want to make you unhappy. I just thought . . ."

"You thought you knew what was best," Hannah finished for her.

"I'm sorry." Megan's voice was very small. "If you think of anything I can do that might help, just tell me. Anything."

"I will." But she was afraid there wasn't anything anyone could do. "I have to get off the phone now." Because her voice was thickening and she'd start to cry if she stayed on any longer. "I'll talk to you again and let you know what's happening."

After she'd hung up she stood for a moment, wiping her palms on her skirt. Megan did sound grieved at the results of her hasty act. Maybe she'd even stop arranging people's lives for them for a bit. But it was too late to undo this situation with Robert.

Hannah went slowly back to the kitchen. She'd like to indulge in a good cry, but that wouldn't mend anything.

And she wouldn't leave Aunt Paula alone to finish the work on her own.

Aunt Paula, her face apprehensive, was watching the stairs when Hannah came down. "Was it bad news, then?"

"Not exactly." She went back to the table, but in her absence, Aunt Paula had finished the bread. Hannah began cleaning up. "It was Megan. She told me she was sorry."

Aunt Paula nodded. "Now that she knows what her careless act caused, she regrets it. She was your friend. What did you say?"

Hannah picked up the bowl and stood holding it cradled against her. "I said that I forgive her. Now I'll try to do it."

"Forgiveness is not easy." Her aunt sighed. "I was a long time forgiving your mamm and daad for going away. It seemed to me they didn't think about the people who would be hurt."

Hannah considered. "I think Mammi didn't really want to leave. She always tried to do whatever Daadi wanted. She'd just go along, whatever it was."

"But if that's so, why didn't she komm back after he went away? Elizabeth must have known I'd have taken her in."

Aunt Paula's obvious distress made Hannah wish she hadn't spoken. Maybe she was as bad as Megan, speaking without thinking about the consequences.

"There was nothing you could have done. If anyone should have helped, it was me, but I didn't understand her depression."

Aunt Paula came to her. She put her arms around Hannah and hugged her close. "It is all right. We both did the best we could."

Hannah's throat tightened. "I should have tried harder to get her to go into the hospital. But she refused, and the suggestion upset her so much . . ."

Her voice trailed off. It was an old hurt, and it had never really left, lingering with what-ifs.

Aunt Paula patted her cheek. "Listen to me, my Hannah. We must forgive other people their wrongs against us. And we must also forgive ourselves. It is God's will, in the end."

"Ja. I know," she whispered. But perhaps that was the hardest forgiveness of all.

The morning rush was over at the bakery on Saturday, and Hannah had taken Jamie out of his play yard to run about in the bakery. He ducked between the tables, giggling when Naomi played peek-a-boo with him around the chairs.

The bell jingled, and a small boy came sidling in, looking shyly toward the counter.

"What is it, Thomas?" Aunt Paula paused, hands full of the whoopie pies she was putting into the case. "Did your mamm send you for something?"

He shook his head, blond hair nearly hiding his eyes. He came forward and held out a note to Hannah. She took it, managing a smile for the boy. "Denke." But a frisson of apprehension slid down her spine.

"Denke, Thomas," Paula added. "Have you room in your tummy for a whoopie pie?"

He nodded, grinning, and took the waxed-paper-wrapped treat. He ducked his head toward Hannah and darted out, apparently not needing to wait for a response.

Hannah ripped the envelope open and scanned the contents, aware of Aunt Paula's gaze on her.

"What is it?" Her aunt slid the whoopie pies into the case and moved next to her.

Hannah handed her the note, frowning. "It's from the bishop. He says he has some early apples you might want, if I'll come by this afternoon and get them." She glanced from her aunt to Naomi, who'd finished wiping the tables and now came closer, face troubled. "What do you think this is about?"

The other two women exchanged glances. "More than chust apples," Aunt Paula said, and Naomi nodded.

"Not anything bad," Naomi said quickly. "If it was, he'd for sure komm here, maybe with the deacon."

Hannah breathed a little easier. The patterns of Amish and black-bumper Mennonites were similar enough here in Pleasant Valley that Naomi would know.

"But what, then?" She stared down at the paper as if it would yield a clue.

"He's maybe heard some talk about Mr. Conroy being here." Aunt Paula sounded tentative, which was unusual for her. But then, the current situation was beyond her normal experience, wasn't it?

"I hope he's not upset about the talk." Hannah pressed her fingers against her forehead, trying to ease the tension there. "Well, I'll have to go." At least when she was out, she wouldn't be waiting and wondering when Robert would pop in with another ultimatum.

Aunt Paula clasped her hand. "Shall I go with you then?"

"I'd better go by myself. But thank you. If you can watch Jamie . . ."

"Ach, don't worry about that." Naomi smiled as Jamie ran into her, holding up his locomotive for her approval. "We will be fine, ja?"

Paula nodded. "Ja. But if you change your mind, I will go gladly."

But it was best that she do this alone. Hannah was still convinced of that a couple of hours later, when she drove her aunt's car into the lane at Bishop Ephraim's orchard. If Naomi was wrong, and this was going to involve a lecture on her behavior, she'd rather not have an audience.

Miriam, the bishop's rosy little dumpling of a wife, came out onto the porch at the sound of the car. She shielded her eyes with her hand, smiling when Hannah got out.

"Ach, Hannah, it is you. Ephraim said you'd be here for

apples this afternoon. He's up in the orchard. Chust go on up." She pointed at the gentle rise behind the farmhouse, where the grove of apple trees spread out. "And stop in for a glass of lemonade when you're done, if you have time, ja?"

"I will, denke." Hannah started back toward the narrow lane that led to the orchard, moving quickly. Maybe she was trying to outrun her apprehension, but if so, it wasn't working.

Bishop Ephraim was on a ladder, picking apples into a basket he had hooked onto a branch. He greeted her with a wave and tossed an apple down to her.

"Early apples are ser gut this year. Your aunt will like them for pies and applesauce cake."

"I'm sure she will." Hannah held the apple, warm and smooth in her hand. Inhaling brought its sweet scent wafting toward her.

"There is another basket." He pointed. "You pick the low ones and I'll get the high ones, and we'll soon have a bushel."

Obeying, Hannah took the basket and began to pick, checking each apple to be sure it was ripe. The orchard was quiet, the only sound the plunk of apples falling into baskets and the repeated call of a bobwhite, somewhere in the trees.

The apprehension drained out of her. Nothing in the bishop's attitude suggested that he planned to reprimand her. Maybe this was only what it seemed . . . the neighborly offer of apples.

"I hear you have been working with William Brand, helping him with his stammering." He reached out farther than she thought he should for an apple, and she held her breath for a moment, but he had a firm grip on the branch.

"I offered to help him, because I had studied that in school. He's improving, I think."

"Ach, ja, I know so. I was chust talking to him a day or so ago." He chuckled. "I hear it's made him a bit more outspoken with his brother, as well."

She nodded, not sure what to say to that.

His hands slowed in their picking, and he looked down at her. "I also hear that your father-in-law is here visiting."

Her stomach twisted. *Visiting* might not be the right expression for what Robert was doing. "He says he'll be leaving on Monday. He lives in Arizona."

"A long way." Bishop Ephraim's tone was casual, but he studied her face. "His life there must be very different from ours."

Hannah suspected most of Pleasant Valley knew Robert wanted her to leave here. And that concern was what had led to this conversation. Perhaps the bishop had been wondering why she hadn't come to him before this.

"Robert has never been around Plain people before. I've tried to explain our lives to him, but maybe I haven't been very successful."

"Sometimes people fear what they don't understand," the bishop observed. "It may be that he fears losing touch with his grandson."

She leaned against the trunk, looking up at him. "I would never do anything to keep Jamie away from his grandfather, but Robert doesn't really seem all that interested in Jamie. He's not one who would get down on the floor and play with him, for instance."

Just saying the words made her realize how much that bothered her. Naomi, Aunt Paula, William, even someone Jamie knew less well, like Caleb, seemed able to relate to him quickly. But Robert didn't even try.

"You think it is that he doesn't want to? Or that he doesn't know how to?"

"That's probably the truth of it. He wasn't around very much when my husband was growing up, and they were never close."

"That is sad. He is the loser, I think."

Hannah nodded. If she were not afraid of what Robert might do, she'd find it easy to feel sorry for him.

She picked another apple and held it for a moment,

frowning. "He doesn't approve of our teachings on nonviolence. He thinks I would bring Jamie up to despise his father's sacrifice, and I can't seem to convince him otherwise."

The ladder creaked. Startled, she looked up to see that the bishop was climbing down, lowering the basket with a rope as he did. He smiled, shaking his head. "My wife insists. She is afraid I will fall if I try to climb down with the basket. Ach, well, we worry about the people we love."

"Yes," she said softly, wondering if he meant Robert. And wondering if it was really worry about Jamie that propelled his actions, instead of just determination to have things his own way.

Bishop Ephraim poured the contents of his basket into hers, filling it to the brim. "There. That is just right."

"My aunt will be so pleased. Thank you, Bishop Ephraim."

He nodded, but she didn't think his mind was on the apples.

"We Anabaptists believe that God has called us not to return evil for evil, but to overcome evil with good. We know the life to which God has called us. But we can still live in amity with our neighbors, accepting that they may hear God's message differently."

He'd said it much better than she ever could. "I wish my father-in-law could understand and accept that difference."

"Ja. Your father-in-law must see that you honor and respect him, but he cannot pressure you to go away from your home."

The bishop picked up the basket, forestalling her effort to take it.

"Some of these apples are destined for the cider press," he said. "They make fine cider." He paused. "Pressing is all right for apples," he said, "but not for people. Not for you, Hannah."

. . .

Despite the fact that so many of the residents didn't have telephones, whispers went around Pleasant Valley at the speed of light, William sometimes thought. By closing time on Saturday afternoon, three different people had managed to drop the news that the Mennonite bishop had spoken to Hannah today.

The knowledge nibbled at William, keeping him from concentrating. When the joint he was gluing slipped for the third time, Caleb took the pieces from his hands.

"Go and see Hannah, then," he said, "before you glue yourself to the chair."

William looked at him, assessing the expression in his cousin's face. "I thought y-you felt m-my feelings for H-Hannah were a mistake."

"Ach, what does my opinion matter? Even a friend would go to see if she's all right, ja?" Caleb slapped his shoulder. "Go on, now. Have supper with us later, ja? We're going to get pizza."

"Denke." William headed for the sink to wash up. At least he and Caleb were still friends.

A few minutes later he was walking quickly down the street to the bakery. They'd be closing, as well, so maybe he could have a quiet word with Hannah, just to be sure she was all right.

Bishop Ephraim was a fair man. Surely he wouldn't blame Hannah for whatever talk her father-in-law was stirring up. Still, if he felt it reflected on Hannah's commitment to the church, it would make her situation even more difficult.

When had it started, this need he felt to pick up her burdens for her? He always wanted to help folks, of course. That was part of his nature, as well as his faith. But it was different with Hannah. It went far beyond wanting. He needed to share her burdens. It was what he'd been put here to do.

The Closed sign was already on the bakery door, but it wasn't locked. He tapped lightly and opened the door.

"C-can I come in?"

"William, for sure you can." Paula was on her way to the kitchen with a tray of dishes. "Hannah will help you." She pushed on through the swinging door.

He turned to Hannah, who was emptying the display case, but before he could say anything, Jamie ran to him and grabbed his leg.

"H-help, my leg is trapped by a b-bear." He bent down, catching Jamie and sweeping him up in the air. "Ach, no. N-not a bear. An eagle."

Jamie giggled and squealed. "More, more!"

William obliged, flying him across the room, loving the sound of the boy's laughter. When Jamie was breathless and limp with giggles, William brought the boy down for a landing against his chest.

"More," Jamie demanded.

"You always want more," Hannah said, coming around the counter to tickle Jamie's chin. "No more roughhousing this close to supper. Go get your train. Show William how the choo-choo goes."

William set him on his feet, and Jamie trotted across the room toward the basket of toys in the far corner.

"I hope I didn't r-rile him up too much." He straightened, studying her face for any clue to what had happened with the bishop.

"He loves it," she said. "I think he understands already that . . ." She stopped, as if not wanting to complete that sentence.

"Every b-boy needs a man in his life," he said carefully.

She nodded. "I thought his grandfather might help fill that gap, but Robert . . ." She shook her head. "He doesn't seem to know how. Jamie got shortchanged in the grandfather department." As if needing to keep her hands busy, Hannah straightened the chairs around the closest table.

"Maybe R-Robert c-could use some encouragement."
He helped her with the chairs. "Your f-father isn't around
at all?"

"I haven't heard from him since he left when I was
thirteen." A shadow touched her face. "I didn't even know
how to let him know when my mother died."

"I'm sorry." William's heart hurt for her. "Sometimes
when p-people leave the church, they j-just get lost."

That was as good a way as any to put it, he guessed. It
was a serious thing, to leave the support and love of the
community. Maybe Hannah's father hadn't realized how
much he had counted on that until it was too late.

He looked down at the chair he was pushing in. Would
he be able to do that? If he had the chance to marry Hannah, would he be able to leave?

His fingers tightened on the chair back. Since he wasn't
likely to be given that chance, he'd best not waste time
thinking about it. Right now Hannah needed a friend, and
that he could offer.

"I hear y-you talked to the b-bishop today."

Jamie hurried back to him, clutching the locomotive in
his hand, and began running it along the table's edge.
William squatted next to him, making sound effects
while he watched Hannah's face for clues.

"Word spread, I guess. I might have known that it
would." But she was smiling a little, and his heart eased.
"Bishop Ephraim wanted to give me a bushel of apples for
my aunt. And he added a few words of support as well."

"That's gut." William didn't realize how relieved he
felt until she said it. "I was afraid—"

"I was, too." She smiled at him, and his heart
seemed to turn over. "He understood. He said I could
honor and respect my father-in-law and still do what I
feel is right."

"And you're s-sure now what that is?" He stood, the
locomotive still in his hand until Jamie snatched it away.

"We belong here." She met his gaze, her brown eyes

steady. "I think I didn't realize how much this place and my faith mean to me until Robert challenged my decision. Then I knew in my heart this is right."

"I am g-glad." He put his hand over hers where it rested on the chair back.

For an instant she looked startled. Then she turned her hand, very deliberately, so that it clasped his.

Warmth and caring seemed to flow between them through their linked hands. Hope welled up in him. He leaned toward her, forgetting where they were, disregarding everything except the longing to touch her, hold her—

"Will!" Jamie shoved the locomotive at him. "Up, Will, up!"

Hannah blinked, as if rousing from a dream, and then smiled. "Somebody wants you."

"Ach, I a-am right here, l-little one." He had to let go of Hannah's hand to pick Jamie up, but that was okay. He loved the boy, too, and not just because he was part of Hannah. "Here we go." He hoisted him to his shoulder, feeling the warmth of Hannah's gaze on them. "How i-is that?"

The door slammed open, its bell clanging as if out of control. Robert Conroy stalked into the shop, his gaze focused on them.

What did he see? Someone else standing in the place that should have been occupied by his son?

"Robert." Hannah smoothed her apron. "I didn't think you were coming by."

"I see that." His voice had an edge. "I came to tell you something. To give you fair warning."

William could almost feel the shiver that went through Hannah. She took a step closer to him.

Conroy's eyes narrowed at that unconscious, betraying movement. "I've been to Harrisburg to meet with an attorney. He's agreed to take my case."

"Attorney?" Hannah echoed the word, probably as confused as William felt.

"You have until Monday," Conroy said. "If I don't hear by then that you're leaving this place and bringing up my grandson the way you should, I'm filing for custody."

He didn't wait for a response. He just slammed back out of the door.

CHAPTER EIGHTEEN

Hannah stood stunned, unable to move. To speak. Worst of all, to think. Her mind had been swept clean of every thought but one.

Robert intended to take her child.

"No." The word ripped from her throat.

"Hannah." William's hand gripped her arm. "You muscht stoppe. Think. H-he can't take Jamie."

His grasp was firm. Strong. It steadied her. Hannah sucked in a strangled breath, then another. She couldn't panic. Now, of all times, she had to be in control.

The kitchen door swung. Aunt Paula and Naomi rushed toward her. Arms closed around her. She was surrounded by love, warmth, support.

"We heard." Her aunt choked on a sob. "It can't be right. He can't do that."

"Ja," Naomi murmured. "Surely he cannot take Jamie away."

Hannah looked up. Jamie still sat on William's shoul-

ders, gripping William's hair, his little face puckering as
if he'd cry, even though he couldn't understand what all
the fuss was about.

William, seeming to read her thoughts, lifted Jamie
from his shoulders and put him into her arms.

The weight of that small little body sent fierce love
surging through Hannah. She held him close, feeling his
breath against her neck when he snuggled.

"It is all r-right. No one will t-take him from you."
William patted her arm.

*Please, Father. Help me to be calm. Guide me to do
the right thing. Please, keep my baby safe.*

Realizing she was leaning against William, she drew
away a step. She had to be strong, for Jamie.

"What can the man be thinking of? Is he crazy, to say such
a thing? The law would not let him take Jamie." Aunt Paula
fussed, but Hannah knew there was fear behind the words.

"I don't know." It took an effort to keep her voice
steady, but Hannah managed. "I wouldn't think so either,
but if a lawyer agreed . . ."

She let that trail off, not wanting to voice the words.
The lawyer must think there was a case, or why would he
or she agree?

"You must talk this over," Naomi said. "Not here,
where anyone can look in the window and see. Upstairs,
ja? I will finish down here."

Hannah nodded, glancing toward the plate-glass windows. Naomi was right. She didn't want to give the community anything else to gossip about.

"Komm." William put his arm around her and Jamie,
urging her toward the steps. "Naomi is right."

Going up the stairs felt like climbing a mountain. If
not for the support of William's arm, she wasn't sure she'd
make it.

There she was, relying on him again. She shouldn't do
that, but she couldn't seem to help it.

"In the kitchen." Once they were upstairs, Aunt Paula

took over. "Jamie will be hungry, and you must have something, Hannah. Nice hot tea is gut for shock. And something sweet to eat, also. That will help you think."

Hannah had a feeling it would take more than that, but she let herself be shepherded into the kitchen. Aunt Paula bustled around, taking refuge from her own fears by feeding people, which was always her first reaction.

William leaned against the counter, watching Hannah. She suspected he'd be by her side if she showed any sign of weakness.

Aunt Paula thrust a mug of tea in front of her and watched her until she sipped it. It scalded her mouth, but it warmed her, too.

Jamie climbed up into his booster chair without being told, and Aunt Paula put toast triangles in front of him.

"I don't understand," her aunt said. "Why does Robert want to do this? He can't imagine he'd be a better parent than you are."

Hannah pressed her fingers against her temples. "He's barely even interacted with Jamie."

"H-he is trying to m-make you afraid. So you'll d-do what he wants."

She nodded. William had it right. That was undoubtedly what was in Robert's mind. "He wants to make me leave Pleasant Valley. Leave the church. Live the way he imagines Travis would want."

"Ach, the man is ferhoodled." Aunt Paula sat down abruptly, as if her legs wouldn't hold her up any longer. "He doesn't want Jamie. He is blinded by the need to control everything."

"He f-feels guilty," William said. "That is it, I th-think. He w-wishes he had been a better f-father, so he's trying to m-make up for that."

Hannah focused on William's words. He was seeing the situation clearly. Robert was driven by guilt as much as anything.

"Well, if he thinks Travis would want that boy taken

away from his mammi, he's crazy, like I said." Aunt Paula's voice was tart with worry and fear.

"You m-must get a l-lawyer, too," William said abruptly.

The advice sounded strange, coming from an Amishman, but Aunt Paula was already nodding.

"Ja, William is right. I know, we don't sue people, but this is different. He is going against you, and you must have a lawyer to defend yourself."

"It will be so expensive. And so ugly to be defending myself in court. If Robert would only listen . . ."

"Well, he won't," Aunt Paula said, her eyes snapping. "You've tried, and he won't listen. We must protect Jamie."

We. She had family now. People who loved her and would do their best to protect her and Jamie.

But to go to court . . . What if she lost? Her heart nearly stopped.

"There i-is the l-lady who helped Sarah," William said.

"Ach, ja, that's so," Aunt Paula exclaimed. "Sarah, the midwife. When the doctor in town tried to make her stop delivering babies, the lady lawyer took her case. She is just the one."

"I don't . . ." Hannah wanted to say she'd think about it. Try to figure out some other way. But in her heart she knew it was no use. Robert wouldn't agree to her plans, so there was nothing else to be done.

Except give in. Give up. Take Jamie away from all that was familiar and try to start over again somewhere else.

"I will go to Sarah." William pushed himself away from the counter. "To g-get the n-name and n-number of the woman."

"Denke, William." Aunt Paula nodded. "That's right. It's the only thing to do."

William was already heading for the stairs.

"I probably won't even be able to talk to the woman before Monday, and that's Robert's deadline."

"All the more reason for William to go right away," her aunt said.

Hannah tried to force a smile, but she couldn't. The truth was that William probably needed to get out of here, and this was a good reason to go.

Something had begun between them. They both knew that. But it was still small and fragile, and all of this pressure was too much, too soon.

William turned at the top of the stairs. "It will be all right. Y-you'll see." Then he hurried down, disappearing from her view.

Anxiety sat next to William on the buggy seat as he drove the few miles to the birthing center. This was a small thing he could do to help Hannah in her trouble—maybe even a needless thing. Hannah or her aunt could have called Sarah to ask for the information, since the birthing center did have a telephone.

Still, going himself gave him the chance to impress upon Sarah how serious the situation was. Hannah, not knowing Sarah, might feel uncomfortable pushing her to contact the attorney on her behalf. William had no such reserve. He'd do whatever he had to do if it got Hannah the help he needed to keep Jamie safe.

Jamie—it seemed he could still feel the boy's weight on his shoulders, hear the gurgle of his laughter. No one should have the right to take Jamie away from those who loved him.

The lane came up faster than he'd thought. The mare must have caught his tension through his handling of the lines. The buggy reached the hitching rail and William jumped down, tossing the line over the rail and hurrying to the door.

This old house had probably seen plenty of people rushing in, filled with anxiety over a baby that was coming. His errand might be different, but it was still about a child's safety.

The door swung open as he approached, and Aaron

looked at him in surprise. "William. I was about to say that Sarah was fetching her bag, but you're not here to call the midwife, are you?"

"No, but I do need to see Sarah."

Aaron waved him in. "Komm, please. We'll be having supper in a little bit. You're wilkom to join us."

He should answer, but his attention was focused on Sarah, just coming into the room.

She looked at him questioningly, maybe reading him better than Aaron did. Sarah always seemed so calm and composed . . . that was probably an asset for a midwife, where nervous parents were concerned.

"Komm, sit down, William. Was ist letz? Tell us about it."

He shook his head to the offer of a chair and instead stood, grasping its back with both hands. "I w-won't s-stay long." He took a shallow breath, remembering all Hannah's teachings. "H-Hannah needs help. Her f-father-in-law h-has gotten a lawyer." It was easier, once he'd started. "He threatens t-to take Jamie away."

There was a shocked exclamation from Aaron behind him.

"Hannah is a g-gut mammi. But he doesn't approve of P-Plain folks. Or our b-beliefs. He's trying to f-force Hannah to leave. Hannah needs a l-lawyer. I thought of th-the one who h-helped you. W-will you call her?"

Understanding filled Sarah's face. "Ja, of course. She is a fine attorney."

"Gut. But it m-must be right away. He gave H-Hannah only until Monday. We can't w-wait."

Sarah shot a glance at Aaron. William knew he was giving away his feelings with every word, but that didn't matter. All that mattered was that Sarah act now.

"I'll call right now." Sarah moved quickly to the door, heading for the phone shanty Aaron had built for her on the porch. "I just hope she's not gone away for the weekend. If I get her, I'll ask her to call Hannah immediately."

She looked again at Aaron. "Why don't you see if William will have something to eat or drink while he waits?"

"I don't need—" he began, but Aaron was already pouring a glass of lemonade.

"Have it anyway, or Sarah will fuss." He took a couple of hand-size molasses cookies from the jar on the counter and put them in front of William. "This is my job now when anxious daads come to the door. I keep them calm while Sarah gets ready."

William took a bite and discovered he was hungry. "It m-must be crazy when a c-couple of bopplis d-decide to komm at once."

Aaron grinned. "That's when I head to the workshop and stay out of the way."

Footsteps drew William's attention to the door. When Sarah appeared, she was smiling. "It's all right. She was there, and when I explained, she said she'd call Hannah right away. Hannah will feel better knowing she has Sheila Downing to help her."

"Gut. D-denke." He set the glass down. "I must go and see what else I can do."

He saw an invitation to supper forming on her face and went quickly to the door. "Denke," he said again, and went out before they could try to convince him.

He couldn't stay. He couldn't sit still that long, not if there was some other way to help Hannah.

He drove back toward town, turning the question over in his mind. Should he tell Hannah's bishop what was happening? But he didn't like to do that without first getting her permission. She might feel the need to consult the bishop herself, especially about hiring a lawyer, something Amish and Mennonites seldom did. This situation wasn't one most folks were prepared to cope with.

He'd almost reached town when another thought occurred to him. Hannah had mentioned how kind Nancy Russo had been, when she'd talked to the woman about her father-in-law. William knew the woman's husband.

Phil was a member of the volunteer fire company, like William, even though he didn't go out on calls much anymore. Phil probably understood Robert Conroy better than William ever could. Maybe they'd be willing to help.

The more he thought about it, the better he liked the idea. But liking it and acting on it were two different things. To go to an Englisch person's house, to talk about something so difficult—for an instant fear took a stranglehold on his throat.

He fought it down, inch by inch. This was for Hannah and Jamie. He would not let them down.

William began rehearsing in his mind what he would say, but the Russo house came up too quickly. Breathing a silent prayer, he turned into the driveway and tied the mare to a porch railing.

He approached the back door, and then realized that he was in town now, not in the country where visitors went to the back door as a matter of course. But even as he thought that, Phil opened the door.

"William Brand! Come in, come in. What brings you our way?" He ushered William into the kitchen. "Nancy, look who's come to see us."

Mrs. Russo he had seen in the shop a time or two, but he'd never actually spoken to her. He took off his hat as she came into the room.

"William, how nice." The woman came straight to him, hand outstretched, smiling warmly. "Is there something we can do for you?"

He swallowed. "I-I w-want to t-talk to you. About R-Robert Conroy." There, it was out, and the rest should be easier.

Nancy and her husband exchanged glances. "You're a friend of Hannah's, I know. Is this about her?"

"Nancy, I'm not sure we should get involved in this," Phil began, his expression uneasy.

"You're the one who got us involved to begin with," she said firmly. She turned back to William. "Go on, William."

He gripped the back of a kitchen chair, as he had at

Aaron and Sarah's. Somehow holding on to something solid made it easier to talk.

"C-Conroy h-has th-threatened H-Hannah. Saying if she d-doesn't l-leave Pleasant Valley, he w-will try to t-take Jamie away."

"But that's ridiculous." Phil's face reddened. "He wouldn't do that. You must have misunderstood."

William let the words wash over him. "I h-heard him. H-he said he had t-talked to a lawyer in H-Harrisburg. If Hannah d-does not agree b-by Monday, he w-will g-go to court."

It sounded unbelievable to William, as well, but it was true. If they wouldn't accept it as true, they wouldn't help.

"I know you are sympathetic to Robert as a fellow vet-eran, Phil," Mrs. Russo said, "but you have to admit that he's not being rational about Hannah's faith. He's a walk-ing collection of all the ridiculous prejudices against Plain people we've ever heard, and you know it."

Phil seemed to deflate as his wife's words sank in. "I've tried to explain to him," he muttered.

"I know you have, dear." She patted his arm. "But we have to do better than that, don't we?"

He nodded, straightening his shoulders. "You're right. Conroy's gone off the rails if he thinks this is the right thing to do."

He met William's gaze. "Hannah can count on us to help in any way we can." He held out his hand. "You have my word on it."

William shook hands, but even as he was thanking them, his mind was jumping ahead. He'd taken a couple of positive steps forward, but was it enough?

The service at the churchhouse had been more meaning-ful than ever before that Sunday morning, Hannah de-cided. She'd prayed her way through the entire worship, feeling the sense of community strong around her. Surely God would show her the way through this trial.

She'd just put Jamie down for his nap, and there had been moments when she'd wanted to crawl into the crib with him. But hiding wasn't the answer any more than running away was. This had to be faced.

"Do you think the lawyer lady will want a cup of coffee? Or maybe iced tea?" Aunt Paula hovered between the living room and the kitchen. "I'm not sure what to offer her."

"Either is fine." What the woman would drink was the least of Hannah's worries, but she knew her aunt was just expressing her own stress by fussing. "It was kind of her to come out here on a Sunday."

"Ja, ser kind. That is what Sarah said about her. I'll have both ready, and some apple crumb pie, as well." The kitchen door swung to behind her.

Hannah still found it hard to believe that the attorney would actually come to the house to talk to her. Sarah must have given her a picture of the situation, stressing that Robert insisted on an answer by Monday. Tomorrow. Hannah's heart seemed to skip a beat.

If she could turn the pages of the calendar back, to before Robert's arrival . . . what would she do? Was there anything she could have done differently from the start that might have prevented this outcome? Maybe it had been inevitable.

The doorbell rang, cutting off that futile line of thought. Hannah put her palm on her stomach, as if that would calm the butterflies there, and went quickly down the stairs to open the door.

The attorney proved to be younger than Hannah had expected, with a sleek, professional air and a cautious smile. She followed Hannah up the steps, talking cheerfully about the drive to Pleasant Valley and the fall colors along the roads.

Only when she had been introduced to Aunt Paula and taken a seat in the living room did she pull out an official-looking pad from the leather briefcase she carried and flick her chin-length brown hair behind her ear.

"Now, then," she said. "I think I have the basics down, from our telephone conversation yesterday. There are just a few more questions I have before we discuss strategy."

Hannah clasped her hands in her lap to keep them from trembling. "I'll tell you anything you want to know, of course."

"As I understand it, you came here to live with your aunt a few months ago. Why was that?" She held a pen poised over the pad.

"I was having trouble making it financially with my husband's army pension and saving anything for Jamie's future, and it was difficult to find someone good to watch Jamie while I worked." She clenched her hands tighter, not liking to remember the panic she'd felt at times. "My aunt is my only family, and when she offered us a home, I knew it was the perfect solution."

Ms. Downing's eyebrows lifted. "Your husband's father had not offered to help you financially?"

She shook her head. "Maybe he didn't realize. He had never even seen Jamie. The only time he came east was for my husband's funeral, and that was before Jamie was born."

"So this visit was the first time he'd met his grandson? Isn't that odd? Had you quarreled with him?"

"I had never quarreled with him, but he and Travis didn't have a very good relationship. We went to visit Robert once after we were married, but that was all."

The woman frowned, and Hannah's stomach twisted. What was she frowning about? Did she think Hannah was in some way to blame?

"And your situation here is working out well?" She looked from Hannah to her aunt.

"Very well," Aunt Paula said before Hannah could answer. "It has been a joy to have them here." She glanced toward the door to Jamie's room, love in her eyes. "I have asked Hannah to be my business partner. It's always been intended that the shop would go to her."

Ms. Downing turned her gaze to Hannah, obviously wanting her to answer as well.

"Jamie and I are very happy here," she said simply. "I am back where I belong. It is home."

The attorney nodded. "Frankly, based on everything I've heard, and the little research I've been able to do, I'd say your father-in-law has no case at all. It's extremely unlikely that the court would take a child away from the mother, particularly as I understand Conroy's only reason for his action is his dislike of your religion."

The knots in her stomach began to loosen. "So we will be all right? Even if he goes to court?"

"Well, no lawyer can guarantee a particular outcome in any case." Sheila Downing smiled. "But this one comes as close to a slam dunk as any I've ever heard of. I mean—"

"That's all right. I know what a slam dunk is." Hannah smiled for the first time in what felt like months.

"Still, the best resolution all around is to persuade your father-in-law to drop the whole idea," the attorney said. "That way nobody has the trouble and expense of preparing a case, and you avoid the publicity that could come up."

"Publicity?" Aunt Paula's face seemed to tighten at the word.

Hannah understood her feelings. It was bad enough to go to a lawyer to settle a family matter. To have it spread all over the newspapers would be horrendous.

"I can't deny that the press finds stories about the Amish and Mennonites newsworthy," Ms. Downing said. "Sometimes that can work to our advantage. It certainly did in Sarah's case. But I do understand your feelings. As I said, it's best for everyone if Conroy forgets this idea."

"I have tried to explain." How often had Hannah said that? Too many times, it seemed.

"Well, we'll have to try again. Maybe I can talk some sense into his attorney, and we can settle this quickly and quietly." Ms. Downing rose. "Call me the minute you hear anything from him. As soon as I know who he's hired, I'll try to set up a meeting." She picked up her case, shoving the legal pad into it.

"But won't you have something to eat or drink?" Aunt Paula was alarmed at the thought of a guest leaving her house without partaking of refreshments. "I have iced tea and apple crumb pie."

"It sounds lovely, but I must be on my way." Ms. Downing shook hands with Hannah. "I know it's easier to say than to do, but try not to worry too much. In all probability, your father-in-law was bluffing. If not, we'll be prepared." She turned toward the stairs.

"I'll walk down with you," Hannah said quickly. She followed the woman down the steps and out onto the porch. "One other thing I wanted to ask you . . . If . . . When I see my father-in-law again, what should I do?"

"Try to get through to him," she said. "I know, you've already tried, probably over and over. But it really is the best way." She smiled. "It's not usually my job to talk my clients out of going to court, but sometimes it's for the best. And it definitely is this time."

Hannah nodded. "I'll try, of course." But she didn't think Robert would listen any more than he had any other time.

She pinned a smile on her face as she watched the attorney back out of the lane, but her heart was heavy. She had no illusions about the cost of a court battle, both emotionally and financially. There had to be another way. But what was it?

CHAPTER NINETEEN

Hannah stood where she was for a few more minutes, wrapping her arms around herself as much for comfort as for warmth. The day had turned cloudy, and the breeze that swept across the backyard felt cool. A few leaves drifted down from the maple tree, which was already showing its fall color.

She didn't want to go back into the house. Much as she loved Aunt Paula, she couldn't deal with her aunt's questions and speculations right now. She needed a short time to clear her head and get a grip on what should come next.

Beyond the garage, the lawn sloped down to the small creek that ran behind the houses on the west side of Pleasant Valley's main street. Hannah walked toward it slowly, head bent. The breeze pulled a strand of hair loose from her kapp, and she tucked it back into place. Her hair still wasn't quite long enough to stay where it should.

If Robert forced her to move back to the outside world with Jamie, that wouldn't matter. She bit her lip at the thought. She could still be a Mennonite, no matter where she was, of course. But she wouldn't be a part of this close-knit, supportive community. She wouldn't have Aunt Paula's love and companionship, or the friends she'd made here. She wouldn't have William.

That was a separate pain, all its own. Hannah pressed her hand against her heart, as if that would help.

She stopped where the ground sloped down to the stream, her gaze on the water. Right now it was shallow and clear, the water gurgling over smooth rocks, their edges rounded by years in the creek bed. Sometimes the creek could overflow, rising to threaten the row of homes and businesses, fierce in its power, carrying away branches, logs, even the occasional chair someone had left out.

That was how she felt—like a branch torn from a vine, carried away to land who knew where. If Robert had his way . . .

Don't think about that. Think about the lawyer's reassurances.

A branch cracked underfoot, and she looked up. William was there.

She turned her gaze quickly back to the stream, afraid he'd see the neediness in her face. But she'd seen enough to know he wore his church clothes—black pants, white shirt, black hat. He must have shed his black jacket after the service.

"I remember wading here once." She nodded toward the stream, still not looking at him. "Probably more than once, but one day is so clear in my mind."

"Ja?" William drew closer—close enough that if she put out her hand she could touch him. "H-how old were you?"

"Small. Four or five maybe." She smiled. "Mammi let me go in by myself, but I slipped on a rock and plopped down. I don't suppose I was hurt, but it scared me."

"Your m-mammi came in after you," he said.

She nodded. "She hurried in, getting her shoes and socks wet when she picked me up. She made a joke of it, taking them off to dry and then playing in the water with me until I wasn't afraid anymore."

There was a brief silence.

"By n-next summer, Jamie will be b-big enough to wade."

"Yes." But fear caught at her. "If we're still here."

"You w-will be." William's voice was filled with confidence. "R-Robert can't m-make you leave."

"That's what the lawyer says. She was very reassuring." She blinked, realizing she'd never thanked him. "Thank you, William. It was kind of you to get Sarah involved."

"Sh-she wants to help. Everyone d-does. Even Phil and N-Nancy Russo."

She looked up at his face, startled to hear their names. "How do you know?"

"I w-went to them."

"You did?" That had taken courage.

"Ja. I told them what R-Robert is trying to d-do. They didn't know."

"I should have thought of that myself. Nancy is so understanding, and Robert is more likely to listen to them than to me."

He nodded. "So y-you shouldn't worry. Folks are on your s-side."

She managed to hold back the words for a moment, but then they broke loose. "That's what the lawyer said, too. Don't worry. But how can I help it? She doesn't think Robert can win if it goes to court, but what about in the meantime? There's the cost—that's bad enough. But the newspapers will pick up the story. People will be talking about us. Aunt Paula—well, it's a poor return for all her kindness."

"Hannah—"

She swept on, not letting him interrupt. "And what if he does win? The lawyer admitted she couldn't guarantee anything. What if—" Her voice broke on a sob.

And then William's arms were around her, and he was holding her close. She turned her face toward his chest, fighting the tears.

With his strong arms clasping her, his heart beating steadily against her cheek, the need to weep slid away. He was here. She was safe.

She couldn't give in . . . couldn't be weak, couldn't depend on anyone else to solve her problems for her. But surely it wasn't wrong to let herself be comforted just for a moment.

William grasped her arms and held her away just enough so that he could see her face. "Hannah, I think y-you should m-marry me."

Her breath caught.

"I-I've been thinking a-about it. If y-you are married, Robert will have less c-claim on Jamie. You w-will have s-security."

Security. The word echoed with a hollow sound in her mind. How long had that been her goal? How long had she thought security equaled happiness?

She'd thought that was all she needed and wanted in life. But she couldn't marry William just to be safe. If he loved her . . .

But he hadn't said anything about love. Only about security.

She seemed to hear Rachel's voice in her mind, telling her how William had proposed to her. *He just wanted to take care of us.*

She and Travis had clung together like two lost children, feeling safe because they loved each other. But they hadn't been safe.

William looked at her steadily, but she couldn't seem to read anything in his normally open face.

"I'm sorry, William." Her voice shook a little, and she fought to steady it. "I can't."

He took both her hands in his. "I c-care about y-you. And J-Jamie."

She couldn't talk about this any longer, because if she tried, she was going to fly into a thousand pieces. "I care about you, too. But I can't marry you just to be safe. I can't."

She pulled her hands free and ran toward the house, managing to hold back the tears until she was inside, the door closed behind her.

Aunt Paula took one look at her and came to put her arms around her. "There now, it will be all right." She patted Hannah's back, her hands and her voice comforting. "It seems hard now, I know. Tell me only if you want. Is it William?"

Hannah nodded, drawing away, wiping her tears with the backs of her hands. "I'm sorry. This is no way for a grown woman to behave."

"Even a grown woman must cry sometimes," Aunt Paula said. She led Hannah to the rocking chair and sat down opposite her. "You have no cause to be ashamed of that. If William upset you . . ."

She shook her head. "He didn't mean to." She took a breath, trying to ease the tightness in her throat. "He asked me to marry him."

Aunt Paula was still for a moment. "What did you say?"

"I told him no, of course. What else could I do?"

"There's no 'of course' about it. William was a kind boy who has grown into a fine, strong man without losing that kindness. You care for each other, ain't so?"

Hannah leaned back in the chair, trying for calm. "What makes you say that?"

"Ach, a person chust has to see William watching you to know how he feels. And the same with you, if a person has eyes."

Hannah rubbed her temples. "I think I gave that away to Robert the day of the barn raising. That's probably why he's so set on getting me away from here."

"Robert Conroy has—" Her aunt stopped, seeming to swallow the words. "Never mind about him. It's been two years since Travis died. You're a young woman. It's natural you should love again."

"I didn't intend it. I thought William was just a friend. But love crept up on me."

"So if that's the case, why did you turn him down?" Aunt Paula shook her head. "Mind, I wish he was Mennonite, but it's not so big a difference. And he's not been baptized and joined the church yet, so there's nothing to keep him from changing."

Aunt Paula had made her smile, just when Hannah thought that might never happen again. "You can stop arranging William's future, because I told him no."

"But why? You haven't given me one gut reason why you shouldn't marry him."

"I can give you several." Her throat was tightening again, aching with tears at the thought of William's face when she'd turned him down. "It's too soon. We've barely realized our feelings. We can't jump into marriage just because of this trouble with Robert. We need time. Besides, William was doing the same thing with me that he did with Rachel—wanting to take care of us. That's not a strong enough basis for a marriage."

"Ach, I see now. William thinks you would withstand Robert better if you were married."

Hannah nodded, suddenly too tired to keep going over it. She'd said no, and that was an end to it.

"Maybe William is right. You need all the support you can find to fight Robert."

"Not that." She put her face in her hands, feeling the weight of her fear dragging her down. "It's just—even if we win, going to court will be so awful. For all of us. Maybe I should just give in. Move away, start over again somewhere else. Then Robert would go away and leave us alone."

Aunt Paula grabbed her hands and pulled them away from her face. "You stop talking like that, you hear? You are a strong woman, Hannah Conroy. You will not be like your mamm, giving in and going along instead of standing for what is right. You will not!"

Hannah could only stare at her. "I never thought I'd hear you tell me not to be like my mamm."

"I loved my sister dearly, but that doesn't mean I was blind to her faults." She flushed a little. "I love you and Jamie for yourselves. You are a strong woman, my Hannah, and you will fight. Ja?"

Hannah nodded. "Ja." She would fight back. But still she prayed that it wouldn't be necessary. That somehow Robert would see that he was wrong.

The phone rang. She started to get up, but Aunt Paula waved her back and went to answer it herself. Hannah heard the murmur of her soft-voiced conversation, background for her own thoughts.

How could she have considered giving up, even for a moment? She was where she belonged.

And if she was right about that, God would surely show her the path.

Aunt Paula hung up the phone, her expression odd, as if she didn't know quite what to make of the caller.

"What is it?" Apprehension rose in Hannah.

"That was Nancy Russo. She says that they have been trying. That we should be at their house tomorrow at eleven to talk to Robert."

So. Hannah didn't know whether to be glad or sorry. Nancy and her husband were trying—she didn't say they'd succeeded.

Now she wouldn't have to wait, nerves stretched, wondering when Robert would turn up. She would see him at eleven, and she'd know, one way or the other.

William had half expected things might be different between him and Caleb when he went in to work on Monday morning, but Caleb was the same as ever. If he'd been offended because William had rejected his advice, he did not show it.

As it turned out, Caleb had been right about one thing. William had gotten hurt. A real pain, this time, not the embarrassment and humiliation he'd felt when Rachel turned him down.

This was an active hurt in his chest, so real that he almost felt like rubbing it, to see if that would make it go away. But he knew better.

Hannah had said no. He had to accept that answer. He didn't have a choice.

William finished assembling the quilt stand he'd been working on and set it aside for the glue to dry before sanding and varnishing.

"Shall I s-start o-on another?" The quilt stands sold well, being small enough for a tourist to easily take home in the trunk of a car.

"How do you feel about rocking chairs?" Caleb grinned, looking a bit like someone who had a secret.

"Ja, I-I like f-fine to make them."

"Gut thing." The grin was even broader now. "Because a store over in Lewisburg wants to start selling them, and they've asked for ten to start with."

"T-ten?" Now William understood the grin. "Th-that's a b-big order, ain't so?"

"For sure. And it's all because of those letters you wrote. I'd never even thought of it, but you were right. He looks like he'll be a steady customer, and who knows how many others will respond, too?" Caleb paused. "That being so, I surely could use you full-time. If you're willing, there's enough work here for both of us. What do you say?"

For a moment William couldn't say the words. Then he smiled back at Caleb, the pain easing a little. "I s-say ja, for sure. That s-suits m-me fine."

"Gut." Caleb clapped his shoulder. "Let's get started then."

They laid out the work, figuring the most efficient way

to put together that many rockers. Caleb was a careful craftsman, and he wanted to be sure they could fill the order quickly without sacrificing quality.

William appreciated Caleb's attitude. He felt that way as well. Nothing should go out of the shop that they wouldn't want to have in their own homes.

Ten o'clock came and went, the time when William usually headed for the bakery and their morning coffee. He didn't move, and Caleb made no comment, asked no questions.

Finally Caleb cleared his throat. "Something I've been wanting to say."

William looked up from his work, waiting.

"I should have said it all yesterday. But the other day, when we talked . . . I spoke out of turn, William. I've been sorry for it ever since. If someone had tried to interfere between me and Katie, I wouldn't have liked it, no matter what their intentions were. So I'm sorry."

William nodded. "I-it's okay."

He wasn't ready to tell Caleb what had happened between him and Hannah. Maybe he never would be. Somehow he didn't see Hannah talking about it either, unless maybe it was to her aunt.

He turned back to the work, trying to focus his attention there. Still, his mind kept straying back to those moments with Hannah beside the stream.

She hadn't said she didn't love him. In fact, she'd admitted that she cared for him. But she wouldn't marry him.

He'd been foolish to think marriage to him was a solution to Hannah's problems. If there had been a chance for them before he spoke, it was blown to pieces for sure now.

If Hannah gave in to her father-in-law, she'd leave. He didn't want to imagine a future without her, even though it was also impossible to imagine a future in which they'd be married and happy together.

She'd intrigued him from the first, her gentleness a contrast to the difficult life he knew she'd had. And then she'd helped him, seeing in him the man he wanted to be instead of the boy others thought him.

She'd given him confidence, setting him free of the fear that used to fill him each time he opened his lips to speak.

If she left, if he could no longer even see her, Pleasant Valley would be a sad place for him.

Someone was coming up the stairs. He and Caleb both looked up, expecting Becky, who'd been cleaning the windows down in the shop. But it was Naomi who walked briskly up the stairs and came to the bench where William was working.

"N-Naomi? I-is something wrong?"

"I thought you should know." Her forehead furrowed, eyes dark with concern. "Hannah and Paula are going over to the Russo house at eleven. Hannah is supposed to meet with her father-in-law there. To try and settle things between them." She paused, studying his face as if measuring the impact of her words on him. "Someone should be there to support them, I think. Paula wants me to keep the bakery open, but someone should be there. *You* should be there, William."

He put down the chair leg he was holding in his hand. "Did Hannah say she wanted me?"

"No." The word was stark. "But she needs you." She stood, waiting.

If he went, uninvited, it might make Hannah angry with him. But did that really matter, if he could help her?

He glanced from Naomi to Caleb. And he knew what he must do.

"Denke, Naomi. I will go now."

He strode quickly to the steps and hurried down. Hannah needed him. He could not stay away.

CHAPTER TWENTY

*H*annah found it hard to let go of Jamie long enough even to put him in the stroller. Logic told her that Robert couldn't possibly succeed in taking Jamie away, but logic couldn't quite overcome the fear.

That task would take faith, perhaps more faith than she had. She gripped the stroller handle tightly as they waited to cross the street, words tumbling over each other in her mind.

Please, Father. You know that I am trying to do my best for my son. You know that I love him more than anything. Soften Robert's heart. Take away the bitterness he feels, and help him to truly listen.

Aunt Paula touched her hand as they started across the street. "I am praying, too," she said softly. "God will surely hear our prayers."

Hannah nodded, trying to picture Travis's face in her mind. If Travis were here, would he know how to reach his father's heart? But if Travis were here, none of this would be happening. She reached down, touching the photo album she'd tucked into the stroller. If William had been right, and Robert was motivated by his guilt over failing his son, maybe the memories Travis had preserved in the photo album could help her now.

She felt Aunt Paula's gaze on her face.

"It will be all right," her aunt said. "God will be with us."

"I know. I try not to worry, but . . ." Just as she tried not to think of William. Of his proposal.

If she'd said yes, William would be beside her now. She could borrow his strength when her own seemed to flag. But she had done the right thing. She had to believe that. She couldn't let William marry her out of need—hers or his.

The walk to Phil and Nancy Russo's house wasn't quite long enough. Hannah felt a flicker of panic as they turned in the front gate. Where were the words that would sway Robert from his course?

Robert's car was parked at the curb in front of the house. He was here already, then. She took a breath, her gaze on the paving stones as they approached the door.

Someone moved, coming toward them across the grass. It was William, and in spite of herself her heart leaped at the sight of him.

"William. What are you doing here?" She tried to sound cool and composed, but suspected she didn't manage it.

"You w-would not accept me as your h-husband, Hannah," he said, his voice steady, his eyes as clear and untroubled as a mountain lake. "What about as a f-friend?"

She couldn't refuse, especially when Jamie was standing up in the stroller, shouting out his happiness at seeing William. Especially when she felt like doing the same. She nodded.

William nodded back, his expression grave. Then he bent over Jamie, his face easing in a smile. "Ja, hush, little schnickelfritz. I see you." He lifted Jamie in his arms and straightened. "R-ready?"

Maybe it wasn't the most conciliating move she could make, arriving with William at her side, but that didn't seem to matter at the moment. She reached for the door-bell.

Nancy must have been watching for them, because she opened the door immediately. "Please, come in." Her gesture welcomed them into the living room at the front of the house.

Hannah stepped inside. Her father-in-law and Phil sat in the two large upholstered chairs nearest the fireplace, almost as if aligned against her. A flicker of fear went through her. What if this was some sort of a setup?

Nancy, who might have guessed Hannah's thought, turned from greeting William and Aunt Paula to touch Hannah's arm, her smile warm and reassuring.

"Please, come and sit down." Nancy drifted about like any hostess, making sure her guests were comfortable.

Hannah ended up on the sofa, with William sitting next to her and Aunt Paula opposite them. Jamie, sud-denly afflicted with shyness, leaned against William's knee, one finger in his mouth. Hannah's heart wrenched at the sight.

Robert's frown deepened. Clearly he didn't take any pleasure in Jamie's obvious fondness for an Amish man. Or would he feel the same about any man?

"I don't see what good this is doing." Robert's tone was almost a growl. "I'm not going to change my mind." His gaze focused on Hannah. "Your friend called me. Tried to talk me out of this. But I've seen for myself."

Hannah stared at him blankly. "My friend? Do you mean Megan?"

"Yes, Megan. I suppose you put her up to calling me, figuring she could get me to change my plans."

"No. I didn't know she was going to call you." But joy bubbled up in her at the thought. Megan had tried to fix this mess. She was on Hannah's side, whatever her reservations about Hannah's choices.

Robert obviously didn't believe her, but Hannah let that slide away. It didn't matter. It was enough to know that Megan had tried to help.

Nancy looked at her husband, and Phil cleared his throat.

"Robert, I haven't known you very long, but we have a lot in common. We retired military stick together, right?"

Robert gave a grudging nod.

"Well, we . . . Nancy and I . . . just want to help settle this so no one gets hurt. That's all."

"It's easily settled." Robert glanced at Hannah and just as quickly looked away. "All Hannah has to do is agree to go back to a normal life, and I'll drop the suit. If money is a problem, I'll even help with that. That's fair, isn't it?"

Aunt Paula swelled, as if about to burst out, and Hannah shook her head. They'd have their turn before this visit was over. But right now Phil and Nancy were fighting the battle for them, and Robert was far more likely to hear what they had to say.

"What is so bad about living here in Pleasant Valley?" Nancy asked. "After all, we live here. It's a pretty nice place to raise a child."

"That's not the point." Robert shook his head irritably, like a horse chasing off flies. "Look at the way Hannah's dressed." He flung out a hand toward her. "The last time I saw her, she looked like any other military wife. Now she's like something out of a history book. You think that's normal?"

Hannah pressed her lips together, reminding herself to take her own advice and let Nancy continue in her own way.

Nancy smiled, shaking her head a little. "You know, Robert, that's kind of how I felt when Phil took me along to his first posting after we were married. Everywhere I looked, all I could see was khaki. I couldn't tell one rank from another—I couldn't even recognize my own husband when his unit marched by unless I was close enough to see his face. It nearly drove me crazy."

Robert looked momentarily buffaloed by the comparison. "But—that's different. A military uniform shows you belong to the service."

"Yes, of course it does." Nancy's voice was gentle, persuasive. "I learned to respect that uniform, knowing what it stood for. Just as I respect the clothing worn by the Plain people, knowing what it stands for."

"That's just my point." The words burst out of Robert. "Those people are against everything my son believed in."

"We're not." This time Hannah had to speak for herself. "We just believe in living lives of nonviolence."

"Same thing. That's like saying Travis's death didn't matter." Robert's tone was harsh, but tears stood in his eyes, and Hannah knew they were near the heart of his reaction.

"That's not it at all." The bishop's words seemed to echo in Hannah's mind, and she tried to rephrase them. "We know that God has called us to live in peace with our neighbors. But we don't judge what God has called others to do. No one in the church would look down on Travis because he was a soldier. No one would deny his sacrifice."

"Your son lay down his life for his friends," Aunt Paula said. Her resentment toward Robert seemed to have vanished, as if she only now saw the depth of his pain. "The Bible says there is no greater love than that."

"Please, Robert." Hannah's heart prayed even as she spoke. "Please understand what we're saying. Don't ask me to leave the love and support Jamie and I have found here."

"If you stay here you'll marry him." Robert jerked his head toward William. "A blind person can see how you feel about each other. What will he teach my grandson about his father?"

Hannah started to speak, but William stopped her with a touch.

"I asked Hannah to m-marry me. She said no." He paused, but she sensed he wasn't finished when he glanced at her, his blue eyes filled with love. "If she changes her mind, I w-would love and care f-for Jamie like my own child. But I would not let him forget his father. I w-would teach him to h-honor his father's sacrifice. And I would want you t-to be part of his life."

Hannah's heart twisted in her chest. She had denied William's love, but still he was here, beside her, defending her. He barely stuttered at all as he spoke what was in his heart.

She wasn't alone in her tears. Robert brushed a tear away almost angrily.

"I don't . . . I can't . . ." He stopped, shaking his head. "I was never there when my boy needed me."

There it was. The stark, simple truth that Robert had been trying to hide, from himself most of all.

"You're wrong, Robert." Hannah took the faded album from the stroller and carried it to Robert. He took it, his eyes evading hers.

"What's this?" His tone was gruff.

"Something your son cherished," Hannah said. She reached out to flip the album open, so that the photos showed . . . photos of the young boy Travis had been, standing next to a man in uniform. "There are pictures here from every leave you ever spent together, Travis said. Those memories were important to him. He was so proud of you. Even when the two of you didn't get along, he never stopped being proud."

Robert stared down at the images for what seemed a long time. His shoulders shook, and a tear dropped onto the page.

William stood, holding Jamie's small hand in his large one, and led her son over to Robert. Then he squatted next to Jamie.

"Grandpa i-is sad," he said, with the gentleness that characterized everything he did. "G-give him a hug."

Jamie hesitated for a moment. Then he held up his arms to Robert.

Robert bent slowly, awkwardly. He hugged his grandson. Then he looked at Hannah, his cheeks wet with tears.

"I'm sorry," he said.

Hannah nodded, her own tears flowing. The battle was over.

William waited behind the bakery that evening, sitting in the swing on the back porch. Dusk came earlier now, and the evening air had a chill to it.

He could see the light from Jamie's bedroom window where it filtered through the trees. Hannah was putting her son to bed. He could wait.

Even as he thought it, the light went off. He sat, the swing creaking slightly. Give her a few more minutes to be sure Jamie was settled for the night, and then he'd knock.

Movement flickered beyond the glass in the door. Hannah opened it and came out, drawing a shawl around her shoulders.

"I thought maybe you'd be here." Her voice was calm and tranquil in the aftermath of the storm.

"I am," he said.

Hannah crossed the porch and sat down next to him, the swing creaking again. She glanced up at the chain. "Will it hold both of us?"

"Ja." He put his arm along the back of the swing, not quite touching her, not wanting to assume anything. "It needs oil. I w-will fix it."

She leaned back, into his arm. "You're good at fixing things."

"I did not d-do much." He didn't pretend not to understand that she was talking about Robert. "He already knew h-he was wrong, ain't so?"

"Probably. It was just as you said. He was blinded by his own guilt. If he had come to me sooner, been a part of our lives, we might have grieved together."

"Ja." He settled her comfortably against his shoulder. "Now I think h-he will try to be a gut grossdaadi."

He felt, rather than saw, her smile. "I'm not sure he knows how."

"We w-will help him. If you l-let me." He waited, and it seemed his breath caught in his throat.

Hannah touched his free hand. "Are you sure this is what you want? When you asked me to marry you, it was because I was in trouble and you wanted to help, but—"

"I w-wanted to help because I love you. That has not changed."

She loved him. He felt sure of her feelings now. But she still might not be ready for marriage.

"I want to m-marry you," he went on. "To be a d-daadi to Jamie. If you are not ready, I will wait."

"Would you?" She didn't look up at him, but he heard a smile in her voice.

"I would w-wait. But sooner is better, ja?"

She tilted her head back to look up at him then, and in the joy on her face he read her answer even before she spoke.

"I love you, William. I thought that it was too soon, that I only felt this way because of the problem with Robert. But now I see that the trouble only showed me the feelings that were already there. I love you, and I'll marry you whenever you want. But . . ."

A shadow crossed the joy, and he knew what caused it. He held her hand in his, cherishing the feel of it.

"I have been thinking on this," he said. "And if y-you gave up driving a car, and I gave up home worship, w-we maybe are meant to be horse-and-buggy Mennonites. What do you think of that?"

The answer had been in the back of his mind for a while. This was the reason he had never felt ready to be baptized—because God had something else in store for him. Probably neither family would be best pleased about the choice, but they would get used to it. More important was what Hannah thought.

Her answer wasn't long in coming. She smiled, and all the hope and joy of a future together seemed contained in that smile.

"I think you are very smart, William Brand." She raised her face for his kiss.

EPILOGUE

*C*ome, Jamie. It's almost time for the parade." Hannah held out a small jacket as William and Jamie came into the bakery from the kitchen.

"Grandpa," Jamie declared, shoving his arms into the jacket's sleeves.

"Ja, Grossdaadi will be in the p-parade," William said, dropping a kiss on Hannah's lips. "You will see him."

Hannah responded to the kiss, her palm against William's cheek, feeling the warmth in her heart that came of loving and being loved. Now that they'd both been baptized into their new church family, their wedding was less than a week away. It would be held in the churchhouse, instead of at home, but their Amish kin would be present, as well as the Mennonites.

"Komm," William said, handing Jamie the small flag his grandfather had brought for him. "You will wave your f-flag when you see Grandpa, ain't so?"

"Ja," Jamie declared. He was talking more every day, it seemed, using Pennsylvania Dutch words as easily as English and often enough mixing them both together.

The three of them went out the front door of the bakery to Main Street, where people were already gathering to watch the Veterans Day parade.

Phil Russo hadn't gotten his wish to have Hannah and Jamie in the parade, but Hannah had persuaded Robert to come for another visit, so Jamie would see his grandfather marching with the valley's veterans.

It was a good compromise, one of many that she and William would make as they built their lives together. Already they felt accepted among the horse-and-buggy Mennonites, a change that was probably easier for her than for William, as the group was so similar to the black bumper Mennonites.

After their wedding, they would move into a house only two blocks from the bakery, with a fenced-in yard for Jamie and an extra bedroom for the other babies they hoped to have. Her life would be full and useful, running the bakery, having a family, loving her new husband.

She studied William's face as he lifted Jamie to his shoulders, ensuring her son a good view of the parade. They could hear the sound of the band somewhere down the street, and Jamie bounced with excitement.

Most of the crowd that had gathered to watch the parade was English, of course. That was only natural. But even as Hannah glanced around, some of the Mennonite and Amish shopkeepers came out their doors, looking down the street for the first glimpse of the parade.

Someone touched her arm, and she turned, barely preventing herself from gasping when she realized it was Isaac Brand. William's brother had come around to accepting their marriage and the changes it would inevitably make in William's life, but she certainly hadn't expected to see him here.

"Isaac, how are you? Do you have business in town today?"

"A few errands, ja," he said. "But since my new little nephew's grossdaadi is in the parade, I thought I would watch." He reached out to pat Jamie's leg, where the boy sat on William's shoulders.

It was an olive branch she hadn't expected from Isaac, and Hannah could tell that William was as surprised as she was.

"That is so kind of you," she said, when William seemed speechless. "Jamie, say denke to Onkel Isaac."

"Denke, Onkel Isaac," Jamie parroted, cooperative at the moment, and she breathed a sigh of relief. He didn't always want to perform when asked to talk, but this was the right moment to pick, because Isaac was smiling and the very air around them seemed warmer.

Or maybe that warmth came from William's hand, clasping hers, hidden by the folds of her skirt. A very un-Amish thing to do, holding hands in public, but maybe William guessed at the emotions tumbling around inside her.

The sound of the high school band grew louder, and it came into view, red-and-white uniforms bright, rounding the corner and heading down Main Street toward the firehouse. Jamie bounced excitedly in time to the music, waving his flag when he saw the color guard with their flags.

A car carrying the community's oldest veterans came next, and a lump choked Hannah's throat. The lump threatened to grow to boulder size when she spotted Robert marching next to Phil in uniform. She fought to keep a smile on her face, but tears weren't far off.

William squeezed her hand, and her racing pulse steadied. Travis was gone, and it was right and natural to grieve him, even to be affected by the sight of a uniform.

But life never stood still, and she moved with it. She glanced up at her son, firmly ensconced on William's shoulders. They'd both moved forward. They'd found a home here in Pleasant Valley, and now they'd found a good man to share it with.

Joy welled up in her, sweeping away the lump in her throat. She had been lost, but now she was found, and she was content.

GLOSSARY OF PENNSYLVANIA DUTCH WORDS AND PHRASES

ach. oh; used as an exclamation

agasinish. stubborn; self-willed

ain't so. A phrase commonly used at the end of a sentence to invite agreement.

alter. old man

anymore. Used as a substitute for "nowadays."

Ausbund. Amish hymnal. Used in the worship services, it contains traditional hymns, words only, to be sung without accompaniment. Many of the hymns date from the sixteenth century.

befuddled. mixed up

blabbermaul. talkative one

blaid. bashful

boppli. baby

bruder. brother

bu. boy

buwe. boys

daadi. daddy

Da Herr sei mit du. The Lord be with you.

denke. thanks (or *danki*)

Englischer. one who is not Plain

ferhoodled. upset; distracted

ferleicht. perhaps

frau. wife

fress. eat

gross. big

grossdaadi. grandfather

grossdaadi haus. An addition to the farmhouse, built for the grandparents to live in once they've "retired" from actively running the farm.

grossmutter. grandmother

gut. good

hatt. hard; difficult

haus. house

hinnersich. backward

ich. I

ja. yes

kapp. Prayer covering, worn in obedience to the Biblical injunction that women should pray with their heads covered. Kapps are made of Swiss organdy and are white. (In some Amish communities, unmarried girls thirteen and older wear black kapps during worship service.)

kinder. kids (or *kinner*)

komm. come

komm schnell. come quick

Leit. the people; the Amish

lippy. sassy

maidal. old maid; spinster

mamm. mother

middaagesse. lunch

mind. remember

onkel. uncle

Ordnung. The agreed-upon rules by which the Amish community lives. When new practices become an issue, they are discussed at length among the leadership. The decision for or against innovation is generally made on the basis of maintaining the home and family as separate from the world. For instance, a telephone might be necessary in a shop in order to conduct business but would be banned from the home because it would intrude on family time.

Pennsylvania Dutch. The language is actually German in origin and is primarily a spoken language. Most Amish write in English, which results in many variations in spelling when the dialect is put into writing! The language probably originated in the south of Germany but is common also among the Swiss Mennonite and French Huguenot immigrants to Pennsylvania. The language was brought to America prior to the Revolution and is still in use today. High German is used for Scripture and church documents, while English is the language of commerce.

rumspringa. Running-around time. The late teen years when Amish youth taste some aspects of the outside world before deciding to be baptized into the church.

schnickelfritz. mischievous child

ser gut. very good

tastes like more. delicious

Was ist letz? What's the matter?

Wie bist du heit. How are you; said in greeting

wilkom. welcome

Wo bist du? Where are you?

RECIPES

Rye Bread

½ cup light or dark brown sugar
½ cup shortening
½ cup molasses
1½ tablespoons salt
2 teaspoons caraway seed
2½ cups scalded milk
2 packages active dry yeast
¾ cup warm water
2 tablespoons grated orange rind
3 cups rye flour
5½ cups white flour

Mix the brown sugar, shortening, molasses, salt, and caraway seed in a large bowl. Add scalded milk and stir, then cool to lukewarm. Meanwhile, add the yeast to the warm water until it's bubbly. Add the yeast/water mixture to the brown sugar mixture, then stir in the grated orange rind, the rye flour, and the white flour until the mixture forms a smooth ball. Turn it out onto a floured board and knead until smooth and elastic. Place in a greased bowl and let rise in a warm, draft-free place until it doubles in size, about 1½ hours. Punch the dough down and shape it into three loaves. Place in loaf pans and let rise for about 1½ hours, until each forms a rounded top above the pan. Bake the loaves at 350°F for 30 to 40 minutes, until lightly browned.

Walnut Streusel Cake

FOR STREUSEL:
½ cup light brown sugar
2 tablespoons softened butter
2 tablespoons flour
½ cup chopped walnuts
1 teaspoon cinnamon

With two knives or a pastry blender, cut the streusel ingredients together until they form fine crumbs. Do not use mixer.

FOR BATTER:
1½ cups flour
¾ cup sugar
2½ teaspoons baking powder
½ teaspoon salt
⅓ cup melted butter
½ cup milk
1 egg
1 teaspoon vanilla

Preheat oven to 375°F.

Combine dry ingredients. In a separate bowl, beat the wet ingredients together. Add the dry ingredients and mix thoroughly. Pour half of the batter into a greased 8-inch baking pan. Sprinkle with half the streusel mixture. Pour in rest of batter and sprinkle with rest of streusel mixture. Bake at 375°F for 25 to 30 minutes.

Pretzels

1 cup milk
½ cup butter
1½ tablespoons sugar
½ teaspoon salt
1 package dry yeast, dissolved in ¼ cup warm
    water
1 egg white, beaten
3¾ cups of flour
1 egg yolk, beaten
coarse salt, for sprinkling

Scald the milk, and then add the butter, sugar, and salt to the pan, turning off the burner and letting the mixture cool to lukewarm. Add the yeast/water mixture and the egg white, and then stir in the flour, using enough flour to make a soft dough. Knead the dough on a floured surface until smooth and elastic. Place the dough in a greased bowl, cover, and let rise in a warm, draft-free place until it doubles in size, about 1½ hours. Punch the dough down, turn it out onto a floured board, and roll it out to a large rectangle. Cut it into twelve strips about 1 inch wide and shape each strip into a traditional pretzel shape. Let them stand on the board until they begin to rise. Meanwhile, fill a large, shallow skillet half full with water and bring almost to a boil. Drop the pretzels in and cook about 1 minute on each side. (It may take several batches to do all of them.) Lift each pretzel out carefully with a slotted spatula, letting it drain before putting it on a greased baking sheet. Once all the pretzels are on the baking sheet, brush them with the beaten egg yolk and sprinkle with coarse salt. Bake in a preheated 425°F oven for about 10 to 15 minutes, until brown. Remove and let cool on a cooling rack. Makes 12 large pretzels.

Dear Reader,

I hope you've enjoyed another visit with the people of Pleasant Valley. Although the place doesn't actually exist, it seems very real to me, as it is based on the Amish settlements here in my area of north-central Pennsylvania.

I loved writing about Hannah, torn as she is between two worlds. To me she represents all those who are seeking to find the place where they belong. That's never been an easy task, and in today's culture it seems more difficult than ever.

When I was growing up, I had several friends who were Old Order Mennonite, and I cherish the ways in which we learned to appreciate each other's differences. Some of my Plain friends left that way of life at some point just as Hannah did, but I believe all of them, again like Hannah, carried that heritage with them wherever they went.

I would love to hear your thoughts on my book. If you'd care to write to me, I'd be happy to reply with a signed bookmark or bookplate and my brochure of Pennsylvania Dutch recipes. You can find me on the Web at martaperry.com, e-mail me at marta@martaperry.com, or write to me in care of Berkley Publicity Department, Penguin Random House, 1745 Broadway, New York, NY 10019.

Blessings,
Marta Perry

Read on for an excerpt from

Naomi's Christmas

Pleasant Valley
BOOK SEVEN

by Marta Perry

Available now
from Berkley Books

Naomi Esch froze in her seat at the family table, unable to stop staring at her father. Daadi had just tossed what felt like a lightning bolt into the middle of her thirtieth birthday celebration. Around her, she could feel her siblings and their spouses stuck in equally unbelieving attitudes.

"Ach, what is wrong with all of you?" Daadi, eyes narrowing, his beard seeming to bristle, glared at his offspring. "This is a reason to celebrate, ain't so?"

Lovina, her brother Elijah's wife, was the first to recover, her sweet, heart-shaped face matching her character. "We wish you and Betty much happiness." She bounced baby Mattie, who'd begun to fuss, in her arms. "Wilkom, Betty."

Betty Shutz, a round dumpling of a woman with a pair of shrewd brown eyes, nodded and smiled, but the glance she sent toward Naomi was cautious.

Isaiah, the youngest and most impetuous, said what

everyone must be thinking. "But what about Naomi? If you and Betty are marrying, what is Naomi to do?"

The question roused Naomi from her frozen state. What was she supposed to do, after fifteen years spent raising her siblings, tending the house and garden and her beehives, and taking care of Daadi?

Daadi's gaze shifted, maybe a bit uneasily. "Naomi is a gut daughter, none better. No one would deny that. But newlyweds want to have time alone together, ja? So we . . . I was thinking Naomi would move in with Elijah and Lovina. They are both busy with the dry-goods store and three young kinder besides. It would be a big help to you, ja?"

Elijah and Lovina exchanged glances, and then Lovina smiled at Naomi. "Nothing would please us more than to have Naomi with us, but that is for her to say, ain't so?"

"Denke, Lovina." Naomi found that her stiff lips could move after all. "But what about my beehives?"

Odd that her thoughts had flown so quickly to her bees in the face of this shock. Or maybe not so odd. The bee-hives were the only things she could call truly hers.

"I've already talked to Dick Holder about the hives, and he'll be happy to give Naomi a gut price for them." Daad spoke as if it were all settled, her life completely changed in a few short minutes.

"I will not sell the hives." Naomi could hardly believe that strong tone was coming out of her mouth. Everyone else looked equally surprised. Maybe they'd never heard such firmness from her.

Daad's eyebrows drew down as he stared at her. "Komm, Naomi, don't be stubborn. It is the sensible thing to do. Betty is allergic to bee stings, so the hives cannot stay here. And Elijah's home in town isn't suit-able. The money will give you a nice little nest egg for the future."

A babble of talk erupted around her as everyone

seemed to have an opinion, but Naomi's thoughts were stuck on the words Daad had used. Her future. He clearly thought he knew what that future was to be. She should move from one sibling to another, helping to raise their children, never having a home or a life of her own.

She was engaging in selfish thinking, maybe, unfitting for a humble Amish person. But . . .

She looked around the table. Elijah, the younger brother she'd comforted when bad dreams woke him in the night. Anna and Mary, the next two in the family. She'd taught the girls everything they needed to know as Amish women, overseen their rumspringas, seen them married to gut men they loved. And Isaiah, the baby, the one whose first stumbling steps she'd guided. Were they to be her future, as they had been her past?

Much as she loved them, her heart yearned for more. Marriage might have passed her by during those years when she was busy raising her siblings, but she'd looked forward to a satisfying future taking care of Daad, tending her hives, enjoying her part-time work at the bakery.

Amos, Elijah's middle child, just two, tugged on her skirt. A glance at his face told her he'd detected the strain in the air. She lifted him to her lap, running her hand down his back, murmuring soothing words. He leaned against her, relaxing, sucking on two fingers as he always did before going to sleep.

Lovina met her gaze from across the table and smiled. "Naomi is wonderful gut with children."

"For sure," Betty said, her first contribution to the conversation. "A widower with kinder would do well to have a wife like Naomi."

Somehow that comment, coming from Betty, was the last straw. Naomi had to speak now, and quickly, before the rest of her life was set in stone by the family.

"You are all ser kind to give so much thought to my life. But as dearly as I love my nieces and nephews, I have no wish to raise them. And I will not give up my beehives. So I think I must find this answer for myself."

She took advantage of the ensuing silence to move the sleeping child to his father's arms. Grabbing a heavy wool shawl from the peg by the back door, she walked out, closing the door gently behind her.

Ready to find
your next great read?

Let us help.

Visit prh.com/nextread